VISION OF VIRTUE

What Reviewers Say About Brey Willows's Work

Song of Serenity

"This was a fun introduction to a new series in a world I already love to bits, and I'm looking forward to meeting the other eight muses in upcoming books."—*The Good, the Bad, and the Unread*

"*Song of Serenity* is an all-around fun read. …Willows is an auto buy author with me because she consistently puts out original stories that stay vivid in my mind long after I've finished the book."—*Lesbian Review*

"The story was filled with passion, tension, and a wonderful sense of a believable kind of magic."—*Lesbireviewed*

Changing Course

"Cosmos dust and prowler balls, this was good. The romance is exactly what a good love story should be like. …This was an exciting adventure with a satisfying romance. A quick read that kept me turning pages. A story with a lot of heart."—*Bookvark*

"*Changing Course* is a wonderful book about intergalactic love between two people who were never supposed to meet and how a once chance meeting changed the course of both their lives forever."—*Les Rêveur*

"Ms. Willows has done an excellent job of world building which is essential for a story like this. The alien world and the different types of people are so vividly drawn that they seem real to the reader. The characters, both main and secondary are very well developed. The story begins with a bang and never lets up. …This is a fantastic novel and is going into my favorites category. It has my highest recommendation."—*Rainbow Reflections*

"No matter what genre Brey Willows turns her hand to we can count on meeting incredible characters, falling into a mind-blowing world and being swept away by a wonderful story."—*Beyond the Crime Scene Tape*

"[A] beautifully crafted sci-fi story with exquisite world-building. ...The romantic element was touching and the sex was so hot— but it takes something special to blend that with a fantastic story. *Changing Course* does all of that. I loved it."—*Kitty Kat's Book Review Blog*

"Imagine if you will, the pairing of a lesbian Jenna Stanis (from *Blake's 7*) and the lesbian answer to a young Han Solo. Throw in a thrilling crash landing and a whole host of dangers on the planet itself and you have the makings of something quite, quite special. ...I really, really enjoyed this book. It had all the elements I loved in the books I loved as a teenager and then some."—*The Good, The Bad and The Unread*

Spinning Tales

"I love what the author has done with traditional fairy tales, and I appreciate the originality of the new characters and elements to classic stories."—*Kissing Backwards*

"This was a charming read! I liked the main character and the way the fairy tale realm works. I also found some of the problems and solutions to be quite funny and fun to read. This is a good read for those who like fairy tales and retellings."—*Fierce Female Reads*

"The story was wonderfully, magically imaginative. And you know, I didn't doubt for a minute that the cottage existed exactly where she said it did! ...I loved the story and the imagination behind it but most of all I was enthralled by the use of language. It was beautiful and poetic and lyrical. ...*Spinning Tales* is excellent and I highly recommend it."—*Kitty Kat's Book Review Blog*

Fury's Bridge

"[*Fury's Bridge*] is a paranormal read that's not like any other. The premise is unique with some intriguing ideas. The main character is witty, strong and interesting."—Melina Bickard, Librarian (Waterloo Library, London)

Fury's Death

"This series has been getting steadily better as it's progressed." —*The Good, the Bad, and the Unread*

"The whole [Afterlife Inc. series] is an intriguing concept, light and playfully done but well researched and constructed, with enough ancient and mythological detail to make it work without ever becoming a theology lesson. If you believe in a higher being how would you react to God or Jesus, Jehovah or Mohammed, being available by email? If you don't believe, how would you feel if the gods—all of them—materialised? ...The romances are well done, unusual issues when eternal forces fall for mortal humans and mental concepts collide. But while the romances are central, the stories are far bigger, dealing, albeit lightly, with the constant battle between good and evil, forces of Chaos and destruction wanting humanity to destroy itself while the gods make a stand for peace, love and ecological sanity."—*Lesbian Reading Room*

Fury's Choice

"As with the first in the series, this book is part romance, part paranormal adventure, with a lot of humor and thought-provoking words on religion, belief, and self-determination thrown in...it is real page-turning stuff."—*Rainbow Reading Room*

"*Fury's Choice* is a refreshing and creative endeavor. The story is populated with flawed and retired gods, vengeful Furies, delightful and thought-provoking characters who give our perspective of religion a little tweak. As tension builds, the story becomes an action-packed adventure. The love affair between Tis and Kera is enchanting. The bad guys are rotten to the core as one might expect. Willows uses well placed wit and humor to enhance the story and break the tension, which masterfully increases as the story progresses."—*Lambda Literary*

Chosen

"If I had a checklist with all the elements that I want to see in a book, *Chosen* could satisfy each item. The characters are so completely relatable, the action scenes are cinematic, the plot kept me on my toes, the dystopian theme is entirely relevant, and the romance is sweet and sexy."—*Lesbian Review*

"This is an absolutely excellent example of speculative dystopian fiction. …The main characters are both excellent; sympathetic, interesting, intelligent, well rounded within the context of their situation. Their physical chemistry is great, the slow burn romance which follows behind is a wonderful read, and a great cliff-hanger to match the will they/won't they of the Chosen. Whether you like fantasy or not you should give this book a go. The romance is spot-on, the world building excellent and the whole is just speculative fiction at its best."—*Curve*

"The romance is spot on, the world building excellent, and the whole is just speculative fiction at its best. I loved Brey Willows's Afterlife Inc trilogy, but this is on a whole new level…"—*Lesbian Reading Room*

"I recommend this to anyone that likes to take a look into the possible future of this planet and its inhabitants."—*scifislacker.com*

Visit us at www.boldstrokesbooks.com

By the Author

VISION OF VIRTUE

by
Brey Willows

2022

VISION OF VIRTUE

ISBN 13: 978-1-63679-118-0

THIS TRADE PAPERBACK ORIGINAL IS PUBLISHED BY
BOLD STROKES BOOKS, INC.
P.O. BOX 249
VALLEY FALLS, NY 12185

FIRST EDITION: SEPTEMBER 2022

CREDITS

EDITOR: CINDY CRESAP
PRODUCTION DESIGN: SUSAN RAMUNDO
COVER DESIGN BY TAMMY SEIDICK

Acknowledgments

Writing isn't done in a vacuum. Even the blood and sweat and swearing bit often includes other people, willing or no. I'm incredibly lucky to be surrounded by a community of people who not only listen to me woe about deadlines and blocks, but who encourage me and, eventually, even read the books.

Thank you to BSB for taking a chance on me and the somewhat off kilter things I write. Sandy, your professionalism is matched with your kindness and your willingness to tell me when things are very much not right. Thanks to Cindy, who sends me innumerable lovely words in an email before I get to the edits, and whose wisdom is always appreciated. To the readers, my heartfelt thanks for sticking with me all these years. And to my wife, who laughs with me, sings wrong lyrics with me, and puts a flower next to my bedside every week: you are my heart.

Dedication

To my buddy of all things,
my reason for getting up each day.
You have given me a world full of magic.

CHAPTER ONE

*H*OW MANY DEMIGOD BABIES ARE OUT THERE
NOW? NO ONE KNOWS AND THE GODS WON'T SAY.
Clio Ardalides pushed the newspaper from the makeup table
into the trash. Another passive-aggressive act by her stylist to remind
her that the world still had difficulties even though the immortals
had merged with the world. As though she needed to be reminded.
As though a *muse* was unaware of suffering.

It was her *job* to know humans. But her show wasn't about
suffering and sadness and all that stuff. Selene's show was where
the gods went to talk politics and answer serious and never-ending
questions surrounding existential angst. Clio's show was about fun,
about the light side of life. Why couldn't some people understand
that?

She sighed and brushed at the strands of light, dyed hair around
her face. Sure, she stayed away from humans for the most part these
days. Her role didn't allow for that kind of thing now. But that
didn't mean she didn't *know* things. She just chose what to focus on.
Nothing wrong with that.

The door opened. "Five minutes, Clio." The gofer shut the door
before she could acknowledge him.

She refreshed her lip gloss and smiled widely at the mirror.
She'd already said hello to tonight's guests and now all she had to
do was shine. As always.

She left her dressing room and let the bright purple chiffon
dress flow around her, giving the impression she was gliding. She

knew it did because she'd practiced extensively to get the effect just right. What was the point in being an immortal in front of the camera if she didn't play the part?

The music came on and she closed her eyes. Deep breaths. One…two…three. She stepped on stage to loud applause, both from the audience and supplemented by the sound crew. She waved and twirled and batted her false lashes, which felt heavy with glue tonight. She sat primly in her high-backed chair and leaned toward the audience.

"Don't you all look gorgeous!" She scanned the crowd, looking for a kind face to focus on. It helped the ever-present nerves, even after all this time. But tonight, not one gave the impression, the *feeling*, she needed. Unsettled, she sat back and focused on the camera instead.

"I've got two super special spectacular guests tonight." She looked into camera two, to get her good side. "Adorable cherub of cheer, kid of kindness, Cupid is here to spread some love!" The cheers were somewhat lackluster, and she worked to smile bigger, her cheeks already growing sore. "And his lovely competition, the stunning and strong, the willful and wily, Skadi!"

The gorgeous Norse goddess strode onto the stage, her short white tunic showing off her long, strong legs. Cupid, red-faced and leering, rode on her shoulder, his bow and arrow cocked at the audience. The audience would have no idea that he was red-faced because he'd been drinking some foul-smelling bourbon since he'd arrived and was half out of his head drunk. And a drunk Cupid had done plenty of damage in the past.

Clio stood and held her hands out to Skadi, who took them and rolled her eyes slightly, her back turned to the camera.

"Get this little shit off my shoulder before he pisses himself and ruins my dress," she hissed, still smiling, though her eyes were narrowed.

Clio reached up and plucked Cupid from Skadi's shoulder, holding him away from her in case Skadi was right about his need to relieve himself. "Isn't Cupid just the cutest thing?"

The audience tittered and gasped as Cupid let loose a haphazard arrow that fortunately didn't hit anyone. It stuck in the carpet and a crew member quickly swept down and grabbed it before an audience member did. Gods only knew what a human would do with an arrow of love. Or loathing. Whichever he'd loaded up this time.

She set him on the floor and tried not to kick him away when he leaned against her leg and caressed her calf.

"Tonight, we're going to watch these two run the gamut, and of course, it will end in an archery contest!"

The crowd's approval was louder this time. The giant screen behind her showed the obstacle course. "First, they have to make it through the bouncy castle highway, then they have to swim across the lake of pudding. Once they're back on shore, they have to climb to the top of Mount Olympus, where they'll be ready to shoot at the moving targets."

Skadi began to stretch like she was going into an actual obstacle course and not something designed just for some lighthearted connection with the gods. Cupid swayed and sat on his fat little behind, drawing a soft "aww" from the audience. Clio nudged him with her purple stiletto. "And as you all know, the one rule of this obstacle course is that no god can use their powers. They have to do it the mortal way or no way!" The audience chanted that phrase with her, and there was no question that beneath it simmered some resentment.

She steeled herself and ignored the pain in her cheeks. "So, let's see our contenders get dirty!"

Skadi left the main stage and headed off to the obstacle course. Cupid tottered after her, gas coming from both his mouth and his rump as he climbed onto the obstacle stage. Clio wondered if he was so drunk that he'd forgotten he had wings. It was highly doubtful he'd listened to a word of the rules and was simply taking them seriously.

The gong rang out, reverberating around the room, and Skadi jumped into the first of four bouncy castles, all set to high bounce. As she went up, her tunic did too, and quickly showed that she didn't have any underwear on. The audience went insane.

So, too, did Cupid. He looked up right as she was at her highest, and the little toad clambered into the bouncy castle, only to be flung into the air when Skadi landed. He bounced behind her like a red-faced beach ball, and Clio had to wipe tears of laughter from her eyes as he turned a sickly green color.

When Skadi made it out of the bouncy houses and into the pool, he scrambled on hands and knees behind her, albeit more slowly. She moved solidly through the thick chocolate pudding, chest deep. He, on the other hand, flopped onto his back and used his hands and feet, both of which were strangely large, to push himself through the gloop without sinking. Skadi made it to the other side just before him.

From there, it was no contest. Skadi's long legs carried her up the "wall" of Mount Olympus easily, and she had plenty of time to steady her aim and take her shot through the small ring of fire and into the giant moving cloud target beyond, where she put the arrow directly in the middle of the painted smiley face. Cupid sat down at the bottom of the wall and scooped a cup of pudding from the pool with the little chalice he kept on his belt, and then proceeded to drink it. Some of it, anyway. The rest dribbled down his fat pink belly.

The crowd oohed and aahed, and Clio turned back to them. "Clearly, we have a winner!"

Skadi leapt from the top of the makeshift mountain to land next to Clio. She accepted the little glass trophy, and they went to a commercial break.

Clio's team came out and smoothed her hair and makeup, and they brought Skadi a wet towel to quickly wipe herself down. Cupid waved off the team and curled into a ball around his pudding cup and fell asleep.

"Thank you for coming out today. I know that wasn't a competition." Clio knew full well that many of the gods felt her show was demeaning.

"I'm a lesser goddess who was selling potatoes from my farm. I'll take what I can get." Skadi shook out her hair and grimaced. "But actual mud was easier to deal with."

Clio turned away like she had something else to concentrate on so that the goddess didn't see that her words stung. Initially, it had been a big laugh, but lately, the laughter had died. The cameras rolled again, and she turned to smile brightly. As long as she could keep focusing on the positive, the other gods' opinions didn't matter.

❖

She waved as Skadi got into a Rolls Royce and drove off, and she watched, bemused, as Cupid was carried out to his garish pink Cadillac. The driver didn't seem at all fazed when Cupid was put, unconscious, into the back seat. Clio shook her head and went back to her dressing room. As she was about to pass the staff room, she stopped to listen. It sounded like several crew members were making plans, including her own stylists.

"I can't wait for that beer tonight," someone said.

"Seriously. What a shit show. If people saw half the crap we saw here, they'd never pray to these assholes again. What is Clio thinking?"

"Clearly, she isn't. I mean, aren't muses supposed to be all about inspiration? The only thing she's inspiring me to do is drink away my depression about working here."

Pain burned in her chest and her eyes teared up. She lifted her chin and walked quickly past the staff room, not bothering to look in. Letting them know she'd heard them wasn't an option. When she made it into her dressing room, she shut the door quietly and leaned against it. Only then did she let the tears flow.

When she was done crying, she picked up her phone and opened her social media account. "Perception is what life is all about. If you perceive beauty, then life is beautiful." She hit send and watched the likes and hearts pour in. It might have been a little trite, but she believed it with her whole heart. She continued to type. "If you don't like working somewhere, you should leave and find something that makes you happy. Don't stay in a shit show you don't believe in." Her finger hovered over the send key, but she deleted the post. Passive-aggressive behavior wasn't her style, and it didn't make the world a better place. Instead, she wrote, "I hope you're still loving the laughter and light my show puts out into the world. Perceive beauty!"

It was kind of just a repeat, but she was gratified to see the outpouring of love for the show. Maybe some of the staff were jaded, but the audience was still out there. She set her phone aside so she could still see it, and then she began the arduous task of taking off the thick makeup her stylist insisted was necessary for the camera. It felt so good when it was off that Clio ran her fingertips over her cheeks, feeling the soft, wrinkle-free skin of her ageless face. When she opened her eyes, she almost didn't recognize the tired looking woman in the mirror. She turned away, not wanting to analyze why she looked so hollow.

Once she'd changed into comfortable designer jeans and a form-fitting sweatshirt, she left her dressing room to find it dark. The crew had left and turned everything off, not bothering to see if she was still there. Tears filled her eyes again and she brushed them away. She couldn't tell herself she didn't care, that they didn't matter, because she did, and they did. She wanted them to like her, and at first, they'd all seemed like a big happy family. But three years on, that family had turned into a feuding faction of friction. How she wished it could be like it had been before.

She slowly made her way out the back door and into the crisp night air. San Francisco was her haven, her own special muse. Creativity thrived in the city and fed her soul the way Italy did. And she had an apartment in Monte Castello di Vibio, the home of the arts, although she hadn't been in a long time. San Francisco in this century called to her, and like any good muse, she listened to things that called to her. Of course, many of the gods lived in the Afterlife compound in Santa Monica, and that made it easier to get them on the show, since it was a simple trip up the coast. Not that they couldn't travel anywhere at the drop of a hat, but... well, perception and reality were a thing for the gods, too. If they perceived something to be a hassle, then it was. So she worked to take the hassle out of it.

She briefly thought about heading to the Academy in Big Sur, her special project where creative people from all over the world came to study with not only the muses, but also with the brightest and best of the humans. But that was a long drive, and she was weary. And when her place in Seacliff came into view, it made her happy the way it always did. The lights were on a timer, since she hated coming home to a dark house, and light spilled from every window, welcoming her home. The gravel drive crunched beneath the tires of her convertible, and she hurried inside, chilled by the fog rolling in off the water.

She went in and hung her long coat on the peg in the hallway. Not for the first time, she thought how lonely it looked there, all by itself. She shook the thought away and went upstairs, where she put on her oldest, most comfy sweatpants and her favorite T-shirt, emblazoned with a Care Bear and the words "Believe in Yourself" across the chest. Cozy socks completed the homey feeling and she went back downstairs to make herself a microwave dinner.

The phone rang, breaking the silence, and she leapt for it.

"I don't know why, but I had a feeling you'd be home."

Eris's voice, low and husky, always made Clio smile. "And where are you that you're able to call me on a Friday night, sister dear?"

Eris laughed. "At the club. Where you should be shaking your ass and finding a warm body to keep you hot in that gorgeous house of yours." She laughed and said something Clio couldn't hear to someone else. "I had a feeling you needed me."

Not alone after all. Clio held back the tears, not wanting Eris to worry. "I did, and I feel a million times better just for hearing your voice."

The background noise on Eris's side faded. "What's up? Talk to me."

Clio launched into the story of that day's show, and ended lamely with, "And then my crew went out for drinks and didn't invite me."

Eris was quiet for a minute. "Clee, maybe you need to change things up. A little less flash and a little more substance, you know?"

"You're one to talk." Clio went to the floor to ceiling window and looked out, but there was nothing to see but fog. "I don't recognize this world anymore, E. It's moving so fast, and there's still so much darkness. If I don't succeed, if I don't bring some lightness to it, I worry…"

"You worry what?"

"That the darkness will just eat up all the light." She swallowed hard. "That sounds silly, doesn't it?"

Eris sighed deeply and Clio could picture her, sitting at her desk, her feet propped on the edge, her eyes closed.

"It doesn't sound silly at all. I get it. But, sis, you're not happy. And if you're not happy, then the people around you aren't happy. That's the way we work, right?" There was an explosion of noise and music, and someone called her name. "Look, I've got to go. But think about what I've said, okay?"

Clio blew a kiss and ended the call. She fell backwards onto the couch and lay there in the silence. She was the muse of history and virtue. Neither of those things seemed to matter in this world. So where did that leave her?

CHAPTER TWO

This is Kit Kalloway, reminding you to always spot the truth."

Kit's friends raised their glasses and cheered as Kit signed off on the huge TV screen on the wall of the bar. She smiled and took their ribbing in the humor it was meant as she raised her glass too. The show that aired tonight had been shot last week, and even her closest friends didn't know how much makeup it had taken to cover the dark circles under her eyes so they wouldn't show up on camera.

"I thought for sure that god was going to smite you when you said he was being cuntish," Barb, Kit's best friend, said.

"Do gods still smite people? Seems like they wouldn't, you know? With all the cameras on them all the time. Would be bad press, right? And are you even allowed to use the word cunt on live TV?" Jim, Barb's long-term boyfriend, had a beer mustache he didn't wipe away.

"And that's the thing, right? It's all about the press." Kit tried to keep the venom from her tone, but it was getting harder every day. "When it's considered hard-hitting news, they'll let me get away with just about anything."

"I think smiting is probably too old-fashioned for this era's gods. Like, they're too cool for that now." Trish, Kit's ex and close friend, nodded wisely. The commercials ended and the next show came on. "Speaking of. Talk about cool."

Kit lowered her head to the table and closed her eyes. "For fuck's sake. Not this. Anything but this."

"I love this show. Clio is so gorgeous, and I love the way she's kind of poking fun at the gods. Like, she seems so down to earth." Trish rested her chin in her hands and watched the TV as Clio smiled and batted her eyes.

"That's what you call down to earth? Some woman in a purple tutu from head to toe? She looks like the Purple People Eater. She's supposed to be the muse of history and virtue, and she's up there pretending like she's showing us that the gods have this fun, normal side. It's as fake as she is." Kit got up and moved around the table and shooed Barb from her seat. "Let me sit with my back to the TV so I don't vomit on the table."

The conversation went on around her, but she sipped her beer and drifted into her own thoughts, as she often did when waters got shallow around her. She had no interest in small talk or the gods playing stupid games. And she certainly had no interest in the host of a show that pandered to the lowest common denominator in society. Which, in Kit's opinion, included the gods.

"What would you be, Kit?" Jim's words finally penetrated her train of thought.

"Would I be, what?" she asked. "Sorry, I wasn't listening."

Barb smiled patiently. "If you hadn't been a reporter, or if you could retrain as something else, what would it be?" She pointed at Jim. "He'd be a pro football player, which is a little cliché, but that's okay. Trish would be a gynecologist, which I think she wouldn't be after she saw one too many with problems. And I'd be an astronaut."

Kit looked at the three of them. "Jim, you have the worst knees in history, and you hate pain. Trish, Barb's right. One too many STDs and you'd never want to see a pussy again. And Barb, you get motion sickness. Falling from space wouldn't be good for you."

They all laughed but Barb looked at her somewhat seriously. "But what about you? If you could retrain, be something else. What would you do?"

Kit sipped her beer and thought, then shrugged. "I've never wanted to be anything other than what I am. I wrote for the school paper when I was six. I can't imagine being anything other than a reporter." Why did that thought fill her with angst? It was true.

Barb's gaze was searching. "Always asking questions, never satisfied with the answers."

Kit flicked a bit of beer foam at her. "That's because there are always more answers out there."

"Too deep, too serious. Let's go dancing." Trish stood up and tugged on Kit's arm. "You're so intense all the time. You think we don't notice, but you look like you've been dragged down the freeway backwards. You're always rumpled like someone forgot you in the dryer, and you've got eyes a panda would envy." She draped her arm around Kit's shoulders. "Let's take you out, get you drunk, and get you laid. That should help with at least one of those issues."

"Which one? I doubt it would unwrinkle me. Thanks for that, by the way. And I'd still be tired if I stayed up fucking all night, so it wouldn't help with the panda eyes either." Kit swallowed the last of her tepid beer. "Thanks, but with your vote of confidence, I'm pretty sure I wouldn't be picking up any women tonight. I'll head home to my cat."

"If you had a cat, we'd give up on you altogether, my lonely handsome friend. Even wrinkled and bleary-eyed, you're still the hottest butch on the dance floor." Trish tugged again.

Barb reached over and gently took Trish's hand from Kit's arm. "She's right, babe. Kit needs sleep and quiet, not a woman demanding a mind-bending orgasm." She kissed Kit's cheek. "Head on home to Buster. We'll take Trish out and make sure she doesn't go home with anyone we wouldn't do ourselves."

Kit laughed and kissed Barb's cheek. "Thanks for understanding. Trish, I promise I'll go out with you soon, okay?"

Trish's pout was fake, and she quickly broke into a smile. "I'm going to hold you to that."

They made their way from the bar together and the other three turned left, while Kit turned right. It was still fairly early, but she was dead on her feet and wanted nothing more than to curl up on the couch and listen to some music before bed.

She headed to the train and took it back to Noe Valley, her home away from home, far enough from the bustle of the city to be quiet and have a neighborhood feel. She stopped into the Whole Foods for a few ingredients and then walked halfway up the hill to her home, a pale blue house stuck between a yellow and a pink home on either side.

Before she opened the door, she set down the grocery bag and planted her feet. As soon as it opened, a big furry head pushed through, and a brown heap of fur leapt on her.

"You're getting way too big for this, boy. Maybe I need to put you on a diet." She buried her face in Buster's thick brown fur and laughed as he danced, practically hugging her and very nearly her height. "Come on. Let's get dinner."

He raced back inside, and she picked up the groceries. The house smelled of cookies and she moaned loudly. "Will you marry me?"

Abel snapped his book shut and bit into a cookie pointedly. "You're late. And you'd make me a terrible husband."

She blew him a kiss and set the groceries on the counter. "Was Buster good for you today?"

"I think you're the only non-rich person in all of San Francisco with a nanny for your dog." Abel stretched, his T-shirt pulling tight against his biceps. "And of course he was. He's the best dog ever born to this world."

Apparently agreeing, Buster jumped up on the couch and stuck his head on Abel's lap.

"Well, I can't have a dog and leave him home alone all day. That would be cruel. I feel bad enough keeping a Newfoundland in a house this size. He should be running around open fields, chasing birds or sheep or whatever it is they chase in the wild." She got out the food and started chopping. "Sorry I'm late."

Abel shrugged and left the couch to sit at the breakfast table. "I'm not going out till around midnight, so it's not like I needed to be home yet." He waved his hand in front of his face. "This is pretty enough without a lot of preparation."

They continued to chat as she cooked, and when she served up the katsu curry dish, he was appropriately impressed. "It's a good thing I walk your horse of a dog every day, or I'd get fat off your cooking."

"If you didn't walk my horse of a dog every day, you wouldn't be here to enjoy my cooking." She nodded toward the tray of cookies on the counter. "And then I wouldn't get to indulge in your baking experiments." She gave Buster a piece of chicken with the spicy breading taken off and he took it gently from her fingers.

Abel watched like an indulgent parent. "It always amazes me how a one-hundred-and-fifty-pound dog can be that gentle." He gathered their dishes and started loading the dishwasher. "Are you going out tonight?"

She pointed at the clock. "It's ten at night. Why on earth would I go out now?"

He rolled his eyes. "You're so damn old. How are you so old when you're not old yet?" He looked her up and down. "If you were a guy, I'd be all over you. You should definitely have some woman here fawning over that body you work so hard on."

"If I did, you wouldn't be here. Be glad I don't."

When they were done cleaning up, he picked up his coat and bag, but stopped and looked uncharacteristically serious. "You know I love you, Kit. And our arrangement couldn't be any more perfect for me. But you're working yourself to death, and I'm worried about you."

Touched by his genuine concern, she pulled him into a gruff hug. "I'm fine, Abel. I promise. Just busy."

He held her at arm's length. "At some point, you're going to burn out. All this anger you carry around, all this guilt. It eats a person up inside, you know? And taking on the gods is sexy in a hero kind of way, but in a reality kind of way, it might get you dead." He cupped her cheek. "And if you die, I'm taking Buster."

She shoved him toward the door. "He'd be lucky to have you, but don't go killing me off yet. I've got plenty of work to do to expose the gods as the eggplants they are. Colorful and tasteless, and not actually very useful."

He laughed and shook his head as he bounded down the stairs to the street. Buster came and sat at her side and put one paw in the air as though waving to Abel.

"See you Monday, hot shot. Call me if something comes up. I might answer."

Kit went inside and lowered herself onto the couch. Her muscles were stiff, and she'd need to get to the gym to work out the stress. Buster huffed onto the sofa beside her and set his head on her leg. She closed her eyes and breathed deeply, letting the silence of her home fill the spaces inside her that felt so hot and angry all the time. Deep down, she knew her friends were right. She'd been burning the candle at every end available since the Merge, and there was no question she was pissed off all the time. "Good thing I'm not one to take it out on the people I love, huh, Buster?" She ran her hand through his thick fur and smiled when he flipped onto his back and started to snore.

Maybe taking on the gods wasn't a great idea. And no, maybe it wouldn't change anything in the grand scheme of things. But she wasn't going to be silent, and she wasn't going to back down. Someone had to hold them accountable, and she had the position and experience to do it. She reached under her coffee table, receiving a grunt from Buster, and opened the old, faded photo album with the gold crest on the front. Photos of her parents, from the time they were young and full of idealism to the month just before the accident, made her smile.

"I miss you guys so much," she said as she traced her mom's face. "You told me I could change the world, and I'm trying. But you have no idea how much it's changed since you left." She closed the album and set it aside. Did they know? Were they in an afterlife they'd chosen, as so many did now? They'd been atheists, but apparently there was some kind of space for atheists, if they wanted to be there. But her parents had died before the Merge, so where did that leave them? As desperately as she wanted to believe they could hear her and were looking out for her, she couldn't. They hadn't wanted an afterlife because they believed that what a person did with their life while they were living it was more important.

She tried to have conversations with them sometimes, imagining what they'd say about the state of the world today. It was part of what drove her, what fired her. They'd want the gods to be accountable too. They'd want answers, and they'd never doubted Kit's ability to dig for the truth.

She gave Buster a brisk belly rub. "Bedtime, buddy."

He groaned as he flipped himself over and slid off the couch before he led the way to the bedroom. Kit turned off the lights and got ready for bed. When she crawled in, the sheets were cold, and she briefly thought of Trish's proclamation that she should get laid. The last woman she'd been with a few months ago had made a big deal of sleeping with a celebrity, and Kit had wanted rid of her not long after the third noisy orgasm. The last thing she needed was someone who wanted to be seen, who wanted notoriety just for existing. If Kit could do her job as well from the shadows, she would. But there was no question that people believed what they saw, and by being on camera and showing them exactly where the gods were failing, she was helping spread truth and balance. She didn't care about the fame or the money, or the women who wrote her letters asking for dates. Several had even said they'd be good wives for her and had gone into a kind of résumé of their qualities. One had included photos. Apparently, she was quite flexible.

Kit liked her space and her quiet. She loved her dog, and she loved her job. Most of the time, that felt like enough. But tonight, as she shivered in the cold sheets and hugged a pillow, it didn't feel perfect.

CHAPTER THREE

They what?" Clio set her cup down hard enough to splash coffee all over the counter. "Do they know who I am?" She flinched at the cliché coming out of her mouth, but she couldn't help it.

The show's producer sighed deeply. "They do, which is why you've still been on air this season. But, babe, ratings don't lie. The numbers are way down, and if it was anyone but you, they would have canceled it last season. They won't keep it going at a loss."

Clio's hand shook as she mopped up her coffee. "So that's it? It's over?"

"Not necessarily. They've given us till midweek to think of a new angle, something to draw viewers back in. Between us, we'll think of something. I think we need something with more substance, that's all."

Clio's breath was shaky, and she curled her feet under her on the couch. "Selene already has that covered with her show. It's all about the serious side of things. Our show was supposed to be lighthearted and fun. It was supposed to focus on the good stuff." She wiped a tear away. "Maybe the show has run its course."

There was a long moment of silence as Clio looked out at the fog swirling lazily above the water. She felt almost as insubstantial.

"Don't give up hope yet. I have a kernel of an idea, but I need to think on it some more. You do so as well, and we'll touch base on Monday, okay?"

She agreed and hung up. Only a few days to save her career. She considered calling one of her sisters, but she wasn't in the mood for a lecture. Impulsively, she jumped up and went to her room, where she changed into a sweater and jeans, pulled her hair into a fashionably messy bun, and grabbed her guitar.

The night air was cold and damp, which matched her mood. But when she pulled up to Neck of the Woods, her spirits began to lift. The doorman greeted her like an old friend and radioed that she was heading downstairs. By the time she made it to the intimate staging area, Kulitta was waiting, her arms open wide.

"It's been too long, beautiful one." She embraced Clio hard. "You only come now when something weighs on you."

The stage was empty, with a soft blue spotlight on the single stool in the center. "Do you mind if I play tonight?"

"My love, if I had Hathor herself on stage, I'd kick her off so I could listen to you instead." Kulitta waved toward the stage. "Go. I'll have your drink brought over."

Clio went to set up. This was the only place where she wasn't concerned with the size of the crowd or who was in it. Ever since the Hittite lesser goddesses Kulitta and her sister Ninatta had taken over the club, Clio had felt comfortable going there to play. And Kulitta was right. She only came to play when she needed to work something out. She used to play all the time, whatever her mood.

She tuned the guitar and strummed, and then began singing a song she'd written herself many years ago. It was a story of love lost and found again, about finding your way back to the person who held your soul in the palm of their hands. The words slid through her, and the more she sang and played, the better she felt, even as tears fell slowly down her cheeks. The music filled her, spilled from her, entwined with the being she was and infused her soul with passion once more. After two more songs she was restored and the weight on her chest was gone. There was nothing in life that couldn't be worked through. Feeling so lost and desolate was a human trait, not one meant for a muse or an immortal of any kind. It was good to remember that.

She smiled at the small audience she couldn't see thanks to the spotlight and left the stage to soft, but genuine, applause. Here, dressed down and without a ton of cameras and make-up, they probably had no idea a muse was on stage. She was just another amateur singer enjoying the atmosphere and the opportunity to play. That was how it should be.

She held her drink up in thanks to Kulitta, who nodded from where she was in conversation with someone at the bar. Clio sipped the strawberry mojito and listened to the person who'd taken her place on stage, a folk singer with funny songs and a mellow voice. Another mojito joined the one on the table and she looked up.

"Your voice is incredible. And it's like that guitar is part of your soul." The tall woman with dark skin and a bright, sexy smile looked down at her. "Can I join you?"

Clio pushed out the other chair with her foot. "Sure."

She sat down and sipped her own drink, something short in a rock glass. "I've never heard someone sing like you. You're an immortal, I take it?"

Clio looked into the woman's deep brown eyes and didn't see any cunning or judgment. "Yes. Does it matter?"

The woman's laugh was full and easy. "Nah. There are so many of you running around now that it makes no difference." She leaned forward and gave Clio a smoldering grin. "Except, if you don't mind me saying so, you do tend to make better lovers."

Clio's clit twitched in response to the overt come-on. How long had it been since someone had flirted with her like this? Too long. "Yes, we do. As long as we stay happy. Otherwise…"

The woman nodded sagely and lifted the amber liquid to her lips again. "I've heard stories. Are you one of those types? Do I need to worry about being turned into a frog if I don't propose in the morning?"

Clio shook her head and downed the rest of the first mojito, then pushed it away and pulled the other one forward. "No. Most definitely not." She smiled. "And that's quite an assumption, that there will be an 'in the morning.'"

It took only a moment of unspoken agreement before the woman stood and held out her hand. Clio took it, and they left the club together.

❖

"See? I told you there'd be an 'in the morning.'"

Clio rolled over and slung her leg over the woman's. She had yet to ask her name. There was something sexy about not knowing. As far as she knew, the woman didn't know hers either. "It was still a lot to presume." She kissed her shoulder. "I could have told you to bugger off."

"Bugger off? Isn't that something they say in England?" She ran her fingertips over Clio's collarbone.

"It is, but I've always thought their way of swearing was far better than the American way."

A phone vibrated on the nightstand and the woman rolled over to check it. She read the screen and then sat up. "I'm sorry, but I have to take this."

Clio pulled the sheet up over her chest and watched as the woman left the bed. She was so sexy she might well have been an immortal herself, if it weren't for the fine lines around her eyes that suggested the very mortal issue of aging. She climbed out of bed and slipped her clothes on, glad that she'd been wearing something casual the night before. It always felt a little lurid having to put on a party dress the next morning.

The woman leaned against the doorframe. "Heading out?"

Clio kissed her cheek. "I am. And you'll be glad to know you won't be turned into a frog today."

The woman laughed and then pulled Clio in for a soft, sweet kiss. "Good to know. I hope to see you again one day."

Clio tapped her lips with her fingertip. "You never know."

She walked out, feeling lighter and more at ease than she had in a long time. The woman had been an excellent lover and the number of orgasms had been just right. And really, it had been a bit of connection she'd needed to get her feet on the ground again.

She waved as she pulled away, and she laughed when she saw the woman step out to wave, still butt naked. The sight nearly made Clio turn around, but she knew better than to get involved with a mortal. Thanks to Aphrodite, that always turned out badly.

Once she was home, she took a long, hot shower and ate breakfast on the balcony. A pod of dolphins swam past, and she smiled at the memory of her and her sisters playing with dolphins when they were children on the shores of Greece. The thought made her a little homesick, so she picked up the phone.

"Hi, Dad."

"My favorite daughter. How are you?"

Zeus's booming voice came through loud and clear, and she held the phone away from her ear, laughing. "Please don't ever say that in the presence of any of your other numerous daughters. I don't think my sisters would mind, but Athena might get her panties in a bunch."

"I doubt she even wears them." He laughed. "What makes you call?"

"Do you ever miss home?"

He paused. "You mean Olympus?"

"Well, I meant Greece, but yeah, Olympus works too."

There was the sound of a candy wrapper and him munching before he answered. "I go back to Olympus pretty regularly at the moment. Hera and I are trying to work some things out. She and Ama went shopping the other day, which is beyond strange. And my temples in Greece are being lit again, so I go there often too. Why don't you come with me next time?"

She had difficulty picturing Zeus's wife and mistress having brunch but such was the world of the immortals. "I'd love that. Everyone else is too busy, and I hate taking trips on my own."

He laughed. "You always have. Of all your sisters, you're the most like me. Lots of flash, and you're a fan of the limelight, just like your old man."

She winced slightly at the thought that she could be so like him. As much as she loved him, he had a reputation for cruelty when he didn't get the adulation he wanted. At least she could console herself that she was never mean to anyone.

Someone spoke in the background.

"Sorry, honey, I have to go. These damn furies and their wives mean I don't get any downtime anymore. It's always do this, do that, stop turning people into birds, don't have any more demigod babies." He groaned dramatically. "I never get any me time."

She laughed. "Somehow, I doubt that's true, but if anyone can keep you in line, they can. Love you. Let me know when you're going to Greece again."

"Will do. I'm COMING!" he shouted as he hung up.

Clio looked out at the water as she sipped a cup of red bush tea. Was she too much like her father? She thought again of the possible cancelation of the show and how that made her feel. Her whole identity was tied into the persona she'd built in this era. If she no longer did that, she could definitely go back to the ACA and be more hands-on in running the college. As much as she loved that, though, it didn't call to her now that it was running so smoothly.

She spent the rest of the day relaxing and reading a new historical novel by a leading author. While the author had clearly done her research, there was no question she hadn't lived in the era. It was too clean, too polished. The actual time period had been stinky and dirty. Even the aristocracy had hardly ever bathed since it was considered bad for a person's health. Science and indoor plumbing had made a beautiful difference to the world. It might be a little more sterile, but it was certainly better smelling.

The romance of the story made her sigh happily when it ended. In truth, she'd seen many heartbreakingly beautiful relationships in her many years on the planet. There'd been plenty of bad ones, too, but that was the thing with human relationships. They were so wonderfully complicated and messy. Their emotions were never simple, and they created chaos where often there didn't need to be any. But they also loved fiercely, and they were capable of such deep, abiding passion.

Or, they used to be. She set the book aside as the warmth of that happy ending faded. Now, she wasn't so sure. There was so much anger, so much desperation and entitlement in the world. She brushed the thought away like an errant fly. She needed to spend her time thinking of something to save her show, not brooding on the state of humanity. She was already doing her best to help them. She just needed to do more.

Chapter Four

"You can fuck right off. There's no chance in hell or anywhere else in the universe. You're clearly out of your goddammed mind." Kit tossed the sweaty, wet towel against the wall, narrowly missing another gym goer, who threw her a dirty look. She threw one back.

"Kit, listen to me—"

"No. If I need to come say it to your face, I will. But you don't want me to do that." She punched the locker, startling the woman across from her, who scurried away.

"Kit, I'm not asking as a friend. I'm telling you as your boss. This is going to happen, so suck it up. The muse's show is tanking, and they need a new spin. Your show is doing okay, but it could do a hell of a lot better. Pairing you up makes sense. It'll give both of you a new spin that audiences will eat up."

"So, because her shit show is doing shitty, I have to give up my show, which isn't shit. That's what you're saying?"

"Kit." His tone was bordering on patiently patronizing. "Your show is good, but feedback shows that the audience finds you really intense, and sometimes they don't want really intense. They want the information without it being so…intense."

She exploded. "The world is fucking intense! Have you not noticed? There are fucking gods walking around, and we still have poverty, and death, and violence. Unlike fucking Clio Ardalides, I know it isn't all fucking unicorns shitting rainbows and puking lollipops."

"I'd like to see that one day. Maybe it'll happen." His tone softened. "I know you don't want this, and frankly, I get it. But we're going to have to bend on this, Kit. It's coming from way higher than either of our pay grades."

"And if I refuse? If I quit?"

He was silent for a moment. "That's your choice, but you signed a contract, and you'd be in breach. We could fight it, but we'd lose."

She slumped onto the wooden bench between the lockers. "God damn it."

"We'll meet Tuesday morning to iron out the details. My office, ten."

"Yeah. Okay. Sorry for being a bitch." She stared at the towel she'd thrown at the wall. She too felt sweaty and thrown against a wall.

"I'm used to it after all these years," he said and ended the call. She rested her head in her hands. "God damn it."

Tuesday morning came around too soon. "Do you want a police escort? Move!" She yelled at a driver who couldn't seem to use the gas pedal. Truth Spotter headquarters was in the Embarcadero, and although she loved her job, she found the high-rises that were often shrouded in fog oppressive. She hit the elevator button for the tenth floor and looked up from her scuffed old Nikes when she heard someone call for her to hold the doors. When she saw Clio hurrying toward her in a cloud of yellow material, she jammed the close button repeatedly and shrugged apologetically as the doors closed just as Clio got there.

She allowed herself some measure of pleasure as she stepped out of the elevator and into the lobby. She waved at the receptionist and then made her way to her producer's office. Jameson Jagson, or Jag, as everyone called him, was a golden boy who knew just how to get what he needed from people. He was sought after and well respected. Right now, Kit wanted to push him out the window.

She looked in his office, but he wasn't there, so she headed to the conference room. Probably the only room big enough to handle Clio's ego. She entered and saw Jag sitting with two other people. He stood and shook her hand. "Kit, this is Clio's agent and her show's producer." They shook her hands in turn, and she got the usual read on them. Industry professionals with the warmth and charisma of wet sand.

She poured herself a coffee and smiled to herself when she heard the door open and Clio come in, sounding irritated. She turned and gave her a smile over the coffee cup, but Clio just glared back at her before turning away to shake Jag's hand.

"Sorry I'm late. Traffic, and then I missed the elevator." A chair pulled out noisily as Clio dragged it from under the table. "Can I get a coffee too, please?"

Kit pointedly sat down and sipped her coffee without answering.

Jag rolled his eyes and got up himself. He took care of everyone's drinks as the others sat there in silence. Once he'd sat back down, Clio looked around.

"What is this about, then? Why are we meeting?"

Kit spluttered on her coffee and looked at the other three. "You haven't even told her yet?"

Clio looked at Kit. "Told me what?"

Kit tilted her head at Jag. She wasn't about to be the one to break the good news.

The producer of Clio's show gave her a smile as fake as his hair plugs. "Clio, as you know, the ratings for your show have dropped drastically—"

"I'm aware." Clio crossed her arms. "I was told we had time to figure out our next move."

He nodded, seeming unperturbed by her interruption. "And that was true. But we've come up with a solution that will make everyone happy."

Kit grunted and played with a sugar cube, spinning it around on the table.

"I know who you are," Clio said, staring at her hard. "You're the reporter who goes around picking at everything, making it look like nothing in the world is good anymore."

Kit leaned forward. "Nothing *is* good anymore. You're the one with the show that hides the ugly truth that the gods are next to useless. Your bias is unbelievable."

Clio's cheeks turned pink. "How dare you talk about bias? You only show the bad, never the good. It's like you go out of your way to show the darkness. At least I bring some light."

"Your light, as you put it, is as good as those old fluorescent strip lights that give people migraines."

"I give people hope." Clio was half standing now as she glared daggers at Kit. "I make them laugh."

"And you leave out anything that doesn't make your guests look good. Famine and plague? Let's skip over that and talk about how cute their cats are. For the muse of history, you damn sure have a narrow view of the present." Kit, too, was standing now, her palms hard on the table.

Jag cleared his throat loudly. "And now our reason for being here." He waited, but neither Kit nor Clio sat down, and they continued to glare at one another. "Please. Don't make this harder than it is."

They sat and Kit leaned back. "This isn't going to work."

Clio's agent looked vaguely apologetic. "Clio, honey, we're combining your show and Kit's. *Clio and Kit's Truth Hunt*. Doesn't it sound great?" She winced when Clio just stared at her. "The thing is, like you've both just said, you approach the gods and what they do in very different ways. And that's fire, which people will love. On screen, you're going to absolutely pop together. Clio, you'll continue to have lots of fun with the gods, and, Kit, you can jump in and ask them what they're doing now and dig into the meat of the story. It will be fantastic."

She enunciated the various syllables like she was trying to weave a spell of agreement over them.

Clio looked stunned, and she stared from person to person until she got to Kit, which seemed to snap her out of her trance. "No. Absolutely not. You said we had time to work something out. Merging our shows isn't an option. It's…it's…"

"Ludicrous? A money grabbing ploy to keep viewers? A desperate decision made by people who don't want to upset an immortal by telling her that her show is shit and she should go back to being what she really is? Whatever that may be." Kit tilted back in her chair. "I agree completely."

Clio stood slowly, draping her obnoxiously large handbag over her arm. "I assume I don't have to agree to this right this instant."

There was silence, and Kit laughed. "See? They don't want to stand up to you in case you turn them into some fruit or vegetable. But I've already been told it's happening, whether we want it to or not." She tilted her head. "Looks like you're stuck with my special brand of reporting."

Clio took a deep breath. "I'm going to go home and consider my options. I don't need to spend my existence beside some negative nelly who will undo all the good work I've done."

Kit shook her head and closed her eyes, and then yelped as she fell backwards in her chair thanks to the tip of Clio's heel tipping it over. Clio stood over her as she lay on the floor. "I'll let you all know my decision." She walked out in a cloud of yellow gauze, like the sun leaving the office in a tantrum.

Kit righted herself and sat back down in her chair. "Well, that was fun. Why on earth didn't you tell her before she got here?"

Clio's agent motioned toward the door Clio had just gone out of. "As you can see, she might be a little resistant to change. But we thought maybe once you two were in the same room, she might change her mind."

"Why?" Kit asked, genuinely curious. None of them answered, and she finally said, "Jag?"

"They haven't said it outright, Kit, but I think it's because you're attractive, and if I'm not mistaken, you're very much Clio's type. I think they were hoping it would sway her."

Kit stared for a moment and then gave a hard laugh. "You tried using my looks to get a three-thousand-year-old muse to do what you want her to do? Jesus H, guys. Even I'm not that egotistical." She pushed up from her chair. "Let me know what she says. I'm gone."

BREY WILLOWS

"Kit, wait. Look at it as a kind of undercover operation. Clio can get you closer to the gods, to all the immortals. You'll get to look behind the curtain, and if there's a way to expose the wizards, that's going to be how you do it." Jag got up and shook her hand again.

She nodded, impressed at that bit of extra marketing. It held some truth, maybe, but she got plenty close enough. Any closer and she might lose the scope of her investigations. Like Clio, who was clearly right up the gods' butts so she couldn't tell the right from the wrong.

Kit made her way back down to the lobby and out onto the street. The sun was just cresting the buildings and she turned her face toward it. She missed open sunshine and quiet countryside. Her stomach rumbled and she decided to head to JT's for breakfast. She wanted some time to think, and JT's had great pancakes.

But when she went in, there was no way to miss the yellow cloud sitting at a table, alone, in the corner, like a rainbow being punished for being naughty. Kit was about to turn away when she saw Clio wipe her eyes.

Damn it all. She was a sucker for a woman in tears. She closed her eyes and told herself it was a bad idea, and then made her way to Clio's table. "Space for one more? I'll cry into my coffee with you."

Clio looked up and gave her a small, teary smile. "At least you could still drink yours. Mine will have mascara in it." She moved her handbag off the opposite seat. "Go ahead."

Kit went to the counter and placed her order, then went back to the table. Clio was staring out the window, and Kit couldn't help but notice how pretty she was when she didn't know she was being watched. Her skin was porcelain smooth, and her blue eyes were like the summer sky. "Want to talk about it?"

Clio didn't turn away from the window. "It feels surreal. I've had lifetimes to do all kinds of jobs. But this one felt special. And now no one likes what I'm doing, and it feels…personal. Like it's me they don't like, not just the show."

Kit shifted so they could put her pancakes down in front of her, and then she began eating. "That's a hell of a lot of importance to put on a job when you're immortal. I mean, if you only get a few measly decades, I would get it, but it's not like you don't have time to do other shows. Or other things that make people like you."

Kit wondered if she'd hit a nerve when Clio almost seemed to flinch at her words. She kept eating and waited.

"You don't want to do this either. Why are you going along with it?" Clio asked, finally looking at Kit.

She swallowed her pancake. "Because I love what I do, and I don't want it taken away from me. If working with you means I get to keep doing what I love, then so be it. Nothing is forever, at least, not for those of us who die. So, I'll suck it up and work with you until something else comes along. It isn't the end of the world. Change is inevitable."

"How pragmatic." Clio looked into Kit's eyes as though she was searching for something, an answer to a question she hadn't asked. Finally, she looked out the window again. "I'm not sure I can be so rational."

Kit shrugged and poured more maple syrup on the last of her pancakes. "Up to you. If you decide not to go ahead, then I'm in the clear. My show will keep going, and I won't be in breach of contract for jumping ship." She chewed, thinking of what Jag had said right before she left. "But if you do stick around, you'll still get to be in the spotlight, and you'll double your audience by doing it with me."

"You assume our audiences are different."

Kit scoffed. "Please. Of course they are. Your audience wants tripe. My audience wants steak."

Clio tilted her head and stole a piece of bacon off Kit's plate, nearly getting a fork in the top of her hand for her audacity. "Do you always see things in such a black-and-white fashion? Do you ever see shades of gray? Overlap?"

Kit shook her head. "Nope. There's right and there's wrong. There are good decisions and bad choices. Things are good or they're bad."

Clio finished the strip of bacon and wiped her fingertips daintily on the napkin. "I think we're going to fight a lot."

Kit pushed her plate away. "Yeah. Well, at least we're not married. We'll be able to leave one another at the end of each day so we can punch walls and drink away our sorrow at being forced to work together."

Clio laughed, and it made Kit smile. It sounded a little like soft bells. Kit stood and held out her hand. "So, should we go back to the office and tell them they've got a firestorm on their hands?"

Clio hesitated, and then she took Kit's hand and stood. "I have conditions."

Kit rolled her eyes and let go of Clio's hand, which was too small, and too soft, and fit too well in her own. "Of course you do."

They walked back to the office, and Kit noticed the looks Clio got along the way. Most were admiring, a few were confused, probably by the outfit of yellow puff, and a couple were disparaging. Kit was used to blending in for the most part, preferring to keep the camera on whatever news story she was focused on, and the attention Clio garnered was a little unsettling, given the nature of their upcoming venture.

They took the elevator up to the office, and Kit asked the receptionist if Jag was available. She called his office, and they were told to go in.

He was sitting at his desk, and Kit didn't miss the tired look in his eyes before he masked it with a smile. "I definitely didn't expect to see you both again today. And not together."

They sat opposite his desk. "Kit has convinced me that this isn't a good idea, in any way, but it's one we have to run with anyway."

Jag frowned, obviously bemused. "Not exactly a ringing endorsement, but okay."

"And Clio has *conditions*," Kit said.

Clio threw her a mildly dirty look before turning back to Jag. "Do I need my agent here, or can I trust you to take down my requirements and pass them on to her and the producers?"

He picked up a pen and pulled a piece of paper forward. "I'm at your command."

She held up her finger. "First of all, I want it noted that we're both doing this because we've been forced to. That if it weren't for that, we'd be continuing with our own shows."

Kit very nearly mentioned the fact that Clio wouldn't have a show at all but bit her tongue when Jag gave her a warning glance.

"Second, I want the shows pre-recorded. That way if something happens that I don't agree with, or if Kit gets too gloom and doom, we can edit it."

"Hey now. You don't get to decide which version of the truth people see. They see it all, or they don't see any of it." Kit tapped the desk hard.

"Fine. We'll make it benefit you as well." She looked at Jag. "Kit, too, has the option to edit the video if she feels I've taken too optimistic a view on things."

"You mean if you've whitewashed things and sandbagged the ugly history and truth of the present." Kit broke the pencil she was playing with. "Fine. I agree to that."

Jag's eyebrows were raised as he wrote so fast it looked like chicken scratch. "What else?"

Clio hesitated. "If the show doesn't do well, then I'm the one to leave. Kit goes back to having her show on her terms."

Kit looked up from the broken pencil, surprised. "That's magnanimous of you."

Clio looked hurt. "Despite what you may think of me, I'm not a bad person. And it's my show which is in trouble, not yours. You don't deserve to go down with the ship, if that's what happens."

Jag waited for Kit to nod, and then he wrote that down too. "Next?"

Clio seemed to be thinking, so Kit spoke up. "I want access. Not just to some powdered version of whatever it is we're covering, but to the deeper stuff too. I want to be able to ask direct questions."

Clio hesitated. "I can only agree to that to a point."

Kit started to argue, but Clio held up her hand.

"Not because I don't want you to ask questions, but because some of the gods or immortals we talk to might be...impulsive when it comes to sensitive questions. I need to be able to stop you if

I think you're placing yourself in danger. I have it on good authority that living as a sentient tree is unpleasant."

Once again, Kit was surprised by Clio's forethought. "That's fair."

Jag wrote it down. "We can talk paychecks and all that in contracts. Is there anything else?"

Kit looked at Clio, who shook her head. Her shoulders were slightly slumped, and she looked tired. Why did she feel the need to bundle her up and take her somewhere she could get comfortable? Instead, she stood, nearly knocking her chair back. "Then we're done. I'm going to go to the gym to punch a bag really hard. Let me know when we're meeting next." She looked down at Clio. "Maybe this won't be so bad, huh?"

Clio gave another tremulous smile. "No. Maybe not."

Kit gave a quick thumbs up and left, wondering what possessed her to give a thumbs up like some frat boy. Working with a muse would be interesting. Would it up her game? That's what having a muse did, wasn't it? But then, Clio wasn't *her* muse. She was just *a* muse. A beautiful, soft, surprisingly considerate woman who happened to be immortal. She rubbed her temple and headed toward the gym. She had a feeling the punching bag was going to get a lot of use in the near future.

CHAPTER FIVE

C lio sat at the first-class airport bar, sipping a glass of champagne. It was their first foray, and she checked again for her passport and the script she'd prepared.

"Why do immortals need passports?" Kit asked as she slid onto the stool beside her. "Can't you all travel on clouds or poofs of air or something? And who is going to tell you that you can't enter a country? Or a country's clouds, or whatever?" She ordered a beer.

Clio looked her over. Her shirt looked like it had been trapped under a tire overnight, and her shoes had mud on them. "Did you sleep in an alley last night?"

Kit looked down and tugged at her shirt. "My maid was too busy cleaning the eleven bathrooms in my house to do the ironing too."

Clio shook her head and turned back to her drink. "Immortals have passports because we do travel among you. Sometimes one god needs to go to another god's domain, and it's simply a courtesy to use a passport so that god is alerted to the other god's presence. It helps keep the peace."

Kit sipped her beer and Clio tried to ignore the way the wrinkled shirt pulled at her rather developed biceps.

"But you're a muse. That's a whole different thing, right? Aren't you allowed to travel anywhere you want?"

Clio pushed her champagne away. Clearly, talks with Kit were going to require a clear head. "Yes, I am. But the Merge agreement says that all immortals are tracked when they're planet bound, as a way to keep everyone safe and to avoid inter-religious strife. That includes me and my sisters, even though we don't have powers typically associated with immortal beings as a whole. And yes, newbie gods all have passports too. Explaining at security that you're an immortal is time-consuming. Better to just have the right paperwork."

It looked like Kit was about to ask another question, but the flight attendant came over and touched Clio's shoulder. "It's time to board, Clio. Is this your guest?"

Clio picked up her bag. "This is Kit. She's going to be traveling with us for the foreseeable future, Sian. Please treat her as you would me." She gave a wicked grin. "But not exactly as you'd treat me. I don't like to share."

Sian laughed and shook Kit's hand. "Sorry to say you're not my type. But I'm glad to have you on board, Kit. I'm a big fan of your show, I hope you don't mind me saying. I'm Clio's personal flight attendant. Anything you need, you just let me know, and if I can't get it, I'll find someone who will."

Kit looked a little bewildered. "Personal flight attendant? You fly with your own staff?"

Clio frowned. "Well, I can't very well attend to my own flight, can I?" She followed Sian out the doors and onto the tarmac, where her personal plane was waiting.

Kit grabbed her arm. "What is this?"

Clio pulled away. "It's a plane. Were you planning on walking to Milwaukee?"

"I have tickets for United. This isn't United."

Clio shuddered. "Gods. Why would I fly in a plane full of people when I have one of my own?" She pulled Kit's ticket from her hand and flapped it at her. "You're welcome to go catch your flight full of germs and body odor. I can, however, tell you that my plane smells lovely, has gorgeous staff, and will give us the quiet and the room to work while we travel so that we're not wasting time." She turned and walked away. "Your choice," she called over her shoulder.

She climbed the steps and smiled when she felt the reverberation behind her telling her Kit was following.

"Are you serious?" Kit stood in the aisle looking around. "This is a flying living room."

Clio put her handbag in the locker beside the couch and sat down on the white leather. "What's the point of having your own plane if you can't fly comfortably?"

Kit continued to mutter and shake her head as she too stowed her hand luggage in the locker and sat on the sofa opposite Clio's.

"Does the extravagance bother you?" Clio asked.

"Yeah, it does. Think of how much you could have helped some village somewhere with the money you spent on this, just so you don't have to fly with other people." Kit folded her arms and glared at her.

"I'll have you know, I've done my fair share of helping villages and people all over the world. In three thousand years, I've seen and done more than you ever could." She pulled out a file and slapped it on the desk. "And if you're going to be all judgy, feel free not to travel with me. We can meet up at the interview sites. You can travel with the camera crew. I'm sure you'd find their company more to your liking."

Kit's jaw clenched as she sat there, her arms folded. She looked like she wanted to swear and hit something but wasn't giving in to either impulse. They were silent until the plane was in the air.

Sian came over and placed Clio's favorite drink when she was flying in front of her and then turned to Kit. "How about for you?"

"Whisky?" Kit said, blatantly looking Sian over.

"I've got two on board today. I'll bring them over for you."

After she left, Kit focused on Clio. "So that's your type, huh? Short hair, big smile?"

Clio looked back at Sian, who was placing bottles on a tray. "I've had different types over the years. But yes, that's been my type for some time. But it isn't just the hair, or the muscles, or the fact that she has the stamina of a train." She glanced at Kit and saw her roll her eyes, a habit she seemed to have. "She's also kind. She has this lightness about her, and everything just rolls off her back. Nothing is ever a problem and she's always happy to see me."

Sian came over with the trolley, and there were two bottles on it. She picked one up. "This is the Dalmore 62. It's over a century old, and the decanter itself is made of platinum and crystal." She held up the other bottle. "And this is the Highland Park Old Twisted Tattoo, a more recent one but damn near as good, if I do say so myself."

Kit shook her head. "I'm definitely not drinking a whisky that it would take the lotto to buy. I'll have the Highland, thanks."

Sian poured it into a rocks glass and smiled at Clio. "Lunch will be in about an hour, if that's okay with you?"

Clio returned Sian's sweet smile. "Perfect. Thank you."

Sian left them, and they stared at one another for a long moment. Kit took a sip of her whisky and made an appreciative sound.

"She's right, this is excellent." She nodded at Clio's glass. "I assume you're having some kind of champagne made from the tears of baby rabbits and the sap of trees on Olympus?"

Clio laughed at the description, even though it was insulting. "It's ginger ale, smart-ass. My stomach always gets a little funny when I fly, so I sip really cold ginger ale. It helps." She tilted her head thoughtfully. "Although creating a drink like the one you suggest would probably be a gold mine."

Kit looked suitably chastised. "I'm sorry, Clio. I'm not usually such an ass." She tilted her glass toward her. "But you do have a whisky on this plane that would sell for thousands."

Clio shrugged. "I do. But the thing is, I bought it the year it was made. It cost about thirty dollars, in today's money. I like collecting different types of alcohol from every century. I don't really drink, but I love the artistry and care that people put into it, year after year." She drew shapes in the condensation on her glass. "They're little reminders of history, of the people who have lived before."

Kit didn't seem to know what to say to that and Clio took a moment to enjoy having finally stumped her. "Anyway, shall we discuss today's interview?" She opened the file and handed over the photo. "That's Joan of Arc Chapel, where the meeting is being held."

Kit looked up from the photo. "It isn't a meeting, Clio. It's a protest."

Clio sighed. "Do we need to argue over every word?"

Kit took a big swallow of her whisky. "We do. How can you, someone who has witnessed history, not understand the importance of words? Of nuance?"

It was a stab, a simple one that cut deep, but she wouldn't let it show. "Fine. It's a protest." She flipped her notes sheets. "We know the Christian and Catholic gods' representatives will be there—"

"But not God himself. As usual."

Clio closed her eyes and forced herself to count to ten. "I'm not going to discuss immortal politics with you, Kit. Can we just do this?" She waved a page of notes.

Kit shrugged and leaned back against the couch without saying anything else.

"Anyway. Also in attendance will be Penia, the spirit of poverty. She's long been retired, but she has come out of retirement to become politically active, along with her sisters, Ame and Tok."

Kit grinned. "Fighting on my side."

Clio shook her head. "We're not on different sides."

Sian came forward and topped up Kit's whisky after getting a nod of thanks, and she added a bottle of water to it. "Wouldn't want you to get dehydrated before you get to work." She winked.

"Hey, let me ask you, Sian. You've worked with Clio for a long time, right? And I assume you've gotten to know some of the other gods?"

Sian nodded, but Clio didn't miss the flash of discomfort in her eyes. "I have."

"Would you say we're on different sides? That when it comes to things like poverty and pandemics and politics, that we see things differently from them?"

Clio smirked. She knew full well what Sian would say. She'd always been on Clio's side.

Sian held up her hands. "Hey now, buddy. Don't go getting me fired. I like this lifestyle." Her laugh was uneasy. "I'll go see how lunch is coming along."

Clio grabbed her hand before she could walk away. "Sian? Do you truly feel like there's that kind of divide?" After all the intimacy they'd shared, she couldn't believe it.

Sian covered Clio's hand with her own. "Sweet thing, I try not to think about it, honestly. But you have to know we're different, right?" She kissed Clio's hand. "It's not bad, or wrong. It just is." She let go and headed to the back once again.

Clio sat back and tried to blink away the tears. She thought she'd known Sian so well, and to find out she thought like Kit did hurt in a way she wasn't prepared for. She turned back to the file. "Milwaukee is the fifth poorest city in the US. The protest is being held to ask why poverty still exists." She closed the file. "I suppose you'll have plenty of questions of your own."

Kit just raised her eyebrows in response.

They sat in silence, and Clio couldn't say anything more that wouldn't bring on the tears. Sian came out with the trolley again, this time with two large plates piled high with colorful food.

"Salmon with a blackberry coulis and boiled potatoes for you," she said as she set down Clio's plate. "And for you, black truffle mushroom risotto with a generous helping of parmesan." She set down Kit's plate and looked between them. "Anything else for the moment?"

Clio shook her head and picked up her fork, though she wasn't hungry now.

Kit sat still, looking at her food. "What's this?"

Sian smiled but looked a little confused. "It's black—"

"No. I mean, how did you know I liked this? It's my favorite dish." Kit looked at Clio.

She concentrated on her salmon. "I called your agent and asked so that you'd have food you liked on the trip. It's one of the perks of having a private plane." She spoke softly, still stung from what felt like betrayal. Did no one actually like her for who she was? For what she was? The tears began to fall, and she wiped them away with her napkin.

Sian sat beside her and pulled her into a side hug. "Clio, I'm sorry if I hurt you. Can we just blame the irksome reporter?" She kissed Clio's temple. "I don't care that you're immortal and see things differently. You're sweet, kind, and generous. It isn't your fault if other people can't see that." She nodded at Kit. "They will, if they get to know you like I have."

Clio could breathe again. She understood better now what Sian had meant, and it was true, it was Kit's fault. "Take her dinner away from her, would you, Sian? Troublemakers don't get to eat."

Sian laughed and stood. "She's already started eating, so I'm afraid you'll have to save that punishment until we're headed home. I'll make sure she doesn't get the lemon meringue pie you ordered for her."

Kit looked up from the risotto she was practically inhaling. "I love lemon meringue," she mumbled around a mouthful of food.

Clio shook her head and continued to eat. The food was exquisite, as always. When Kit was done, she groaned and sat back with her hands over her stomach. "That was the best risotto I've ever had."

Her food half-eaten, Clio pushed the plate away. "I'll let Edesia know the next time I see her. She's the go-to for all of us who travel a lot."

Kit nodded and slipped sideways on the couch after kicking off her boots. She closed her eyes and tucked her hands behind her head. "Thank you, Clio. It was really thoughtful of you." She opened one eye. "Please don't take away my lemon meringue."

Clio laughed. How could she continue to be angry at an extremely sexy woman with a sharp wit and the body of a gym rat? "Fine. But I'm letting you know now. Food will always be held to ransom on these trips. Behave, or you eat peanuts."

Kit closed her eye and yawned. "Deal."

If only it would be that easy. Clio knew full well that nothing would stop Kit from getting at whatever truth needed to be uncovered, no matter how messy or uncomfortable it might be. She stared out the window at the thick cloud layer below. But things weren't that simple. They never had been, but the world had changed so drastically that it was especially true now. She glanced at Kit when she heard her shift. She was lying on her side, one arm bent beneath her head. She looked serious even in her sleep, but now Clio could take her time and really look at her.

Her brown hair was cut short around the sides but left a little long on top and was obviously professionally done. Likely a result of her career rather than any desire to pay attention to her appearance. Her biceps pushed against the arms of her shirt, which had ridden up just enough to show a flat, muscular stomach. Her legs, encased in worn jeans that fit her just right, looked strong.

"I think sex would make our relationship difficult, but if you look at me like that any longer, I'm going to show Sian how it's really done."

Clio's gaze snapped up to Kit's face, and her face heated when she saw Kit staring at her with a little wicked grin.

"I was trying to figure out how to get the dirt from your clothes out of my white sofa," Clio said, turning away. How mortifying.

"Yup. That's what your expression said, for sure." Kit flipped onto her other side. "Now you can stare at my ass."

Clio threw a throw pillow at her, making her laugh. Under different circumstances they might have been able to develop something. If they weren't always at one another's throats. She took a quick peek. It really was a very nice ass.

CHAPTER SIX

K it took in the atmosphere of the protest. There was nothing like a group of people gathering to demand answers, to demand better, to demand change. The air crackled with electricity, and she gripped her notebook hard. The camera crew had already been there for hours, shooting extra footage, and she checked in with them and had a look at what they had so far.

Strangely, Clio hung back. In her navy-blue skirt suit she didn't stand out the way she usually did, and it occurred to Kit that she wasn't being her usual flamboyant self. Soon, though, some people recognized her and crowded around. A few asked for autographs, and some took selfies. But then the protesters got involved and the atmosphere changed. They started shouting questions at her, asking how she was making the world better.

Kit moved to Clio's side and held up her hand for their attention. Clio leaned into her. She looked calm enough, but Kit felt her arm tremble. "Hey, all. You're asking the right questions, and Clio and I are so glad we're here to cover your protest."

Murmurs went through the crowd as they recognized Kit, and she gave them a quick smile. "Remember where to focus your anger, though. Clio isn't in charge." Kit pointed at the chapel. "Those guys in there are the ones you need to get answers from."

The crowd seemed to turn as one, and the chanting and sign waving resumed. Kit felt Clio's body relax slightly.

"Thank you." She squeezed Kit's hand quickly. "I haven't been in the midst of real turmoil in a long time. It took me by surprise."

Kit searched Clio's expression. "Are you okay now?"

Clio took a shaky breath. "I am. I just have to get used to this new role, don't I?"

"We both do." They looked up when a bell sounded. "Let's go inside."

The camera crew followed them into the chapel, which was fit to bursting with all the people stuffed inside. The protesters were all outside, however. Inside were a motley crew of politicians and civil servants, along with three women who were clearly part of the immortal set. When they saw Clio, they came over and gave her the kiss of greeting on both cheeks.

"Kit, I'd like you to meet Penia, Ame, and Tok. The spirits of poverty, lack of resource, and begging."

Kit shook their hands. "I didn't know such a thing existed."

Ame frowned. "I'm not sure we're things, but we do exist."

Kit held up her hands. "My apologies. That came out wrong. I love that you're leading this protest, and I love your shirts."

Their T-shirts were made up of artful statistics about poverty and race that formed a peace symbol.

Penia looked tense. "Thank you. We're selling them outside if you want one. The money we raise will go to helping the local homeless shelters."

Kit nodded, impressed. Why hadn't she come across this type of immortal before? "Can I ask you something? Why are you retired? Doesn't that mean you don't work anymore?"

Tok, who never seemed to stop looking around, answered. "No. Gods and spirits retire when people stop believing in them, when they stop being paid attention to. And people stopped caring about poverty, resources, and beggars a long time ago. But that doesn't mean we're not doing what we can."

Penia nodded. "Now that we don't have to hide that we're immortal, we can be out on the streets doing real good."

Kit wanted to punch the air. "Fantastic. And how do you—"

"Isn't this fantastic?" Clio stepped past Kit and tugged at Ame's T-shirt so it could be seen clearly by the camera crew. "I think every city needs something like this to raise awareness. We can start raising money right now!" She looked directly at the camera. "If you're in the area, come grab one of these fantastic T-shirts. If they run out, I'll be sure to get some more, and you can contact the show directly to get yours."

Clio's focus on fashion stalled the conversation, and Kit had to find her train of thought again. But before she could, Clio turned and motioned at the chapel.

"Isn't this stunning? I remember when it was built. Do you, girls?" They blinked at Clio without answering but it didn't put her off her stride. "I can't believe they moved it stone by stone from France. Isn't it wonderful how history finds a way to survive?"

The bell tolled again, and the room grew silent. Clio moved to Kit's side while the three sisters took their place at the front of the room. The raised stage made it possible to see from anywhere, and when the two people moved to stand on the stage, Kit nearly laughed out loud.

Two angels stood there in plain black suits trimmed in white, with white wings outspread, looking for all the world like they were bored shitless. They didn't even pretend to look down at the people watching. Rather, they focused in on the three sisters. "We're here to take your questions on behalf of our Fathers."

The sisters stood together. "This is the fifth poorest state in America, one of the largest sectors for Christianity. We want answers as to why poverty, the lack of resources, and the need to beg remain issues."

There were shouts of agreement from the crowd. The reps barely blinked. "The two gods have agreed on the following statement." They both raised their arms like they were delivering a sermon. "We are not to blame for the politics of your country which keep you bound to a system which feeds on itself like a snake eating its tail. You cannot pray to be lifted out of poverty. Not enough of you pray for the same thing, and so those prayers go unanswered because they are unasked. The same goes for resources. Which resources would you have replenished? And for whom? They will simply be taken away again by the political system you have put in place. Fix the political system and the issues you complain about will resolve themselves in time."

They lowered their arms in a choreographed movement and stepped back, lowering their wings. The crowd, silent while they listened, began to rumble, and then shouts began in earnest. Fury and incredulity were flung at the reps like knives. But they'd clearly completed their duty, and they turned to leave.

Kit grabbed Clio's hand. "We need to interview them before they leave."

Together, they pushed through the crowd and out into the open, the camera crew right behind them. They moved quickly around the side of the building. There was no guarantee they were still around, but Kit had to try.

There was no one at the back door. "Fuck," Kit said.

But Clio was looking around, her head tilted almost like she was listening to something. "This way. I can hear them talking." She turned and headed down the tree lined path that led away from the chapel. It opened onto a large walkway, and across from it, standing beside the statue of Mary, were the two reps.

"Are they smoking a joint?" Kit asked as one rep passed it to the other.

"I'm sure it's just a cigarette. Or something holy, like…sage."

Kit looked away from the reps to stare at Clio. "Yeah, because so many people smoke sage."

They walked toward the reps, one of whom quickly threw the joint down and ground it out with his pearly white boot.

"Hey, guys. Kit and Clio from *Truth Hunt* here. Do you have a second?"

They looked like they were going to say no, but then one focused on Clio. "Hey. You're the muse with the TV show. The one that makes us laugh." His voice was husky and most definitely lacked the gravitas it had held only minutes ago. "We'll totally chat. Want us to do something funny? Look, I can do a handstand on my wings!" He proved his claim by dropping into a handstand, and then using the points of his wings to hold himself up. Until, that is, he lost his balance and toppled over at Mary's cement feet.

The other rep began laughing so hard he was snorting. "That was awesome."

"Guys, if we could just ask you about that protest and what you had to say?" Kit tried again.

The guy at Mary's feet struggled into a sitting position. "Go for it. Clio's awesome."

"And so pretty." The other rep batted his long lashes at her.

"Aw, aren't you sweet," Clio said with a saccharine smile. "Can you tell us a little about what you said back there? Maybe explain what the bosses mean about political systems?"

The rep still standing frowned like he was trying to make sense of the world around him. "I don't really know, you know? You know how they talk up there, all riddles and mysteries. Like it makes them sound extra smart or whatever." He shrugged and plopped down on the statue's base next to his friend.

"But *you* know, Clio. Right? You know." The other rep nodded. "They can only make certain changes, and the prayers have to be really specific, and they only work for big change when enough people come at it from exactly the same direction. But humans…" He shook his head, his expression suggesting it might be the saddest thing ever. "They don't get it, right? They can never agree on anything."

The other nodded. "So, round and round they go."

Kit stepped forward. "You're saying that it's people's own fault that they live in poverty? That they're reduced to begging?"

They both frowned at her, and the one with his handstand wings fluffed them. "See? You humans don't listen. It's not the poor people's fault. It's the fault of the people in power who make things all unequal and stuff. Get rid of those people and that system and change is inev…inevet…" He sighed. "You've killed my buzz. Let's go."

"Inevitable," Kit said as she and Clio and the camera crew watched the reps fly off, their bright white wings soon lost against the pale blue sky.

"It's sensible," said Clio. "And it's a good answer that people probably needed to hear from a higher power. Change has to happen here, where it matters. Democracy is a beautiful thing, and if employed right, things will be different." She smiled brightly. "The protest worked, and now there are some answers to be thought through. What a great day!"

Kit stared at her, baffled. "Is that really how you see it?" When Clio looked at her blankly, Kit pinched the bridge of her nose. "That wasn't an answer at all. It was the gods passing the buck, blaming humans and telling them to fix things themselves. What good are they, what good is prayer and belief, if the gods don't do a damn thing to help people?"

Clio squared off with her. "But they have helped. They've provided a pragmatic solution. And you heard the reps—"

"The high as a kite reps?"

"Again, we don't know what they were smoking." Clio glared at her. "Prayer must be specific and clear from a large group of people. Surely there isn't an entity who could grant everyone who ever prayed to win the lottery what they want? It wouldn't work. So it needs to be clear and from enough people so that the god can step in."

"What do you call all those people in there?" Kit pointed back at the church, where chanting could still be heard.

"I call it a group of people who got an answer they aren't sure what to do with yet. But they all come to the question from very different backgrounds and needs." Clio looked at the camera, her expression sweet. "Sometimes parents have to make us do things for ourselves so we can keep that going into the future."

"Jesus H Christ." Kit stared up at the statue of Mary. "Could you sound any more patronizing?" She turned to the camera crew. "Come on, let's go back to the protest and do some interviews there."

They walked back to the chapel without speaking. As they made their way through the crowd, talking to protesters and getting snippets of people's stories, Kit noticed that Clio hung back. When the crowd had thinned and they had enough footage, she turned to find Clio sitting at the base of a tree.

"Did you just give up? Or did you decide that asking what designer label people were wearing wasn't going to work here?"

Clio pulled at the grass and let it fall through her fingertips. "This isn't going to work."

Kit groaned and leaned against the tree. "This again?"

Clio shook her head. "You don't understand. I don't have a place here. I don't want all this ugliness. I don't want anger and desperation. I've had my share. There aren't words that are going to help this situation. At least, not any from me." She pushed up from the ground. "Can we leave?"

Kit nodded. The camera crew said they'd get a few more shots and then head back to the airport. Clio got into the back seat of the black sedan that had brought them to the chapel and Kit followed. The ride to the private plane was made in silence. Kit wasn't sure what to say. She felt bad for the jibe about Clio not having anything to say, and her sadness was almost palpable. Handling emotions in high pressure situations was one thing. Handling them coming from a sad muse was like withholding love from a puppy.

They got on the plane, and Sian clearly read the situation quickly. They got strapped in, and then were quickly airborne. Once they were at altitude, Sian brought out a strangely colored blanket which she draped over Clio, who smiled at her gratefully. Kit mentally traced the pattern until she figured it out.

"Alice in Wonderland?"

Clio smoothed the blanket over her legs. "That's what the world feels like. Upside down and inside out. The blanket is a kind of comfort thing. It helps me remember that it's all an adventure, even when nothing makes sense."

Kit shook her head when Sian held up the whisky bottle. "Cherry Coke, if you have it?" Sian nodded and brought back Clio's ginger ale and Kit's Coke, then she made herself scarce.

"What did you mean back there?" Kit asked.

"When?" Clio had her eyes closed and her head rested against the soft leather.

"You said you'd had your share. What do you mean?"

Clio's eyes opened. "I'm the muse of history, Kit."

"Yeah, but what does that mean? You don't create history. You don't influence people who are going to make history, right?"

"I inspire those who record history to do it well, and with as little bias as possible. Some bias is always inevitable, but still. I inspire people who have written down other people's words, other people's ideas, and the nature of other people's lives. It's those people who need me, who use what I am to guide them into the truest version of history they can record. I also help with the creation of things meant to live on into the future, like the Joan of Arc chapel, or the basilica in Milan. I inspire the creators to build the most perfect version of what they can imagine."

Kit pondered that while sipping her drink. "So, what did you mean?"

"History isn't exactly full of roses and lavender, is it?" She pulled the blanket tighter around her. "It's full of war, and strife, and death. It's full of humans being unbelievably cruel to each other over everything from land and power to wanting a parking space at Christmas. I stand with the people who record history, and if there isn't anyone, I do it myself." She looked at Kit, her eyes tired. "I recorded the plague. The Black Death. World Wars. Vietnam. Civil wars. The witch trials all over the world, where I heard the women screaming as they were burned." She closed her eyes again. "Blame me if you want to, but I'm tired of the ugliness of this world. I just wanted to bring something good to it. Maybe you're right. Maybe there's nothing good left."

It was so unlike the Clio that Kit knew, this depressed version. Not once had she given any thought to what Clio might have experienced in her lifetime. Of all the muses, maybe being the muse of history was the worst.

Sian came over and placed a huge slice of lemon meringue pie in front of her. "It's best to let her process when she's like this," she whispered. "Let me know if you need anything else," she said in a normal tone.

Kit nodded and saw that Clio had moved to a large leather recliner. She put it almost all the way down and then curled up under her blanket with her back to Kit.

The lemon meringue pie was the best Kit had ever had, but she couldn't enjoy it fully. She hated that she'd made Clio feel bad and seeing Clio so morose was like seeing a depressed kitten in a pound. She finished her pie and then took the recliner opposite Clio's and closed her eyes.

She checked her watch when she woke to turbulence and saw that they were nearly back. Clio was still lying down, but now she was facing her.

"Sorry for being an Eeyore. It just gets to me sometimes." She spoke softly, her gaze open and trusting.

"I get it. I'm sorry for making it worse." Kit barely kept from reaching out to touch Clio's soft-looking cheek. "Can I ask you something else?"

Clio nodded and pillowed her cheek on her hand. "Sure."

"What is virtue?"

Clio laughed. "What do you mean?"

"I mean, what is it? I know the dictionary definition, I think, but what does it mean to you?" Kit hoped she wasn't opening another can of stupid.

Clio thought for a moment, her gaze unfocused. "Marcus Aurelius once said, when we were discussing this very question, that virtue meant a life lived with courage, purpose, and devotion. I think that's true. But I think it's more than that. It's caring about the world more than yourself. It's helping people even if it inconveniences you or if it doesn't benefit you. It's having the backbone to stand up for people who can't stand up for themselves." She focused again, this time on Kit. "It sounds a little simplistic, but that's how I see it."

Kit thought about it. "So, how are you a muse of that?"

"I bring it out in people who already have those elements in place. And in people who don't, maybe I can help add it to their world in some way."

"And is it automatic? Like, just being around someone makes it happen? Or do you have to focus it on someone?" It was strange to think that being around Clio might change her. She wasn't interested in changing.

"Both, I guess. When I spend a lot of time in large groups, I can effect small changes in everyone there. For instance, I spent time in ancient Greece listening to the great philosophers of the time. Their ideas of virtue were discussed at length and their desire to record things word for word was influenced by me. But the crowd who listened were able to more accurately absorb what they were saying because of my presence too, even though I wasn't focused on them."

Sian came out to let them know they were about to land, breaking the conversation and giving Kit time to think about what Clio had shared. Again, what did that mean for their time together? Even though the changes Clio brought about in people were, in theory, good ones, she didn't like the idea of someone changing her without her having any say in it. But what choice did she have? They were stuck together. She'd simply have to be aware of anything out of character. Easy.

CHAPTER SEVEN

I can't believe the producer let you pick the next interview." Kit had been in a sour mood from the moment the car had pulled up.

"It's a good one, I promise. And remember that this is a combination of our shows. Not me just tagging along on your super downer sessions."

"And why can't I know where we're going?" Kit folded her arms and glared across at her.

"Because it's a big secret." Clio glared back. "Or maybe it's because I enjoy getting under your skin and showing you that you can't control everything." She opened the divider between them and the driver, and he handed back two drinks. "Here, grumpy butt. Mocha, no foam."

Kit took hers and sipped but continued to look cranky.

Clio shook her head and sipped her cherry latte while she flipped through the latest fashion magazine. She loved the creativity of the designs, even if many were impractical and downright odd. Like the person covered in multiple pillows. While Clio could see how that would benefit someone with narcolepsy, it wasn't terribly flattering in a more general sense.

"Sorry," Kit said a little while later. "I really hate mornings, and I hate feeling unprepared for an interview. It irks the living fuck out of me."

Clio grinned. "I know." She set the magazine aside. "Remember one of my conditions, the one about keeping you safe?"

Kit's eyes narrowed. "Yes…"

"This is going to be one of those situations where I need to take the lead. We're going to be in my territory, and I need you to be careful what you say. You can be extremely rude."

Kit's eyebrows shot up. "Rude? Direct, maybe. And I don't pull punches, sure. But rude implies—"

"It doesn't imply anything. You say things because you want to say them, and you don't care how it makes people feel or whether it might be politic to say it differently. With your black-and-white attitude and your razor-sharp sense of humor, you throw words out there like you're entitled to air your opinion without consequence, even if it hurts people." Clio seldomly told anyone off, but it needed to be said. Today's excursion could get Kit killed. Or worse, turned into some kind of flora or fauna. Or a combination of the two.

"Wow." Kit looked genuinely stunned. "That was harsh."

"See? I'm capable of being blunt too." Clio checked her watch. "We're nearly there."

The atmosphere was tense, but Clio wasn't going to back down. When the car stopped though, she smiled. "I can't wait." She threw open the door and stepped out into the dirt parking lot.

Their usual camera crew was waiting near a tree that looked as old as time itself. They waved and Clio and Kit started over.

"Where are we?"

The camera crew began to shoot.

"Welcome to Archimedes International." Clio waved at the small green hills in front of them. "This is reclaimed land, and it's being used for something really special."

They walked up the dirt path over the green hill and stopped at the top. Below was a long row of squat cement buildings, many built directly into the hillside. Laughter and noise rose from the groups of kids playing outside the buildings, along the dirt paths, and even down on the beach below the cliff.

They continued walking. "This was once called Battery O'Rourke, a fort built in the early 1900s which was closed and abandoned in 1945. After the Merge, there was a surge in youth depression and anxiety. Existential angst isn't only for grown-ups these days. Today's kids are super aware of the world around them, and while they seem to take many things in stride, they have a higher rate of suicide and self-harm than ever before in history."

"So you gave them a place to hang out? Isn't that a bit of a pat on the head?" Kit asked.

Clio glanced at her and then back at the camp they were approaching. "It isn't just a place to hang out. It's a summer camp for at-risk youth."

They arrived and the kids grew quiet as they approached.

"What the fuck," Kit murmured. "Is that a god?"

Clio waved and ran forward. "Boreas!"

He wrapped his big purple wings around her in a hug. "Welcome, sweet muse! It's good to have you here. Maybe you can inspire some of the young ones toward a more virtuous state of being."

Clio smiled and stepped back, hoping her impostor syndrome didn't show in her expression. "Thanks so much for letting us shoot today. I think the world needs to see what good work you're doing."

Boreas turned to Kit and held out his beefy hand. "Nice to meet you. I liked the work you did in Goa last year."

Kit, usually so implacable, looked taken aback. "You watch my show?"

He laughed and his wings kicked up some dust as they moved gently. "Many of us do. You're good at digging down to the core of an issue so we can understand it better. It helps us put things in motion, when we can."

If Clio could have bottled the wonder in Kit's expression, she'd have done it and kept it to look at for the rest of her days. "Not so black-and-white after all, is it?" she asked softly before turning to Boreas. "So, tell us what's going on here."

He tucked his wings back as they walked beside him toward the largest of the buildings. "When Death and her consort called a meeting to let us know about the surge in youth suicide, we knew we needed to take action. But we needed plenty of space, and we needed some time to let the Merge settle into place." They stopped as a group of teenagers ran past, shoving and laughing. One of them gave Boreas a high five as he went. "We met with the muses, all nine of them." He laughed again and winked at Kit. "If you ever want to feel outnumbered and inadequate on a whole new scale, sit with all of them at once."

Kit grimaced. "One is enough, thanks."

"The muses had some fantastic ideas, and one of them came off the back of the ACA, in Big Sur."

"That's the Ancient College of the Arts, right?" Kit asked.

"Clio's baby, if I'm not mistaken." Boreas draped his arm around her shoulders. "And that's where this place was born. The ACA is for people who want to develop their creative talents. But Archimedes is about asking questions and learning all kinds of things. And we bring in both gods and philosophers to help teach. We make it fun, too."

They stopped walking and Clio pointed. "Looks like they're having fun down there."

Kids were in the water with snorkels. A woman was in the water with them, and they seemed to be listening avidly.

"Does she have horns?" Kit squinted and held her hand above her eyes to block out the sun.

"Crab claws where you'd normally find horns. She used to only wear seaweed for clothing, but that stuff stinks and puts people off. I convinced her to use a wetsuit, and she loves it. Says it makes her feel like a dolphin." Boreas smiled fondly. "As a water deity, she's teaching them all about sea life and tides, but she's doing it in a hands-on way that the kids love."

"And they can ask her any questions they have, right?" Clio asked.

"Right. And it doesn't have to be about her specialty. The kids are encouraged to ask anything they want to of any of us, and if we can answer, we do, and as honestly as possible."

"What do you teach?" Kit asked, not taking her eyes off the water ahead.

"As a god of wind, I teach about wind." He laughed once again, and it filled the air. "Technically it's called anemology now. But I show them how winds can change weather patterns, how it helps them sail, fly, and how to make wind work for them."

They continued toward another building. "How do you choose which kids get to come here? I assume it costs a fortune, to get to study with the gods." Kit's tone was even, but there was a hint of venom beneath the surface.

Boreas raised his eyebrow and his wings twitched. "I hadn't given much thought to what it would be like to be on the receiving end of your talents, Ms. Kalloway."

Clio's pulse sped up and she moved in quickly. "And that's why you watch her show. If she didn't make people want to punch her, she wouldn't be doing her job."

He laughed and his wings relaxed. "Good thing you're here to protect her."

Kit's head snapped around and Clio gave her a friendly shrug that was a clear warning.

"In answer to your question, Kit, no. This isn't an institution based on finance. It's by recommendation. Teachers and counselors from every single school in the nation are asked to draw up a list of names of students they feel might be at risk or who need guidance. Those students are then invited here. There's no cost to them. We cover travel expenses and everything included in the week."

"And there are two other Archimedes centers going, right?" Clio asked.

"Yes! We have one on the coast of Spain, and one in Norway. We're working on putting one in Australia. We're trying to reach youth all over the world."

Kit shoved her hands in her pockets. Her brow was furrowed, as if she was trying to find the loophole.

Clio stepped to the edge of a hill and breathed in deeply. "I love the sea air." She turned to Boreas, knowing full well that she was perfectly lit by the sun. "What do you think this place offers, Boreas? If you had to sum it up."

He made a point of looking around before he answered. "Hope and understanding."

"Can you expand on that?" Kit asked, like she was ready to pounce.

"The kids who come here feel lost and alone. They don't understand the world, and it's a complicated one. Nothing is simple, and in this age of technology that should be connecting us, it's also serving to alienate us." He lifted his arms and wings, the sunlight making the purple in his feathers dance. "Here, they learn they're not alone. They can ask anything they want, and they can talk to one another about those questions. They develop compassion for each other and for themselves. The gods who teach here do it because they believe in the children, and they want to help them. Help the kids, and the world will be better in the long run. We all get hope for the future, and we learn to understand one another better." He gave Kit a meaningful look. "And ourselves, too."

She frowned and was about to speak, but Clio cut her off. This was going well, and it didn't need to take a serious turn.

"Beautiful. Now, you told me we could join in. What are we going to do today?"

He motioned and they headed down the path toward the shore. "Kit, we did a little research, and we found out that you're originally from Minnesota. So we've set up something just for you."

Clio realized she'd fallen into the trap of thinking everyone she met in California was from California. She hadn't given a thought to where Kit actually came from. It was a reminder how little they really knew about each other.

They arrived at the shore and rounded the bend, and Kit gave a startled laugh. "I had one just like it back home."

The little skiff had Kit's name on a placard in big bold letters. It was the first in a line of them, and Clio's name, too, was on another.

Boreas smiled down at her. "I know. I used to blow the wind for you on Island Lake." He walked off toward the skiff.

Kit stood staring after him and jumped a little when Clio touched her arm. "Are you okay?"

She shrugged. "It's weird, I guess. To think a god was watching you. I mean, you're always told they are, but you don't really believe it. But hardly anyone knows how much time I spent on that lake."

Clio took her hand and tugged her toward the little boat. "I think it's sweet."

A group of kids were gathered and greeted them shyly.

Boreas held up his hands. "This is Amphitrite. She's our sailing tutor, and today she's set a challenge. You two against the youth she's trained. No sails. Just good ol' arm power." He grinned at the kids. "I have faith that our kids will leave you an ocean behind."

Kit picked up the paddle beside the skiff with her name on it, holding it almost tenderly. "I think you'll find I'll give them a run for their money."

There was plenty of jeers and banter which Kit took well.

"They've been taught by the queen of the ocean, Kit. I'd say you're outmatched." Clio bowed her head respectfully to Amphitrite, who gave her a nod and smile.

"Let's see what you've learned, kids. To your paddles!" Amphitrite shouted, and the kids raced off to their individual skiffs.

Clio went to hers and gladly took Kit's outstretched hand to help her balance as she got into the little boat. "I haven't done this since the eighteen hundreds."

Kit gave her hand a little squeeze. "You say these things like they're so ordinary. You have no idea, do you?" She turned away and practically leapt into her skiff, quickly pushing it back into open water.

Clio fumbled a little with the oar when it got caught in her loose sleeves, but she got the hang of it and lined up with the other boats. There was a light in Kit's eyes she hadn't seen before, and she looked so at home with the paddle resting across her lap, her legs splayed a little. She was always sexy, but in that moment, she made Clio shiver a little.

Amphitrite stood before the line of boats, her feet just below the water, though she wasn't standing on anything. "This is the finish line. You'll race out to the checkered flag, go around it, and then come back. Nice and simple." She pointed her trident at the group. "No rough stuff. Fair play only."

There was plenty of laughter at that, and more than one red-faced kid who obviously hadn't taken well to falling behind before this. Amphitrite waved her trident, an arc of water flew over the boats, and they were off.

Clio hadn't laughed so hard in a very long time. At one point she had to lay her paddle on her lap and drift because she couldn't see through the tears of laughter. Amphitrite's admonition about no rough stuff had absolutely no effect. The kids shoved each other's boats with their paddles, and then they quickly ganged up on Kit, who was pulling ahead thanks to their lack of focus. She swatted at them, splashed them, and urged them onward. When one kid's boat looked like it was going over, she shoved out her oar to steady him, and his friend raced past. "Sucker!" he yelled, and the boy she was helping grinned fiendishly. Kit stuck her paddle under his boat and flipped him, and then set off after his friend.

Clio gave up and slowly paddled back toward the finish line, making sure to stay well out of the way of the fracas. And from a distance she could watch the joy and total relaxation in Kit's expression, which made her heart ache. The camera crew, in a skiff lazily blown by Boreas himself, stayed just far enough away to keep from getting wet, but close enough to watch Kit play with the kids.

She got back to the finish line where Amphitrite was waiting.

"You gave up, little muse." She didn't sound in the least upset about it.

"Sometimes it's better to watch than participate."

There was a shout as another boat tipped and the rest of the skiffs went around the checkered flag before setting course back to the finish line. Kit was in line with four others, and the messing around had stopped now that they were headed back. They all paddled furiously, and Kit could be heard cheerfully egging them on.

Clio was holding her breath as the skiffs sped toward them. And then something strange happened. Kit seemed to lose her balance, and she dropped her paddle in order to grab the side of the skiff. Her paddle was quickly lost in the wake behind her, and she threw up her hands and groaned loudly. The other three skiffs passed the finish line almost at the same time, and Kit joined the others in applauding.

Boreas and the camera crew floated up beside Clio. "Odd," he said. "In all the years I've been watching her, I've never seen her drop a paddle."

Clio nodded. "Strange how things happen sometimes." Her heart swelled with admiration. Kit wasn't about to outshine the kids who'd been working so hard here. *What is virtue, Kit?* So often, really good people had no idea how good they were.

One of the kids coming up behind Kit scooped up her paddle and handed it over after shaking some water at her. She paddled to the finish line and back to shore, where she let her fingers glide over the side of the skiff after she got out. "Thank you," she said to Boreas once she was back on shore. "That was the most fun I've had in ages."

"We think fun is important. It makes learning and compassion easier." He winked at her. "And even though you've lost, we have something for you." He accepted a little trophy from one of the kids. "For participating and doing your best. Too bad you weren't taught by the queen of the sea, eh?"

She accepted the trophy and held it aloft. "Maybe not, but I had a god of wind looking out for me, so that's pretty special too."

Boreas patted her on the back and swiped at his eyes. "Well now. That's enough. We don't need any rainstorms." They walked back to the main building. "You're always welcome here. If you have questions of your own, if you need someone to talk to, or hell, if you have a subject you'd like to teach, it would be wonderful to have you back."

He shook Kit's hand, and then took Clio in a tight embrace. "That goes for you too, little sister," he whispered. "You're not alone out there." He let go and stepped back. "And now I need to go show the kids how storms develop. Safe winds home." He flapped his enormous purple wings and launched into the air.

Kit and Clio, followed by the camera crew, made their way back to the parking lot.

"So? What do you think?" Clio asked.

Kit leaned against the car and studied her little trophy. "Honestly? I think I need to process it. But there's no question they're doing good in the world, and that those kids are massively benefiting from the program." She frowned and twirled the trophy between her hands. "But how does it help them in the long run? Once they're adults facing real issues?"

Clio leaned against the car beside Kit, taking in the warmth of the sun and the body beside her. The cameras, as always, were still running. "Knowledge is power. You never know how the kids will put what they've learned to use. Hydropower, maybe? They might be able to help with climate change because of what they learned here. Or they might grow to understand how to develop better ways to treat people from the plants the nymphs teach about."

"And they might never have had the opportunity to learn these things had it not been for the program." Kit nodded and turned to face Clio. "All right, muse. You've won this round."

Clio's stomach dropped. "I wasn't aware we were competing."

Kit pulled open the rear car door. "Weren't you?"

Chapter Eight

The car ride back to the station was far more relaxed, and she and Clio laughed about the kids' antics.

She didn't want to analyze why it felt good to have Clio watching her, cheering for her, laughing with her. Part of her had wanted to win just to make Clio proud of her, but she had a feeling Clio knew she'd dropped the oar on purpose. So maybe that was even better.

"Thank you," Kit said. "I'm not the easiest person to deal with, and I appreciate you setting up today." She leaned her head against the headrest. "I think you're right. There's nothing wrong with a bit of fun."

Clio's smile was sweet and soft, not like the practiced one she used for the camera. "It was fun, but I think it was also necessary. It's important to see that good things are happening too." She touched Kit's leg. "And it's important they see the not so good stuff. Sometimes."

It felt like a milestone, and Kit's shoulders relaxed even more. "I think we might be a good team after all, Clio."

"Maybe so." Clio grinned when Kit's eyebrow went up. "Maybe we'll be a solid influence on each other."

They arrived back at the station and got out. "Do you have plans tonight?" Kit asked, though why she did was beyond her.

Clio hesitated. "No, not tonight. I think I'll relax with a glass of wine and some music. You?"

Kit rolled her eyes. "My friends and I have a thing where we meet up on Tuesday nights to talk about our week. If you want to join us—"

Clio shook her head. "Thank you, that's really sweet. But I'm pretty tired, and alone time helps refresh my batteries."

"Oh. Yeah, of course. Okay, well, see you Friday." Why was it disappointing that Clio had turned her down so quickly? One good day didn't make up for the diametrically opposed outlooks they had on life.

Almost like she knew what Kit was thinking, Clio put her hand on Kit's arm. "Really, thank you for the invitation. I don't have many friends, and I bet your friends are wonderful. I just need a little me time. Please ask me again sometime."

Kit relaxed. "Yeah, of course I will."

Clio squeezed her arm, lingering for a little longer than usual. "Thanks for today." She finally let go, slowly, and stepped back, her gaze staying on Kit. Then she quickly turned and headed into the parking garage.

Kit blew out a long breath. What was that? If it had happened in a bar, she'd have asked the woman home with her in an instant. But this was Clio. She wasn't bar fodder. She was an immortal, for Christ's sake. She took her keys from her pocket and headed down the street to her car. A good drink would sort out whatever confusion was going on in her weirdo brain and she'd be back to normal by tomorrow.

By the time Kit met up with her friends at the new bar she was irritated by the traffic and the rain. They were waiting at a table near the stairs and waved her over. She hung her jacket on the back of the chair and shook the water from her hair.

"What are you, a dog?" Trish held her hands up to ward off the flying droplets.

"I've been accused of that before, yes." Kit grinned and gratefully took a large gulp of the beer already waiting for her. "Thanks."

They dove straight into conversation about how her new shindig with Clio was going. She told them about the day hanging out with the god of wind, and the woman with crab claws on her head instead of horns. They were full of questions, and she found that her shoulders relaxed the more she talked about Clio

"Sounds like you're having a good time," Barb said.

"We've only done two shoots, but I can see how it might work now." Hopefully, she wasn't being too optimistic.

"And?" Trish asked. "Have you done the deed with her already?"

Kit flicked beer foam at her. "Do you honestly think I'd sleep with one of them? They're nothing like us. It would be like sleeping with a different species." Not that it hadn't occurred to her when she'd seen Clio looking so lovely when she'd woken on the plane. What would it be like to wake up to that beautiful face every day?

"I'd totally go there." Trish sighed dramatically. "I bet the sex is amazing."

Kit shook her head. "No thanks. Way too many complications. At least with a human you can age together. You can joke about gray pubes and wrinkles. Imagine looking at someone next to you who never ages while you're getting all wrinkly and cranky."

Barb laughed. "You may have a point there, although you're already wrinkly and cranky."

It was a good thing Clio hadn't accepted her invitation to join them tonight. This way, she could speak her mind without worrying about offending her new co-worker. It had been foolish to invite her in the first place. Better to keep their personal and work relationships separate, so they could, like she'd said, blow off steam about working together. Still, she had a feeling that for all of Clio's bubbly facade, she was lonely. Or maybe she was projecting.

She focused on her friends and joined in the banter. Staying focused on the here and now was what life was about. As long as she could remember that, life would stay just the way it was.

CHAPTER NINE

I think the producers want us to kill each other. On screen, preferably." Chloe stared out the window at the world thirty thousand feet below. "Why would you choose this of all places?"

Kit sipped the drink Sian had brought over. Non-alcoholic mojitos were pretty good. The last thing she needed was a hangover when they arrived. "Our first interview was pretty tame. The second was a lot of fun, I'll grant you that. But we need meat, and this is where we're going to find it."

"Along with death and destruction. Charming."

"How long has it been since you've been to Mexico?" Kit asked. "I've been a lot and I think it's a beautiful place."

Clio glared at her. "Of course it's beautiful. It's stunning. And I was in Oaxaca well before it was Oaxaca." She looked back out the window. "I was there when they spoke another language altogether and they'd created the most magnificent pyramids. I helped inspire them to build something that would really last and show the beauty and intricacy of their culture. Of course, they didn't have written language, so their history was lost. Except for what I wrote in my own journals, of course."

Kit leaned forward, intrigued. "You never talk about the history of stuff. Not the really important bits. What was it like back then?"

Clio rested her forehead against the window and drew circles in the condensation with her fingertip. "The forest stretched as far as the eye could see. Birds of the kind you've never even thought of filled the trees with so many songs it sounded like a choir from dawn to dusk. They had running water. They kept some rooms cool and others hot, all through natural means. The tribes in Mexico were astounding in their innovation. You humans have lost so much in your hurry to move forward."

"And?" Kit asked when it seemed like Clio wasn't going to continue.

She sighed deeply. "And like you humans always are, they were bloodthirsty and wanted power. I left when they began to talk about conquering instead of creating. The same reason I've left so many places. It's always destruction. Humans are never satisfied."

Kit was quiet as she pondered that. There was depth to Clio that was well hidden, and she liked this side of their conversations, as contentious as they might become. "But isn't that dissatisfaction what keeps us innovating?"

"It is. It's also what keeps you from knowing when to stop, when enough is enough. If we hadn't had the Merge, you would have taken the earth beyond the tipping point. You would have destroyed the only place you have to live because you couldn't be satisfied."

Kit wasn't sure what to say to that. Everyone was fully aware that the climate change tipping point had become almost inevitable, and the predictions had been dire. But once the gods stepped in, climate had been the first thing they'd dealt with, directing their followers into better ways. The world had still warmed, but nowhere near as fast and at a more natural rate. She hadn't really considered that aspect of the good they'd done.

"I chose Mexico because it's one of the last big holdouts. But they have a new goddess, right? And yet, things are still bad there. The ten different drug cartels are out of control. Over a hundred thousand people died last year in cartel-related violence. And the mineral mining is unregulated and now using child labor. We need to draw attention to it so we can work out how to fix it."

Clio turned in her seat to more fully face her. "And you think that can happen?"

Kit drummed her fingers on her thigh. "Honestly? I don't know. I do know that working with you is already making me see things a little differently, and that makes me uncomfortable. But reminding me that good stuff is happening makes me wonder if more good stuff could happen." She shrugged. "I don't know."

They landed just outside Mexico City, and when they got to the bottom of the metal stairs, Kit looked up when she heard Clio let out a high-pitched laugh.

"Dani!" Clio launched herself at a tall, dark-haired woman who caught her and swung her around. "I can't believe you're here." She looked over her shoulder and waved Kit forward impatiently. "Dani, this is Kit Kalloway. Kit, this is Dani. You know her as Death, or Santa Muerte as she's called now that she's a big old god."

Kit blinked and involuntarily took a step back. The tall, handsome butch with the gentle dark eyes was Death herself. Fan-fucking-tastic. "Nice to meet you."

Dani smiled, and her expression was kind. "Great to meet you too. I've been a huge fan for years."

Once again, Kit was bewildered. "Death watches my show?"

She laughed. "Well, Death isn't really my job title anymore. I had someone step into the primary position once I had to take on the Santa Muerte role thanks to an uptick in followers." She pushed her hands into her pockets. "But most days, I'm just me."

Clio hooked her arm through Dani's and started toward the convertible yellow Mustang. "Don't let her fool you, Kit. When she goes into goddess mode, it's something else. And sorry, I'd forgotten you weren't Death anymore. How is Idona doing?"

Kit continued to listen but kept her mouth shut. How the hell was she supposed to act when she was riding around with a goddess? Clio was immortal, yeah, but she seemed more human, more relatable. Or maybe that was just Clio.

She looked up and saw them watching her. "Sorry, I was miles away. What?"

"I was wondering if you'd like to get something to eat before we go to the hotel. I've arranged the meeting your producer asked for, and we have time to relax a little beforehand."

Kit just nodded, still weirded out by being in Dani's presence. They stopped in front of a little café that smelled divine, and Dani left to have a quick word with the manager.

"Sexy butch goddess got your tongue?" Clio's eyebrow quirked in that way that made her both sexy and irritating.

"I don't know what you're talking about." Kit looked at the menu and realized it was in Spanish. She could make out a few words but not a lot. "I'm just being respectful."

Clio let out a puff of laughter. "Please. Nothing keeps you from asking questions. Zeus himself wouldn't be safe with you." She nodded toward Dani. "But super hottie there comes out and you get all shy. It's adorable."

Kit ran her hands over her face. "She's not my type, I assure you. You can't see how being in a car with Death would be intimidating to a human? Really?"

Clio tilted her head. "You're never weird around me."

"Do you take people's souls to the underworld? You inspire people, you don't end their lives."

"I don't end people's lives either." Dani set down two huge bowls of tortilla chips and a bowl of chunky salsa. "I'm there when people are dying, or when they need something in general, these days." She scooped up a big bit of salsa with her tortilla chip and bit into it. "Idona and her team are there for souls when they're ready to leave their bodies."

Kit blanched. Offending a goddess seemed like a bad idea no matter what she was the goddess of. But Clio didn't look worried, which was a good sign. She'd already said she wouldn't let Kit get turned to stone. "Sorry. My mistake."

Dani reached across and touched her hand gently. "If you don't ask questions, you don't get answers. As you've often said on your show, ignorance and apathy are destructive."

Kit smiled, strangely calmed by Dani's brief touch. "Thank you."

A woman came out carrying a huge tray full of food that she quickly placed all over their table before giving Dani a warm smile and leaving them to it.

"What is all this?" Clio asked, already digging in.

"This is one of the few places that does smaller plates so you can taste a lot of different things. We've got cheese and onion enchiladas, beef tamales, chicken chimichangas, and chili rellenos."

They were silent as they ate, commenting only on how good everything was.

Kit hadn't had authentic Mexican food in forever, and she took her time savoring every bite. She damn near jumped out of her skin when someone dressed in a black cloak and holding a scythe seemed to materialize out of thin air beside Dani. She bent low and whispered in her ear, and then Dani responded in kind, looking thoughtful. Her eyes changed, going black, the whites of her eyes disappearing. Kit scooted her chair back a few inches, her heart pounding.

The person in the cloak vanished as quickly as she appeared, and Kit was glad she was sitting down, or her knees would have given out. Knowing the immortal world was part of this one now was one thing. People with crab claws on their heads or wearing big wings could easily be thought of as in costume. Seeing them appear and vanish at the dinner table was another thing altogether.

Dani blinked and her eyes went back to normal. She sighed and set her napkin on the table. "You might want to put off your interview and come for a ride with me."

Clio's shoulders dropped. "This is going to be ugly, isn't it?"

Dani nodded and stood. "I'll understand if you don't want to go, but I need to see for myself what has happened."

The three of them went to the Mustang they'd arrived in, but Dani was silent, and Kit could see in the rearview mirror how her eyes kept going full black.

Clio reached back from the front seat and touched Kit's thigh. "Are you okay?"

"Why wouldn't I be? Nothing weird about any of this, is there?" She swallowed hard when she met Dani's eyes in the mirror. She picked up her phone and opened the messages. "Where should I tell the camera crew to go?"

Dani gave her the name of a bridge instead of an address, and she quickly sent it, but her finger shook. Everyone knew that in Mexico, a story that included a bridge was going to have a bad ending.

They arrived soon after, and Kit saw their camera crew waiting on the verge, but there was no one else there. "Why aren't there other news crews or onlookers here yet?"

"The Yama, the person who came to deliver the message, felt the number of souls leaving their bodies and came to me right away. This has only happened within the last hour so we're the first people here, other than the Yama who have come to collect the souls."

"Yama?" Kit asked, searching what she could see of the bridge.

"The crew who help gather souls all over the world. They're called Yama Dutas, technically, but they just go by Yamas, or the singular Yama." Dani started to lead the way down the little hill, with the camera crew already filming behind them.

Clio hung back, and Kit turned. "Aren't you coming?"

Her eyes were wide, and her arms were wrapped around herself. "I don't want to do this."

Dani stopped and turned as well, and her expression was sympathetic. "I know you've already dealt with your share of this, Clio. You don't have to come."

"Yes, you do." Kit shoved away the empathy. "This is the point. You can't only look at the good stuff. You have to see the bad stuff too. This is what we do."

She glared at Kit. "When you've lived through nearly every war humans have ever waged, then you can tell me what I need to see and what I don't. But you want me to do this? Fine. Let's do this." She stomped off past Dani, leading the way down the hill but moving carefully in her high-heeled sandals.

Kit shook her head and started after her, but Dani's soft touch stopped her.

"Muses are sensitive creatures, Kit. They feel more deeply than you or I could ever imagine. It's beautiful, but it can also be a curse. Go gentle." She turned to follow Clio.

Kit shook out her arms. The warning was subtle, but there was no doubt it was there. She followed the other two but skidded to a stop when she reached the bottom, near the swollen river that raced past. She squatted, her knees unwilling to support her.

Bodies hung like grotesque swaying pillars from long ropes attached to the bridge. Their feet caught the river like rocks, making it swirl around them. They ranged in height, and there was no question that among the twenty or more bodies there were a number of women and children.

"There's more," Dani said softly, pointing.

What initially looked like a pile of clothing came clear, and Kit turned away to vomit. It was a pile of body parts, a pyramid of death.

There was silence for a long time before Kit stood and steadied herself. She'd been in war zones before. She could take it. But when she turned around to look, she stumbled back.

Dani, the sweet, dark-haired butch, was a good eight feet tall. Her face had become a painted skull, full of swirls and shapes, and her eyes were voids of darkness. She looked at the bridge and fury radiated from her.

Clio, tears running down her face, her beautiful floral sundress incongruous with the scene behind her, turned to the camera. "This is what you needed to see, apparently. The death and destruction that drugs and everything about them bring to the world. The killing of people to prove what? That you have more drugs? That you have more disrespect for humanity than anyone else? Good for you. I hope you're ready for what's coming your way."

Kit turned to Dani. "Are you going to do something about this?"

Dani's eerily empty eyes turned toward Kit and the cameras. "I need everyone who has lost someone to this world of violence to pray to me. Right now. Pray for vengeance. Pray for righteousness. Pray for justice. All of you. Pray to me *now*, so that I can deliver these human scum ponds to your feet."

The words were thunder piercing the air like arrows, and the tone was irresistible. If Kit had a loved one who had been taken by this particular violence, she'd have been on her knees in the mud, her eyes closed and the words rising from her lips.

"You can't do anything if people don't pray to you for help?" she finally asked as she found her voice.

"Gods don't intervene in human affairs unless asked. I need people to come together to ask. And once they do…"

The air cracked with electricity.

Kit stepped out of the camera's range and called the producer. "This needs to go live. Right now. I don't care what show you have to interrupt to do it. Call CNN and have them interrupt whatever the fuck they're showing. Now." She got confirmation and hung up, then told the camera crew, who got set up.

The filming they'd already done ran, and then the cameraman motioned to her that they were live. "Kit Kalloway here, with Clio Ardalides and Santa Muerte." The camera panned first to Clio, who stood staring at the bodies with her arms wrapped firmly around herself, and then to Dani, whose brightly painted skull looked macabre against the hangings behind her. "We're at the scene of something that can only be described as devastating horror. At least twenty bodies are hanging from this bridge behind me, and there is a pile of body parts on the shoreline, which we're not going to show for basic humanitarian reasons." She continued to speak while the camera took in the scene around them. "Tonight, we were supposed to speak with a contact who is deep within the world of the cartels here in Mexico. But nothing that person would have said could match what you're seeing here."

Kit dug her heels into the ground to steady herself. Clio looked so stricken, so utterly despondent, that she wanted to go to her, hold her close and let her cry. Till now, Clio had been a professional rival, someone to prove wrong and have fun with while doing it. Now, though, she just wanted to apologize. She refocused on the camera.

"The authorities will be here soon, I'm assuming. But as you heard Santa Muerte say, if you're tired of this, if you've been hurt by this, you need to direct your prayers to her. No more apathy, no more sticking your head in the sand. Let her stand up for you. ALL of you, pray right damn now."

They cut the live feed when the authorities pulled up, closely followed by other news crews. Many of the new arrivals stopped and knelt where they were, heads bowed before Dani.

Clio walked past Kit, her shoulders slumped, her eyes showing a weariness of soul Kit had never seen before. "I'm glad you got what you wanted," she said quietly. "I want to leave."

Kit watched her walk back to the car they'd arrived in. But it didn't look like Dani was going anywhere. Did you just ask a goddess if you could borrow her car keys? Why the fuck not? She tapped Dani's side, since she couldn't reach her shoulder anymore, and she had to steel herself from stepping backward when Dani looked down at her.

"Sorry to bother you. Can we borrow your car?" Never had anything more ludicrous left her mouth.

Dani's nod was slow, like she was in water. "Keys are in it." Suddenly, one of Dani's death minions appeared beside her.

"Fuck me backwards." Kit held her hand to her chest. "I don't think I'll ever get used to that." If Kit never saw a skull smile again, she'd be fine with it. She shivered at the specter.

"I'd like my Yama to direct you somewhere safe. Things are unstable and you could be in danger."

"Sure. Does she want to—"

"She doesn't drive." Dani turned away, clearly done with the conversation.

"No, of course not. Why would she need to?" Kit glanced at the Yama, but with the face shrouded by the cloak, there was no telling what she looked like. "I mean, you can just pop in and out, can't you?" There was no answer. "Right. No problem." She got in the driver's seat and the Yama got in the passenger side. Clio was in the back, her knees drawn up to her chest as she sat sideways on the seat. She glanced at Kit and then at the Yama and gave a little nod like she already understood what was going on.

"You'll tell me where to go?" Kit started the car and the Yama pointed. At least the finger was fleshy and not bone.

"The theatrics are unnecessary and not really funny right now, Soc."

The Yama threw off the hood, revealing a pretty redhead with a big smile. "Sorry, Clio. I was just trying to lighten the mood. Scenes like that really suck."

Kit let out a huge breath of air. "For fuck's sake. You were just messing with me?"

"I don't get much of a chance to talk to live people. And the dead don't usually have much of a sense of humor when I come across them. Too fresh, you know?" She motioned to the left. "Turn here and head to the end of the alley."

The area looked anything but safe. "Are you sure?"

"This has been my sector for fifty years. I'm sure."

She barely looked more than twenty. The day couldn't get any more surreal. "Okay, right to the end of the alley. To that nice big brick wall." She slowed and wondered how un-butch and unprofessional it would be if she peed herself in the car.

The wall shimmered and disappeared. In its place was a road, along which were tall palm trees. All of them appeared to be dead, as did the grass surrounding the gravestones spread as far as the eye could see.

"C'mon, Soc. That's just sick after what we've seen." Clio's tone was sharp, and she thumped the back of the passenger seat.

"Fine! Sorry. Jeez." She waved her hand and it turned into what looked like a regular highway with sunshine and palm trees. Living ones, this time.

"On we go."

Kit couldn't get her foot to press down on the gas pedal. She looked at Clio in the rearview. "What's going on?"

Clio met her gaze. "Dani wants to keep us safe. And the safest place in the world isn't in the world. We're going to stay in the Deadlands." She closed her eyes and rested her head against the window. "You wanted access, Kit. Welcome to the underworld."

CHAPTER TEN

Clio's heart hurt. It ached like someone had balled it up in their hands and smooshed it back into her chest. All those lives, gone. Children, women, men. The ugliness of humanity had been proven to her over and over again, and eventually she'd learned her lesson. She'd stopped being around them, and this was exactly why.

They got out of the car in front of a beautiful ranch-style house, complete with roses and a wraparound porch. She headed straight to one of the deck chairs and collapsed into it.

"What is Soc short for?" Kit asked the Yama.

"It's a nickname. When I first got here, I spent a lot of time asking questions and analyzing the nature of the Deadlands. Clio started calling me mini-Socrates, and I've been Soc ever since." She grinned. "I love it."

Kit stood with her hands in her pockets, looking as uncomfortable as a living person in the underworld should. "Whose house is this?"

Soc raised her hand. "I'll leave the explanations to Clio. I need to get back to work. See you soon." She turned and headed past the car, and then what looked like a door opened and she went through it and was gone.

"That freaks me out. I'm not afraid to say it." Kit flopped into the seat next to Clio.

"This is a guest house. Dani had it built after the Merge. Her wife, Megara, helped her revamp the Deadlands into something more welcoming. Now they have friends over sometimes, so they built this." Clio's eyes were closed, her knees tucked up under her chin. She didn't want to talk. She didn't want to hear Kit say they'd done something good today, or that seeing the bad was necessary. It wasn't.

The feelings rose and she began to cry. She let the tears flow, one for every soul on that bridge and in that pile. And one for every soul in this world taken by violence. She was barely aware of Kit's gentle hands pulling her from the deck chair and leading her inside to the couch. And she didn't pull away when Kit sat down with her and pulled her into a tight, strong embrace. She cried on Kit's chest, all the loneliness, fear, and disappointment flowing out and soaking Kit's shirt.

Eventually, she grew calm and scooted down so her head rested on Kit's thigh. She murmured gratefully when Kit covered her with a blanket, and she quickly fell into an emotionally exhausted sleep.

When she woke, she felt Kit's thigh flex under her head and she looked up, rubbing her eyes. "I'm so sorry. How long have I been asleep?"

"Only about an hour, I think. It's kind of hard to tell here, and I didn't want to move my arm to check my watch." Kit's stomach rumbled loudly, and she groaned. "I'm so hungry."

Clio struggled to sit up and quickly ran her hand through her hair. "I must be a mess."

"I think you look perfect."

Clio snapped around at the tone in Kit's voice. It was husky, not teasing. And the look in Kit's eyes suggested she wasn't hungry for just food.

"What's going on?" Clio asked.

"You're beautiful, Clio." Kit stretched, keeping her eyes on Clio. "I've always thought so. But there's something about watching a woman sleep. You can see her, without a mask or pretense. And fucking hell, you're so damn beautiful when you let that mask fall."

Clio wasn't sure how to take that. "So, I'm not beautiful unless I'm sleeping?"

Kit laughed and stood. "Are we allowed to eat in the underworld? Or is there no food because we're supposed to be dead? Christ, if we eat something here are we stuck here forever, like that tale about Persephone?" She shivered, only half-jokingly. "This might be safe, but I think I'd rather take my chances with the cartels. I'd rather not come back here until I'm actually supposed to be here."

Clio got up too, letting the other conversation go. Falling asleep on Kit's lap, having someone hold her and simply let her feel, was almost too much to take. It had been so very long. "The cupboards usually have stuff in them."

She went hunting and found enough in the cupboard and fridge to make them a meal. "Relax. I'll have something for us in a jiffy."

Kit sat on a breakfast stool. "A jiffy?"

"When you pick up words throughout the centuries it's sad to let them go. That's one I particularly like." Clio started chopping and dicing. It was nice to be cooking for someone.

"I owe you an apology, Clio." Kit's tone had that husky hint to it again.

"Probably several. But what is it you're apologizing for right now?" Clio shot her a quick smile and didn't miss the heat in Kit's eyes.

"For being stubborn and bull-headed. I haven't considered that you've been through a hell of a lot more than I have. You've probably seen worse than what we saw out there, haven't you?"

Clio nodded but just kept chopping.

"And yet you worked to show people something good. Fun, happy things to take them away from what they see beyond their doorsteps every day. Maybe I don't agree with how you've gone about it, but I've had some time to think, and I kind of understand now." Kit snagged a piece of carrot. "So I'm sorry for being an ass and not considering your feelings."

Clio thought about that. "But you're not sorry for wanting to show people what we saw today."

Kit frowned. "No, I'm not sorry about that. I still think people need to see that there are things that need to be changed, and even Boreas said it was useful. And by doing what we did, we helped give Dani a platform to spread her message. Maybe now she can make some headway against the cartels." She paused. "But she can't actually kill people, can she?"

Clio tilted her head, thinking. "It's hard to say. Gods throughout history have been able to kill people off, but they always do it in creative ways; they use lightning, or turn people into piles of salt, or into trees or animals. But Dani is the personification of death, the actual goddess of death. She's one of the softest, sweetest people I've ever met. But her rage was like sand in the air today. I could feel it stinging me. It'll be interesting to see what she does."

They were quiet for a while longer, and Clio returned to the tone of Kit's voice and the look in her eyes moments before. She'd never once considered that Kit might find her attractive. Kit was all kinds of sexy, but their views were so different. And she knew what it was to love a human.

"That smells good," Kit finally said.

"I learned how to cook in France about thirty years ago. I picked up plenty of great recipes over the years, obviously, but it was only when I was in Paris and I dated a chef that I learned the finer things, like how much of an herb to use and what mixed best with what. I got pretty good before we went our separate ways."

Kit leaned forward. "And what about now? Are you with anyone? Other than Sian, I mean."

Clio stirred the sauce, wondering how much she wanted to reveal in this inevitable line of questioning. "No. I haven't been with anyone seriously for a long time."

"Why not?"

"You're relentless, aren't you?" Clio dipped the spoon into the mixture and held it out for Kit to taste. She shivered when Kit's eyes didn't leave hers as her lips touched the spoon.

"Maybe a little more oregano. And my relentless nature is what people love about me."

Clio laughed. "I'm sure." She added more oregano. "How much do you actually know about me? Not just about the muses, but me in particular?"

Kit tilted her head and stared at the food for a second. "Not a lot, I guess. I read some articles on things you've done, like the Arts College and such, but there wasn't a lot of personal information. Just pieces of mythology."

Clio smiled wistfully. "What you call mythology, I call backstory. Myths are stories told so long ago that people forget they're actually made up of a lot of truth."

"Go on?" Kit asked when Clio went quiet.

"Many, many years ago, I was confronted by a goddess who was being...well, not virtuous. She'd fallen in love with a mortal and was chasing him around like a lovestruck fool. It was unseemly, and the young man didn't return her admiration. Like an idiot, I told her she was behaving like a silly mortal." She tapped the spoon hard against the pot, splashing a little and making Kit jump back. "Sorry. In return for my sage advice, she cursed me. I'd forever only be able to fall in love with mortals, never immortals, so that I'd eventually have to watch them grow old and die. For the rest of my existence."

"Jesus Christ."

"No, not him. He's much nicer than that. Aphrodite, though, isn't a goddess you insult." She shrugged. "What she didn't realize was that I don't fall in love easily anyway. It might seem like I'm the type, but really, I guard my heart pretty well. The drawback of being a muse of virtue is that it's only a really virtuous person who can steal my heart. And there aren't a lot of those out there who also happen to be my type."

"And what type is that?" Kit held up her hand. "Never mind. Sian, right?"

"Tall, butch, handsome, and hot." Clio grinned. "Exactly."

"But you haven't fallen in love with her?" Kit asked. "Shit. Sorry. Totally not my business."

"It's not, but I'll still answer." Clio smiled when Kit gave her an apologetic look. "I love Sian as a friend, and we have some great times together. She's a really good person. But no, I've never been in love with her. That's a spark you don't find with many people. Not the real thing, anyway." She bit her lip, wondering if she wanted an answer to the same question. "What about you? Is there a woman pining away for you at home?"

Kit snorted. "My dog, Buster, probably doesn't count in this instance. Can you imagine anyone pining for my company?"

Clio glanced at Kit's rugged jawline, her strong forearms, her long fingers. Yes, actually, she could. She returned to stirring the sauce that no longer needed to be stirred.

"As you've probably guessed, I'm married to my job. I enjoy dating here and there, and I'm not averse to an occasional one-night stand to scratch a more immediate itch. But love? That will just break you. As you've seen, I imagine."

There was real pain under Kit's flippant words, pain Clio could feel as it swept over her skin. "I think Aphrodite meant that to be true. But what I've found is that when you find real love, it doesn't break you at all. Sure, when you lose it, the pain is unbearable. But the beauty you got from loving so deeply remains always, and the pain fades."

Kit remained quiet, chewing thoughtfully and loudly on a carrot stick.

"I read that you lost your parents when you were young." Clio kept her tone even, conversational. "What happened?"

"Car accident." Her tone was clipped. "When I was twelve. They were my everything. And when I prayed after, no one answered."

Clio looked up. "What were you praying for?"

Kit looked taken aback by the question. "For it not to have happened. For them to come back to me."

Clio set down the spoon and reached across to take Kit's hand. "People can't be brought back to life. Not by any god, anywhere. Accidents are awful, but they're part of life on this earth. You didn't get an answer because there wasn't one to give you."

She started to dish up, and her understanding of Kit grew with every spoonful of food she put on the plate. Kit's anger at the gods and her need to show people that they weren't perfect made sense now. It came from a place of abandonment and anger, as did many people's feelings toward the gods when it came to imperfect mortal existences.

She set their plates down on the table. "Sit. I didn't just slave over that hot stove for nothing."

Kit sat and picked up her fork. "It took you about thirty minutes."

Clio reached for her plate and slid it away. "If you're going to disparage my cooking—"

"No!" Kit pulled the plate back to her. "I was just saying." She took a bite and made a deep sound in her throat. "That's amazing. You can be my housewife pining at home for me anytime."

Clio choked on her drink. "Do I strike you as the pining housewife type?"

Kit grinned and raised her eyebrow, the fork halfway to her mouth. "Wanna find out?"

Clio laughed, and the tension was broken. They spent the next hour talking about their favorite movies, music, and comediennes. Kit got Clio to talk about her favorite moments in history, and Clio asked Kit where on earth she'd most like to go, which unsurprisingly was far away from people.

"Finland? It's beautiful. I haven't spent much time there over the years. The people are naturally kind, and there isn't much need for a muse of history either."

"I want to see the northern lights and pet a reindeer and go husky sledding." Kit's eyes sparkled when she talked about it. "When I retire, that's what I'm going to do."

Clio shook her head as she gathered their dishes and took them to the sink, Kit right behind her. "Why would you wait until you retire? It's such a modern way of thinking, you know. Waiting until some specific point in your life before you go somewhere you've dreamt of going." She glanced at Kit, who leaned against the counter next to her. "Surely everything you've learned in this life has shown you that you should do everything you want to do, whenever you can?" She lightly cupped Kit's cheek. "Life can be unexpectedly short."

Kit's eyes darkened and she put her hand over Clio's, holding it to her cheek. Clio froze, rooted in place, her breathing picking up speed. Kit's eyes moved to Clio's lips, and she darted forward, letting go of Clio's hand and crushing her lips to Clio's.

Clio moaned and pressed her body to Kit's, tangling her hands in Kit's short hair. Kit's thigh pressed between her legs, and she groaned against Kit's mouth at the utterly perfect pressure that was right where she needed it. Kit's tongue sought entrance to her mouth, and she granted it willingly, opening to her. The kiss was all Kit: passionate, raw, intense. Kit's lips moved away from her mouth, over her jaw and down her neck, nipping and kissing a hot trail that set off fireworks in Clio's body and soul.

There was a knock at the door and Kit rested her forehead against Clio's. "God fucking damn all of it to hell."

Clio couldn't help but smile and she slid out from Kit's hold. "It's probably Dani."

Kit bent and rested her head on her arms on the countertop. "Nothing like Death stopping by to kill a vibe."

Clio laughed out loud this time and tried to tame her hair. Her lips felt swollen, and her breathing was erratic. She opened the door and pasted on a smile.

Dani took one look at her and winced a little. "Sorry. I didn't know."

Clio took her hand and led her inside. "Me neither." She smiled at the look of understanding in Dani's eyes.

"I wanted to let you know that things are in motion, but you shouldn't stay in Mexico. If it's okay, I'd like to drive you back to the airport using the Deadlands highway."

Kit crossed her arms. "Are you killing the story?"

Dani's smile was gentle. "I'm not. I don't imagine you've had the time to watch the news." She grinned a little. "But if you did, you'd see that I'm already able to work on clean-up thanks to you airing what you saw, in the raw and open way you did." She hugged Clio to her side. "It was ugly work, but you made a real difference today."

Clio softened under Dani's always gentle touch. "I hated it."

Dani nodded and kissed the top of Clio's head. "I know you did. But part of what made the newscast so explosive was your reaction and how genuine it was. People are used to seeing you bubbly and free, so it was extra powerful." She looked down at her. "It was real."

Clio felt the weight of judgment, even though she knew it wasn't Dani's intention. "Fun and bubbly doesn't mean not real."

"No, it doesn't." She let go and moved toward the door. "But you know what I mean, Clio. If you two are ready, I'd like to head out now. Meg is making dinner and she has a couple of special dinner guests she'd like me to meet."

Clio laughed when Dani blushed, and Kit looked at her with a question in her eyes. "Meg is known for having very *special* guests. Usually extremely attractive ones who are also flexible and not bound by human inhibitions."

"And I understand you've been to more than one of her parties over the centuries," Dani said with a wink. "Before my time with her, that is."

Kit looked between them, and Clio could only imagine what she was thinking, especially after their kiss moments before. "No sense in wasting the life we're given, right?" she said and grinned at Kit when her eyebrows went up. Had she expected Clio to deny it?

"Okay, let's go." Dani picked up the car keys by the door. "Unless you two want to join the party tonight."

"Not me, thanks," Clio said. "I've had enough excitement today." She looked at Kit. "But if you want to?"

"No!" Kit held up her hands. "Sorry, I mean, no thanks. I'm all about wild sex orgies with gods, but like Clio said, I'm tired out too."

Dani laughed. "I'm so glad you both turned me down. I wouldn't want to compete with either of you in the bedroom. You're just Meg's type," she said, looking Kit over. "And Clio would have everyone else's attention."

Kit's mouth opened, but nothing came out. She looked at Clio, who just smiled sweetly.

"Off we go, then," Clio said. "But tell Meg I miss her, and that she should come visit me one day. We'll go shopping."

Kit shook her head as she followed them out to the car. "I feel like I've gone down the rabbit hole."

"Nah. Just the Deadlands. The rabbit hole is somewhere else entirely." Dani started the car and headed down a long road with no other cars on it. When they entered the daylight at the end of the road, they were on the airport tarmac. The plane engines were already rumbling, and the stairs were waiting.

They got out and Clio gave Dani a hard hug. "Thank you, old friend. You reminded me of some things today."

Dani held her at arm's length. "Remember who you are, Clio Ardalides. You're never truly alone." She let go and turned to Kit, holding out her hand. "And you, Kit Kalloway. Be gentle with my favorite muse or you'll see me again under different circumstances."

Kit's eyes widened. "Yup. Okay. Will do."

Dani laughed and pulled her into a bro-hug. "Good. And take care of yourself, too."

They headed up the stairs to the plane and settled in. Clio waved out the window to Dani, who waved back as she leaned against her Mustang, one hand in her pocket, looking for all the world like a bog-standard sexy as hell mortal woman.

Sian leaned down next to her and looked out the window too. "Damn. My competition is getting fiercer all the time. She's something else."

"You have no idea," Kit said from across the aisle.

CHAPTER ELEVEN

K it rolled face down on the bed and punched her pillow repeatedly. The flight back from Mexico had been silent. Not because she hadn't wanted to lay the seats back all the way and pull Clio onto her lap to continue what they'd started, but because Clio had put her chair back, pulled an eye mask on, and gone to sleep, making it oh-so-clear that they weren't going to be doing anything, including talking. So Kit had spent the entire flight bugging the hell out of Sian, asking her stupid questions about flying and regaling her with her thoughts on why bubblegum lost its flavor so quickly, until Sian had given in and brought out a deck of cards just to keep Kit occupied. They'd ended up laughing and ribbing each other relentlessly, which most definitely helped keep her mind off the fact that Clio was lying down not ten feet away.

When the captain radioed that they were going to land, Sian shoved the cards at Kit. "I need to wake her up."

Kit turned to watch, curious. Sian knelt on one knee next to Clio's chair and caressed her cheek, speaking softly. Clio pulled off the eye mask and smiled at her, beautifully sleepy.

It was a tender moment, and Kit didn't like the feeling of insecurity and jealousy that kicked her in the gut. They seemed to have something special. And yet, Clio had been clear in her feelings about Sian. But when Kit looked at Sian's expression, she wondered if Sian was in the same place. It didn't look like it.

Sian left Clio's side and punched Kit in the shoulder as she passed. "Go sit down and strap in, stud. Can't have you falling over and bruising that pretty TV face."

Kit gave her a rude hand gesture in return and then went and did as she was told. "Sleep well?" she asked.

"I'm sorry, but I couldn't stay awake a minute longer. Emotional stuff like that really takes it out of me." Clio's smile was quick and then she started to gather her things. "Were you okay?"

Sian came forward with damp warm towels for their faces. "She was a royal pain in the ass. But I'm going to take her to the gym and show her how to work out so she doesn't look like such a wimp anymore."

Clio looked surprised. "You're going to meet up? Away from the plane?"

Sian laughed. "I don't live on this thing, you know. I have a life beyond it." She leaned down. "In fact, after I'm done wearing her out at the gym, maybe I could come over and do the same with you." She wiggled her eyebrows, but the look in her eyes was serious.

Clio glanced over Sian's shoulder at Kit, who was studiously looking out the window. "I'm afraid I won't be very good company for a while, Sian. But if I change my mind?"

"You know I'll come running." Sian sounded a little sad, but she covered it quickly.

Why was Kit so glad that Clio had turned her down?

The plane landed and Kit gave a sigh of relief. She'd done nothing but replay that hot and heavy moment at the guesthouse for the whole journey home, but she wasn't ready to dissect it or to hear Clio say it had been a mistake, that they were colleagues, and that it shouldn't have happened.

Part of her wanted to ask Clio to come back to her place. Part of her wanted to tell Sian to get off the plane so she could enjoy what they'd started right there on the plane. But the larger part of her knew it would complicate things. She still had pretty intense feelings about the immortals, and Clio didn't seem to share her misgivings. Sure, they'd reached a kind of impasse, but who knew how long it would last?

They disembarked and Sian and Kit traded friendly barbs and agreed to meet up the following day. Clio was a good few steps ahead, like she was in a hurry. Not a good sign.

Clio smiled brightly. "Sounds like you've got some good plans for your days off. I do too, of course. I'll see you at the meeting next week?" She leaned forward and kissed Kit on the cheek, backing away before Kit could turn her face to get more than just a peck.

"Yeah. Okay." Kit hoped she hid the way the dismissal stung. "See you then."

She watched as Clio got into her car and drove off, giving Kit and Sian a little wave as she zipped by.

"Come on," Sian said. "First round is on me. We'll work off the calories tomorrow."

Kit laughed and followed her, but she remained preoccupied with the woman she had no business thinking about outside of work.

"She's hot, intelligent, and she looks past your rather extreme taste in clothing as well as your bossiness. I'm not sure why you'd stay away from her. I'd think you'd bring her home and chain her to your bed. If she's into that. I know you went through your own phase."

"It was the seventeen hundreds and de Sade was all the rage." Clio popped the cork on the wine bottle while holding the phone between her shoulder and her ear. "Anyway, can you see how it would be complicated?"

"No." Eris was blunt, as always. "If she was your boss, maybe, although that's always a hot combination too, until it goes tits up. But she's just a co-worker, and you're both adults. There's no logical reason for you to stay out of her pants or to keep her out of yours."

"And what about how she feels about immortals?"

"Clearly it doesn't apply to you, given that she tickled your tonsils. And you should check out the way she looked at you on camera when you did that segment in Mexico. I mean, if someone looked at me that way I'd run for the fucking mountains, but I happen to know that some women like being looked at like someone wants to protect them from all the bad shit in the world."

Clio frowned and took a sip of wine. "What are you talking about?"

"I refuse to repeat myself just because you're being dense. Watch the segment. Then call her and get your head out of your ass. If you want her, and she wants you, then go for it."

"And Aphrodite?" Clio knew Eris would understand.

"Yeah, that's a shit deal. It would be better if you could fall in love with someone who would live as long as you. But we both know plenty of immortals with mortal lovers now, and they're making it work. You can enjoy the hell out of that body while it's around." Her tone softened. "I know it hurts when it ends, sis, but you know better than any of us that it doesn't mean you don't give it your all."

Clio sighed. "I don't know what's holding me back. I know it doesn't make sense, but I can't seem to get past this sense that I should wait."

"For what? For that perfect body to go to waste? Or worse, to someone else?" There was a giggly, high-pitched voice in the background. "Mortal lives go by in the blink of an eye. I've got to run."

Clio hung up feeling ten times better after talking to her sister. Eris was one to talk, since she had plenty of her own issues around love and relationships, but she was right that time was precious. And yet, when Clio thought of how vehement Kit was about the gods not doing enough, when she thought of the way Kit had looked freaked out when she'd found out who Dani was and when the Yama had come to guide them, she froze. How could she fit into Clio's world? Before the Merge, Clio hadn't told her lovers who or what she was. Eventually they'd known she was special when they aged and she didn't. But that had been between them.

Now, Kit knew exactly who and what she was. They were from different worlds, and Kit wasn't a huge fan of hers. Not to mention she'd always seemed to find Clio fake, something that wasn't lost on Clio. Could she live with Kit's intense desire to show the dark sides of the world to people all the time? And could Kit deal with her desire not to focus on the bad stuff?

There were so many questions, and so few answers. She wondered if Sian and Kit had enjoyed their workout together, and she had no problem admitting to herself that she was glad they weren't each other's type. She hated feeling jealous, and more than once her spontaneous nature had gotten the best of her when it came to jealousy and other women. Who knew that brocade curtains were so flammable?

She picked up the remote control to turn on the news, just to see if she could see what Eris was talking about, but then tossed it down again. Regardless of the way Kit might be looking at her, she couldn't face seeing the horror of what they'd covered. Once was enough.

The phone rang and she glanced at the readout. Why did it feel like a bad omen whenever she got a call from her producer these days?

"Hey, can you come into the office in the morning? The team is gathering and want to talk to both of you."

"Can you give me a hint this time instead of springing something on me?" She'd been less than impressed with the way they'd handled her with kid gloves.

"We want to talk about how great the show did the other night and discuss a couple of things to make it even better. That's all."

"Great. That's all." Cleo hadn't bothered to turn on the TV since she'd been home, focusing instead on music and the sound of the ocean. "I'll be there at ten."

"Perfect, thanks."

She put the phone down and stood staring out at the water. Kit would be there too, presumably. And while she couldn't wait to see her, it also felt a little too much like that first crush excitement, which could lead to way too much complication.

She went to her closet and sifted through the multitude of colors and materials. Her favorites were bright, bold colors that made her feel vibrant and free. But Kit didn't seem overly fond of that part of her. Why did that matter? She tugged out a cherry red pantsuit and matching heels that made her feel sexy and powerful. Changing who you were for other people was disingenuous, and as much as she wanted Kit, and other people, to like her, she couldn't be untrue to herself. It wasn't fair to them or to her.

The next morning, she ran late as usual, but only by a few minutes. When she walked into the office in the Embarcadero everyone was already seated, and there was a steaming cup of coffee sitting in front of the one empty seat. Kit tilted her head toward it. "For you."

She sat down, grateful for the simple gesture. "Sorry I'm late." She looked at the two extra people at the table and smiled at them.

"No problem, Clio." Jag raised his cup to her. "Thanks for coming in on such short notice."

Clio's producer was practically vibrating. "That segment you did the other day was a masterpiece. It was brilliant thinking to go live with it instead of holding onto it like we have the others. Your ratings have soared. People loved it."

Jag didn't look as excited. "I wouldn't say they loved it. We've had a ton of response—"

"Which is what we wanted." Clio's producer looked irked.

"Responses," Jag continued, "which have shown that people are watching to see what you two come up with. But there's no question it was incredibly intense, and a lot of those responses included people who said they felt sorry for Clio."

"And people who said both of you looked exhausted." The woman Clio hadn't met spoke up.

"I was upset because it was upsetting," Clio said, looking around the table. "If I'd been cracking jokes and asking about fashion it would have been..." She shrugged. "I wouldn't have done it."

"And that's why we needed to meet today." Clio's agent motioned toward the two new people. "First of all, you need a stylist with you. Your images need to stay intact, and you both looked simply awful. Tamara here is going to make sure you both look your best from now on."

Tamara gave them a big smile that cracked the makeup in the little lines at her eyes.

"And to help balance you two out, between the sweet and the salty, is Paul. He's a current philosopher at Cal Tech and he has agreed to come on and be a kind of buffer between the two of you."

Clio stared at him, wracking her brain. He seemed so familiar… When she figured it out, she was about to say something, but he gave her the tiniest shake of his head and she stopped. "Nice to meet you both. It won't hurt for us to look good on camera, and for someone to make sure Kit doesn't look like she slept underground for a week."

Kit rolled her eyes and tilted back on her chair. "I get the stylist. But why the buffer?" She glanced at Clio. "I thought we did well together."

"Oh, you did." Clio's agent's tone was irritatingly placating. "But there's always room for improvement, right?"

"You haven't even aired the other two segments we've done. Why not wait to add people into the mix until you've shown those and gotten your *feedback*?" Kit's tone left no doubts as to how she felt about this change.

Clio put her hand on Kit's arm and liked the way her bicep bunched under it. "You never know, Kit. This could be really good."

Kit pulled her arm away, frowning. "Jesus, Clio. Can't you ever stand up for yourself? Do you always have to play the good child?" She stood and left the room, the door silently whooshing shut behind her.

Clio shook inside but wasn't sure if it was from anger or hurt, or some toxic combination of the two. Just when it seemed like she and Kit were getting somewhere.

"Okay, that's settled then. The segments you've already filmed are set to air this Friday and next week, and we'll let you both know when they've been edited so you can come in and give them the green light." Jag pushed himself up from the table like there was a weight on his shoulders.

She got up and moved around the table. Then she took him in a tight hug, which he quickly returned. "Everything will be okay," she said quietly.

He pulled back and looked at her. "You think so?"

The virtue in him, the deep desire to do right for everyone around him, vibrated so strongly she could feel it through the hug. "I do." She put her hand over his heart. "I can feel it."

Tears welled in his eyes. "Thank you, Clio." He released her and blinked quickly before turning away. "Let me know if you need anything, and good luck with the next segment."

Clio nodded, and the others left, with the stylist promising she'd make Clio look all kinds of fabulous the next time she was on air. Soon, it was only Clio and the philosopher left in the room. He continued to sit at the table and smile at her enigmatically.

She went and sat beside him. "Paul?"

"Ridiculous, no?" His accent would be hard to place in this world. "I wanted something so plain no one would ever connect me to who I was."

"But, Anulap, why would you want to hide who you were?"

He stretched his long, thin frame. "There's no reason for them to know. I've gotten used to moving around whenever anyone gets suspicious, and I've found that I like living as a normal person. A pre-fader god gets as much respect as a person who gets an M-Phil instead of a PhD. As though you've done well for trying, but you didn't actually get there in the end."

"But you won't be in the background if you come on the show. You'll be front and center, and there will be people like me who recognize you."

He nodded and took her hand gently. "Yes. But when I saw you in Mexico, and what you were doing there, I simply had to come forward. There's something special between you, absolutely. But it wouldn't hurt to have an old god of magic and knowledge at your side, will it?" He covered her hand with his other one. "I want to be part of what you're doing, Clio. I loved your show of fun and silliness, but you're capable of so much more. The Mexico segment showed that."

She slid her hand away from his. "What it showed was that it hurts me when there's death and violence all around me. If people just want to see me cry in the face of mayhem, then that's not what I want." She got up and squeezed his shoulder. "It will be nice to have someone around who understands our world, though."

She made her way back to her car and stopped to look at JT's café. Was Kit there having pancakes drenched in too much syrup? Should she go to her, the way Kit had done when this thing started? She jerked open the car door as she thought about what Kit had said to her. She could stand up for herself just fine.

CHAPTER TWELVE

A rt." Kit grimaced. "I could be doing a million other things. Doing laundry by hand in the mud would be more interesting and useful."

"Good to know. At least you're not doing this with a muse whose responsibility is art." Clio's shoulders ached from the tense flight to Santa Fe. Tamara had fussed with her hair and made her try on several different outfits, giving commentary on each. Kit had disappeared into the back with Sian after hardly even a hello to Clio. And Paul had sat silently at the front, reading a book.

Tamara tugged a piece of Clio's hair into place as they walked toward the Merging Arts Gallery, and she pulled her head away. "I think it's fine now, thanks." When she'd asked why Tamara wasn't giving Kit the same treatment, she'd said it was a beauty and the beast kind of thing. Clio was the beautiful, put-together muse, while Kit was the down-to-earth, rugged one. Kit had simply shaken her head and gone back to the card game.

She'd done her own makeup for the other sessions, and now it felt like she was wearing a mask again, even though she'd asked Tamara to apply it with a light hand. She was worried that if she blinked her eyelids might stick together thanks to the copious amounts of mascara. It was impossible to be grateful, but she tried for gracious, and Tamara didn't seem to notice the difference.

Kit held the door open for Clio. "Careful you don't float away," she said.

Clio lifted her chin and walked past, the bubble sleeves pressing against both doors as she entered. In truth, she felt like a blimp about to take off thanks to all the material that puffed out around her arms and legs. And the light pink made it worse. She probably looked like walking cotton candy. Why had she let Tamara talk her into this outfit?

"Hey, you made it." A rail-thin young man in low-slung, paint-covered jeans came striding up. He held out his hand. "I'm Red. Come on in and I'll show you around."

Clio took the lead, since Kit looked like she might be mentally washing her laundry. "Tell us all about what you're doing here."

He looked at her with total sincerity. "We're changing the world through art. Having a muse here…" He shook his shaggy hair. "It's so wild. We couldn't be more excited."

Clio's ego swelled a little under his praise. "Thank you. It's good when someone knows the importance of art to the world."

Kit cleared her throat and looked toward the ceiling.

"Totally. Back here." They followed him into a huge studio space with several artists at work. It was quiet except for the sounds of painting—brushes scraping canvas, paints being mixed on trays, and quiet music playing in the background.

"What's this about?" Kit finally spoke up.

"Santa Fe has always been an artsy place. Like, people from all over the world have been coming here for centuries. It's got good energy and artists feel that." He looked at Clio for confirmation and she nodded, although it wasn't quite that simple. It had to do with the lines of energy that ran through the planet and the way they crossed in Santa Fe, but it wasn't time to get into an astrophysical conversation.

"So, after the Merge, this guy calls, says he wants to do something with people to get them in touch with the artists in their souls. And I'm like, yeah, totally, let's do it." He smiled and pointed. "And so he came down from, like, wherever he's from, and set out all these ideas. Then I got a group of artists I know together, and we set things in motion."

"And what are these things and who is that guy?" Kit's tone made it clear she was losing patience.

"That," Clio said, trying to keep her pink bubble outfit from touching any of the canvases, "is Ptah, ancient Egyptian god of craftsmen and architects." She drew up in front of him and bowed her head. "Nice to see you again."

His dark skin had splotches of paint on it, including a blue spot on the end of his nose. "Likewise, muse of history. It is good you kept my name in the books so I would not be forgotten." He looked over Clio's shoulder at the camera crew. "And because you did so, I was able to come here and do what I love."

She looked around, keeping her smile in place for the camera, even though his gratitude made her a little weepy. It wasn't often someone praised her for their continued existence. "And what is that?"

"With Red and the others, we've created a commune of artists, a collective who share their knowledge and passion. One day per week we also have immortals come in who are free to share their tips and do their own paintings as well." He pointed with his paintbrush to a watercolor on the wall in the corner. "Your father did that one."

"Zeus painted a watercolor of pandas?" Kit asked, her voice dripping with incredulity. "I can certainly see how that's time well spent in helping humanity."

"Adding beauty to the world is always a good thing," Clio said, keeping her back to Kit. "And allowing that beauty to come through you is a way to free your mind and find answers you've been struggling with." She glanced over her shoulder. "Maybe you should try it."

"So, anyway," Red said, his eyes darting nervously between the group and Ptah, "people come from all over to paint together, to create together, and it's formed this amazing setup. Paintings sell for loads, and we put that money back into the gallery and into this crazy awesome program called Art for Youth—"

"Clever," Kit muttered.

"That gives kids places to express themselves through art when maybe they can't express themselves through words." He frowned at Kit. "You're kind of a bummer, aren't you?"

She looked startled that he'd called her on it. "Not much of an art person, I guess."

"Yeah, I can tell. You have this whole vibe going on." He shrugged. "It's cool. Takes all kinds, right?"

Clio awkwardly hooked her arm through his. "Show us around and tell us about some of the art. Can you show us any of the work done by the youth group?"

He did as asked, and Ptah continued to paint with one member of the camera crew filming over his shoulder while the other followed Clio around. She asked questions and made a fuss of the kids' work, though some were better than others. She dug a little deeper and got out the information that the kids who worked in the program had been sent there by the county. They were considered at-risk kids who had difficult home lives or who were often in trouble with the law. The difference in their behavior after they'd joined the program was huge, with many of them going on to art school.

"I think a couple have even applied to the ACA," Red said, his expression showing his pride in what they'd accomplished.

"I think that's spectacular," Clio said, turning her back to the camera so she could unstick her mascara and open her eye properly. "What a wonderful thing to offer the world."

Kit stepped forward. "Art isn't going to solve the problem of hunger or help provide resources to the most needy." She crossed her arms. "How are they making the world a better place?"

He looked at her blankly. "It's art."

When it looked like she was going to go on another rant, and just when Clio was wondering if there was enough paint in the pot beside her to dump over Kit's head, Paul stepped forward.

"Kit, one of the difficulties of a logical mind is to find the usefulness of beauty. But beauty is useful in its own way. We need it like we need right and wrong. What is beautiful is not ugly, and because we have both, we know which one we wish for more of." He gave her a small smile and stepped back again.

Kit looked baffled and Clio shot Paul a grateful smile.

"Thank you for the tour, Red. And, Ptah, wonderful to see you again. If we can ever help or get involved at the ACA, please give me a call. The world needs as much beauty as it can possibly get." Clio led the way out of the shop and glanced at the camera. "That's not the only wonderful thing happening here. Next, we're headed to the most spiritual, most delicious shop in all of New Mexico."

She made a simple hand gesture and the crew stopped filming. She winced and squeezed her eyes shut. "Tamara, you have to get this gunk off my eyes. I can barely see."

"But, Clio, it's making your eyes simply pop." Tamara dabbed at Clio's forehead with a blotter. "And if we change it now, it will look strange as part of the segment."

She sighed. "Fine. But next time, go easy, please."

"I know my job. Promise." Tamara's smile was less than genuine.

"And I know whether or not I can see," Clio snapped. "Let's finish this." She looked back at Kit, who was leaning against a wall, smirking. "Will you be getting involved other than as a pain in the ass?"

"Involved, yes. Pain in the ass, always." She pushed away from the wall. "I love chocolate and it serves a purpose in the world. Medically proven."

The cameras started rolling again and they went in. The chocolate shop smelled of earthy cocoa and spices. Kit peered into the cases, her nose practically pressed to the glass.

"Welcome to Mezo Chocolates." The woman behind the counter had thick, long dark hair with beads in her thin braids. Her brown eyes matched the chocolate in the cases.

"Lily, right? It's wonderful to meet you. Tell us about your shop." Clio leaned in to broadcast her interest.

Lily told them about how the shop had been started as a way to remember Mezo American ancestry, and they created drinking chocolate as well as chocolate pieces that came from ancient recipes from all kinds of indigenous cultures.

"And then, after the Merge, we had two of the ancient gods come to us and ask if they could help make the chocolate." Her face lit up with pride. "And now the chocolate that we created from the memories of our ancestors is infused with the special touch of the gods. We're living in total harmony with what we've wanted to do all along."

"That one." Kit pointed at a dark chocolate with a green line running through it. "What is that?"

Lily laughed. "That's our special agave chocolate with a caramel center." She pulled it out and handed it to Kit. "Take small bites so you really appreciate all the flavors."

Kit did as instructed and made sounds that were only this side of sexual. "That was incredible."

"Yes, it certainly sounded like it, didn't it?" Clio said sweetly. "And you have another side to your business now, don't you?"

"We do! We now offer chocolatier mentorship to all indigenous people who'd like to learn how to do this themselves. It gives them a chance to learn more about their culture's use of chocolate and cooking in general, and it allows them to talk to the gods who are part of their heritage. Not just the two who enjoy working here, but also others who donate their time to help others remember who they are."

Clio's eyes watered. "How beautiful. Understanding our history, where we come from and who our people were, can be so powerful. It can show us who we are and what we maybe don't want to be, too." She reached out and took Lily's hand. "Thank you for sharing this with us. We'll put your shop email on the screen when this airs so that people can get in touch with you about the program. As can gods who want to get involved, I assume?"

She nodded enthusiastically. "By all means. And if you and your group would like to try it yourselves, we've got something set up for you."

Clio was surprised. She hadn't been told this would be part of it. Based on Kit's expression, she hadn't either. "That would be incredible. Thank you so much."

Lily smiled as she poked at Clio's bubble sleeve. "I have an outfit that might be more suitable for working with chocolate. You wouldn't want to get that messy."

Clio would be fine with taking it off and leaving it in a whole vat of chocolate. "That's so kind. I do love trying on new clothes!"

Kit's sigh was audible, but Clio ignored her.

As a group, they followed Lily into the back area that was set up with all kinds of trays and spices as well as molds. "I'll take you through the basic process, and then you'll try your hand at it." She motioned to Clio, who followed her into another room. "It isn't as fancy, but I think this would suit you." She handed her a simple black sundress with large red poppies on it. "Please consider it a gift."

"This is beyond perfect. Thank you so, so much." Clio ducked into the utilitarian bathroom and practically ripped off the balloon dress. The sundress let her breathe and she sighed happily. When she came out, she held up the pink monstrosity. "I don't suppose you know any crafters around who could make use of this material?"

Lily smiled knowingly and took it. "I'm sure they'd be grateful for it." She set it on a countertop and led the way back into the kitchen where the others waited.

Clio nearly stumbled when she saw the look in Kit's eyes as they traveled the length of her. It set her on fire and her stomach lit with butterflies. Kit's eyes met hers and she shivered at the intensity in them. "So," she turned away, needing to break the spell, "what do we do first?"

The next hour was full of laughter and playful banter as Clio and Kit, as well as Tamara and Paul, learned a few secrets of chocolate making and design. Clio's were pretty but simple. Tamara's were too big and kept falling apart. Paul's were delicate and looked like they could go into the shop window. Kit's, though, hardly ever made it to the tray. She kept eating her chocolate as she designed it, and then didn't have enough to finish whatever she'd had in mind, so she ate the rest.

"The only one you finally get to the tray in a whole piece and it looks like a log of poo." Clio peered at it.

"It'll taste amazing, just the same." She picked up her icing bag and began to write on it. "Look, it even has your name on it."

Clio laughed when Kit added a lopsided heart above the I. "Gee, thanks."

By the time they left, they had bags of chocolate to take back with them, and Clio had arranged for a large order to be sent to the ACA and to her sisters, as well as a giant gift basket for Zeus.

They walked past other galleries and commented on the different events going on, and Paul shared some information about the nature of art and the chemicals in the brain, which Kit admitted to finding interesting.

Paul stopped in front of a gallery window. "Clio, isn't that you?"

She looked over in surprise at the sculpture of her standing in a chariot, holding a book in one arm. The ornate clock that made up the wheel didn't seem to be working. "I haven't seen a chariot clock like that in ages. But the original was in marble. This one looks like it's metal of some kind."

"Why are you standing in a chariot?" Kit asked.

"I love the way your mind always goes to the logical questions first. Not, who created it and why, but rather, why I'm standing up." Clio shook her head, smiling. "Carlo Franzoni created the original in 1819. He was an Italian sculptor who loved the ancient style, and for some reason he chose me for this one. His sculpture of Justice is in the Supreme Court to this day."

Kit stood there, her hands in her pockets, staring at the sculpture that was just big enough to fit on a mantle. Her expressions flickered in her eyes, but Clio couldn't make them out.

"Unless you want to take in any of the other ninety-eight art galleries in the city, I think we're about done." Clio turned to the camera. "I think today's *Truth Hunt* has shown us how important creativity is in our world."

The cameras stopped rolling and Clio stretched her shoulders.

"Nice final line," Kit said, still looking at the sculpture.

"Thanks. I don't know why I did it, but it felt right." She tugged on Kit's shirt. "You ready to go? Or do you prefer the silent version of me in that clock?"

Kit finally looked at her. "I definitely prefer the real thing."

Once again there was that look in Kit's eyes, and Clio ducked her head and moved away. "Well, the real thing wants food and quiet."

"I'm down with that," Kit said, falling into step beside her.

"Clio, where's your dress?" Tamara asked from behind them.

Clio rolled her eyes and smiled a little when Kit bumped her shoulder.

"Yeah, Clio, where's your dress?"

She managed to pinch Kit's thigh as they walked. "I'm afraid I tore it when I was taking it off. I left it behind for the crafters to use."

Tamara gave a gasp of dismay. "Clio, that was Armani. You can't just give it over to someone to cut up for a quilt."

Kit barely covered her laugh with a cough.

"Actually, it will make a lovely, comfy quilt, I'm sure." Clio disliked losing her temper, but she was quickly growing tired of the drama. And she *liked* the occasionally spicy drama of life.

They continued down the street toward their van and Kit glanced over her shoulder. "Paul is super quiet. I keep forgetting he's even with us until some wise-man nugget falls out of his mouth."

Paul seemed to be listening sympathetically to Tamara's rant about whatever it was she was talking about. "He's unusual, that's for sure."

Kit's eyebrow went up. "Something to tell me?"

Clio nodded. "I'll share, but when it's just you and me."

Kit looked satisfied with that answer. "Clio, look. We knew this was going to be tough. And I'll probably keep apologizing for being an ass, and I admit that sometimes I think you'd be way better if you were more real. But I think it was a good day."

Impulsively, Clio took her hand. "Thank you. That means a lot. Aside from the back-handed compliment, that is."

They got to the van and piled in. At the airport, the camera crew got out first and headed to their area, and then the van took Clio, Kit, Paul, and Tamara to the private plane area, where they boarded quickly. This time, once they were airborne, Kit moved over to share the couch with Clio, leaving Tamara to sit on her own as she flipped through photos on her iPad. Paul, once again, stayed up front reading his book.

"I checked my email while we were at the first gallery. They're going to show the first segment we did tomorrow night. I've already given my go-ahead. I figure it'll be fine, and I don't have the patience to sit through it right now." Kit accepted the Cherry Coke from Sian. "And then they'll show the others weekly."

The words sucked the high of the day away and Clio slumped. "And if the audience doesn't respond, then I'll be out of a job. I'll email in a minute and tell them I give my go-ahead too. There wasn't anything people shouldn't see."

"You could always go back to Santa Fe and model for sculptors." Kit gave her a teasing grin. "I'm sure there's a call out there somewhere for naked muse models."

"How did we go from modeling for a sculptor to modeling naked? I wasn't naked in the chariot. My chiton and cloak were very respectable." The banter made her feel better.

"I think naked is far more interesting." Kit laced Clio's fingers with her own. "You're infuriating. But damn if I'm not glad we're in this together."

The way Kit's hand felt as it held hers made Clio tremble inside. She knew this feeling. She'd avoided it for years. But as she looked into Kit's eyes, there was no avoiding it now. Damn Cupid and his pissed off mother. Falling for a human wasn't in her plan.

CHAPTER THIRTEEN

K it sat on the couch with Buster's big head on her lap. "I should have reviewed the damn footage, Bust." The segment they'd done at the protest wasn't bad, but they'd cleverly cut out the angels sharing a joint as well as their moronic antics trying to impress Clio. They sat at the base of the statue looking sad as they explained what they understood of the god's instructions. So much for the buffoons who'd make the gods look bad. Once again, things had been covered over with varnish to hide the decay beneath.

Clio, with her thick dark hair in simple curls hanging down her back, looked more beautiful than the angels. Her eyes were the color of the sky. At the time, Kit had felt like Clio's saccharine smile would be obvious, but in truth, it wasn't. She looked genuine.

Kit, on the other hand, looked pretty dismal next to her. Wrinkled and grumpy, she looked irritated and tired. "They said we're beauty and the beast, Buster. What do you think?" She scratched behind his ears and received a lick of support. Maybe she should make more of an effort, if only so Clio didn't look like she was working with a pile of angry laundry.

They had several more interviews lined up and she couldn't decide whether or not she was looking forward to them. It was unsettling. She always loved her work and couldn't wait for the next story. But working with someone was hard, not to mention she didn't exactly come off looking great. Without Clio, though, there wouldn't have been much of a story. She was the one who had known where to find the angels. And the three immortals had come right up to talk to her, whereas they might not have done that if Kit had been alone.

Did that mean she wasn't good at her job? "Come on, Buster. Let's go for a walk." Fresh air would help straighten out her thoughts. She hooked on his leash and grabbed a thick sweatshirt to ward off the evening chill brought on by the fog.

As they made their way down the block, she appreciated the way the lights reflected off the shiny sidewalk slick with rain. It made her think of their art segment, and she smiled as she remembered the look of relief in Clio's expression after she'd changed out of the Pepto-Bismol dress. And damn, what she'd changed into had set Kit's body on fire. A particular part of her body, really. The dress had hugged Clio's curves just right, and Kit had wanted to run her lips over the soft skin of Clio's shoulder and collar bone to the swell of her breasts.

They'd never talked about that kiss they'd shared in the house in the Deadlands. They hadn't had a lot of alone time, but neither of them had picked up the phone to chat about it either. She didn't know why Clio hadn't, but Kit wasn't sure what to say. It had been the most sensual, erotic kiss she'd ever had with someone. If she could have thrown something at Dani and told her to get out, without being turned into fireplace ash, she would have. She'd wanted to boost Clio onto the counter and taste every inch of her.

And now, even when they were shooting something she didn't care about or when Clio had on her TV face, as Kit had come to think of it, she still wanted to press Clio against a wall and kiss her that way again.

But it was a bad idea. There were stories out there about people getting involved with an immortal, and there weren't a whole lot of happily-ever-afters. Clio had said as much herself. Hell, to the gods, falling in love with a mortal was considered a curse. The only way Clio could avoid that curse was to avoid letting her heart get involved. And beyond the fact that Kit didn't want to get involved with someone who refused to look at things from a practical perspective, she also didn't want to get involved with someone who couldn't give her whole heart.

It was doomed to fail. She looked down when Buster nuzzled her hand. "Sorry, buddy. I'm not very good company tonight, am I?"

They made their way back to the house and she flopped back down on the sofa. Her phone buzzed and she glanced at the message from Barb, confirming that they were meeting up tomorrow night for drinks as usual, and she gave her the name of the new place they were trying. She sent back a thumbs up emoji. When had she become an emoji person?

A commercial advertising a new pair of shoes in the Jesus line came on and she turned the TV off. Life was so strange now, and she didn't need a fling with a muse to complicate it any further, no matter how insanely hot that muse was.

"How would you feel if I called you before ten a.m. on your day off?" Kit mumbled into the phone, the pillow muffling her words.

"I'd be so stunned I'd probably need therapy." Jag rustled some papers so she could hear it. "The reviews are in from last night's segment. Interested?"

Kit groaned and rolled over and came face to face with Buster's big brown head on the pillow next to hers. His breath propelled her from the bed. "Fine. Go."

"This is exactly what the world needs right now," he clearly read from something. "People from both sides of the Merge taking on the bigger issues to show us that there's hope even when it feels hopeless. Kit Kalloway and Clio Ardalides make a powder keg of a team and don't seem to hold anything back. We can't wait to see what they get up to next."

"Nothing about the beauty and the beast?" she asked as she dumped coffee into the French press.

"That was Clio's people's idea, not mine. They're a little more focused on the look of things than the meat."

"Good thing you're there to be my meat, then."

He laughed. "Not even the weirdest thing you've ever said to me. Anyway, I wanted you to know. It looks good. Keep it up."

Kit put the phone down and wondered if Clio's people had called her with the same news. She picked her phone up again and sent a text.

Hey. Good news, beauty. You're stuck with the beast for a while.

She hit send and wondered why that phrasing had gotten stuck in her craw. She'd been called a beast in bed and in the gym, and she was good with it. Why did it sit like a thorn in her thumb when it came to Clio? Her phone buzzed.

I might have gotten different news.

There was a sad face next to it. Kit hit the phone button. "What's with the sad face?" she asked when Clio picked up.

"I was told that I came off as unlikable, and I didn't have enough of my trademark humor in place. And that in future segments I need to have more fun, or they're going to take me from the show. Well, essentially, they'll pull out, which leaves just you and your show."

Kit leaned against the countertop. "I was just told that the reviews are great, and that we make a great team. Jag said to keep doing what we're doing." Why would Clio's people give her completely opposite news?

"Well, at least someone believes in us, I guess." She sounded despondent.

"I'm really sorry, Clio. I don't get why we got different messages. Want me to ask Jag?"

Clio hesitated. "No, that's okay. We'll just see how it plays out. Thanks for calling."

Kit didn't want to hang up, but she couldn't think of anything else to say. "My friends and I are going to hang out tonight. Want to join us?" What was she thinking? So much for keeping things in the professional realm.

"Thanks for the offer, really. But I think I need some time to myself to figure out what I want from my future."

Kit's stomach turned. "What do you mean? Isn't this what you wanted?"

"The part you've been told? Yes. The part I've been told...I don't know. I wanted fun and light, but that doesn't mean I want to be a laughing stock." She hiccupped. "I'm so confused. Anyway, thanks again for calling and for the invite. Please don't stop asking. I promise I'll accept one day."

"Yeah, of course. Call me if you want to talk anything out."

They ended the call and Kit looked down at Buster, who was a giant ball of gorgeous brown fluff at her feet. "What are we going to do?"

The bar was one Kit had passed several times before but one she'd never stopped into. Barb, Trish, and Jim waved her over from their table near the stairs. There was already a beer waiting for her.

"How is the new cool kid on the block?" Barb asked.

"I've always been cool." Kit grinned and winked at the passing waitress, more out of habit than anything else.

"No, you've always thought you were cool. No one else agreed. But now you're really playing with the cool kids." Trish tapped her bottle to Kit's. "And we're assuming that you're not going to forget your oldest and dearest friends when you start going to all the cool kid parties."

"Do you think one of the gods you know could make me a football player?" Jim asked.

"And what? You'd give up your accounting job?" She looked up from the menu when none of them responded. "What?"

"Come on. Tell us what it's like. You've always got a hard-on for going after the gods, but you've never been this close to any. What's it like?" Barb rested her elbows on the table and waited.

"It's...I don't know. You haven't seen the one at the camp yet, but that was pretty crazy. There's this god with a trimmed goatee and huge purple wings who tells me he watched out for me whenever I went sailing alone—"

"No way!" Trish's eyes lit up. "Did you get a feather as a keepsake?"

Kit wrinkled her nose. "They're a part of his body. It's like asking if I got a lock of hair or a toenail or something. He's not a bird."

Trish sighed. "You're so literal. I would have asked for one."

Was this what life was going to turn into? Her little group of friends asking questions about the people she'd met instead of asking about her? She looked up when someone tapped her on the shoulder.

A woman with a very deeply cut top and very large breasts trying to escape that top held out a napkin. "I'm sorry to bother you, but could I get your autograph?"

Trying not to show that she was thrown, she smiled and signed it and handed it back. Then the woman handed her another napkin, this one with her name and phone number on it. "Just in case you need a friend tonight."

There was no mistaking the meaning in her eyes or her hips as she sauntered away.

Jim let out a low whistle. "I want to be your friend forever."

Barb elbowed him in the side. "Excuse me?"

"Yeah, excuse me?" Kit said, laughing. "The autograph part is new, but it isn't like the phone number part is."

"Dude, your status has just gone up about five levels." Jim put his arm around Barb, who looked slightly mollified. "It must feel good to be recognized."

"You think I wasn't recognizable before Clio?" She frowned and took a long drink of her beer and then motioned for another.

Trish took her hand and lowered it as she was about to take another drink. "That's not what we're saying. But you have to admit that this is going to raise your profile massively. Don't get all stubborn crazy on us, okay?"

Kit let her shoulders drop. "Sorry. Our producers are being hard-asses and learning to work with someone is making me cranky."

"Then tonight is a good night for you to relax." Barb gave her an understanding smile.

The conversation flowed with more ease, and they joked as usual as they caught up on each other's weeks. There was a lull in the conversation and music floated up from downstairs. Kit tilted her head and listened. There was something familiar about it.

"Hey, what's going on downstairs?" she asked.

"They have amateur singers come in sometimes to use the stage down there. Did you want to check it out?" Trish asked, already picking up her glass.

The others picked up theirs too and headed downstairs into the blue-lit smoke meant to provide atmosphere but which really just kept her from being able to see the stage perfectly. They snagged a table while the singer took a break and Kit looked around. There were only about twenty or so people in the audience and the stage was set up for a single singer on a stool. It was low-key, meant to be a place to share music, not really showcase talent. It was perfect.

They continued to talk until a guitar strum broke in and Kit looked at the stage. Her heart leapt and she leaned forward. Clio sat alone, a guitar tucked against her, her head bowed over it as she began to sing. Her voice was beautiful, haunting and sad as she sang about roads not taken and trying to figure out who she was.

"Holy shit," Jim whispered. "Isn't that your co-worker?"

Kit nodded but didn't speak, not wanting to break the spell Clio was weaving with her lyrics and voice. The rest of the room seemed equally as enthralled, and when she finished, there were some whistles along with loud applause. Clio looked startled, as though she'd forgotten there were other people around.

"She looks amazing," Trish whispered.

That was certainly true. She wore tight jeans, black heeled boots, and a tight black T-shirt with a peace logo on it. Kit realized it was a T-shirt from the protest and it made her smile. It wasn't Clio's usual style, but damn was it sexy. Her hair was pulled into a messy bun, with whisps escaping around her face. Kit wanted to jump on stage and pull the bun down so she could lace her fingers in that thick, gorgeous hair.

"You're going to set the stage on fire if you keep looking at her like that," Barb said.

Kit sat back and tried to rein it in, but she had to keep crossing and uncrossing her legs to stem the throb between them. At the end of Clio's next song, a slightly lively one about burning bridges you no longer needed to cross, she gave the audience a quick smile, said thanks, and left the stage.

Kit jumped up and went to the bar. "Can you get a message to the woman who just left the stage, please?"

The bartender looked her over. "You're the one she works with."

Kit nodded. "I'd really like to ask her to join me and my friends." She motioned behind her toward her table, not wanting to seem like she was just there to be a nuisance.

"Sure, I'll let her know." She said something to the other person behind the bar and then walked away.

Kit went back to her table. "I've sent word for Clio to join us, if she wants to."

Trish practically clapped like an excited child. "That's amazing."

Barb looked thoughtful, but Jim looked as excited as Trish, and probably for similar reasons. Unlike Kit, Trish didn't really have a type. She just liked sexy women, and Clio was definitely one of those. A flare of jealousy went through her, and then she laughed. Clio had made it very clear what her type was.

"Hey, fancy seeing you here," Clio said as she came up to the table. Her hands were clasped like she didn't know what to do with them, and she looked adorably shy.

Kit stood. "Hey. I had no idea you were a singer." She pulled out the chair next to her and nearly sighed with relief when Clio sat down instead of saying she had to leave.

"I'm not a singer, not really. I enjoy playing guitar and I love music. Singing gives me an emotional outlet. I use it when I'm trying to work through things." Clio nodded her thanks to the bartender who brought over her drink.

"You sing more beautifully than anyone I've ever heard sing. Ever." Trish was practically vibrating. "I'm Trish. Sorry for Kit's bad manners, although I'm sure you know all about those now." She stuck her tongue out at Kit, who just rolled her eyes. "And this is

Barb, Kit's best friend, and Jim, Barb's boyfriend who we're stuck with until Barb finds someone more attractive."

Clio laughed, a sound Kit wanted to hear forever.

"Nice to meet you all. I didn't expect to see anyone I knew tonight."

"You came alone?" Kit asked.

Clio wrapped a napkin around her glass to soak up the condensation. "I always do."

There it was again, that sound of loneliness that Kit had picked up on before.

"Well, you aren't alone tonight. Cheers!" Barb held up her drink, and the undercurrent was gone.

For the next two hours, Kit was happy to mostly sit back and listen to the conversation flowing around her. Clio was animated and sweet, funny and kind. She listened and asked great questions that kept the conversation going. And it was real, the kind of real that Kit found intoxicating.

"No, really. You put a Popsicle stick in the banana, then you wrap it in plastic wrap and put it in the freezer for a few hours. It's like eating frozen banana ice cream when you take it out." Clio licked her lips and winked.

"Unless it's covered in chocolate, I don't see the point." Barb held her hand over her mouth and yawned. "Sorry, guys, but I think it's time for me to call it. I'm wiped and I have a meeting in the morning." She and Jim stood, and the other three followed.

Kit was behind Clio on the stairs, and it meant she was face to butt, and she wanted to grab it, sink her teeth into it, drag the jeans off it. She tripped on a stair.

"Seriously. Don't be a wet sponge. You've *got* to go for it," Trish said in her ear when they were saying good night. Clio had been impervious to Trish's flirtation and not-so-subtle attempts to draw her in with double entendres. Instead, Clio had seemed to have eyes only for Kit.

Kit and Clio were left standing alone on the sidewalk. She wanted to reach for Clio, pull her close, and kiss her stupid. But she couldn't find the words.

"Come home with me," Clio said.

Kit looked up from her boots. "What?"

"Come home with me."

Kit searched Clio's eyes and saw her own desire reflected back at her. She simply took Clio's hand and followed her to her car. Bad idea or not, she wanted this.

CHAPTER FOURTEEN

Clio threw her head back, giving Kit access to her neck. Something broke as they created a tornado of lust through the house, the sound of glass shattering and something wooden thumping against the floor. She didn't care. The house could fall into the ocean, as long as Kit didn't stop what she was doing.

Kit pressed hot, hard kisses along Clio's throat. Her hands slid under her T-shirt and pulled, and she flung it behind her as she moved lower, sucking and biting the tops of Clio's breasts above the black lace bra. Her teeth closed over Clio's hard nipples, sucking them through the lace, and she cried out, pushing her breast harder against Kit's mouth.

"Fuck." Kit grabbed Clio's ass and lifted her.

She wrapped her legs around Kit and continued the kiss that had started the moment they were in the car. The way Kit had been looking at her singed her soul and made her weak with desire. She hadn't bothered to rethink the invitation to come home with her. She needed this.

Kit kicked open a door and they landed on the bed with Kit on top of her. She shifted and pushed her thigh between Clio's legs, right where she was throbbing so hard it almost hurt. "Please," she murmured against Kit's lips. "Please."

She didn't know what she was asking for, but Kit seemed to. She pulled her top off and Clio kicked off her boots, which were quickly joined by Kit's.

Kit's black, silky sports bra covered perfect breasts and highlighted her solid, flat stomach. She ran her hands over Kit's abs and smiled as the skin rippled under her fingertips. "It's like you're carved from marble."

"I sure as fuck feel as hard as marble right now," she said, lowering herself once again onto Clio. "I need to touch you."

Clio arched into Kit's touch as she squeezed her breasts and tugged at her nipples. She began to beg again and was silenced with a hot kiss. Kit quickly undid her jeans and slid them off, then traced the black lace between Clio's thighs.

"Tell me what you want," she said, her voice husky.

"I want you," Clio said as she looked at Kit, kneeling between her legs, her finger too lightly sliding along Clio's wet panties.

"Tell me." She pressed harder. "What do you want?"

Clio lifted her hips and pressed against Kit's finger. "I want you to fuck me."

The air seemed to leave Kit in a rush, and she pulled Clio's bra down so she could suck on her nipple. With her other hand, she pushed her panties aside and entered her, deep and slow.

"Please," Clio whispered again. "Please fuck me."

Kit didn't need any more encouragement. She pushed in deep and hard, adding another finger, as she sucked and bit at Clio's nipples. She took her harder and faster, responding to Clio's pleas and cries, until Clio cried out and slammed herself against Kit's fingers as the orgasm crashed over her. She held Kit to her by her hair as her body shook.

Finally, she settled and Kit slipped out of her. Kit stood to finish undressing and then got in bed beside her and pulled the blanket up over them both. Clio rested her head on Kit's chest and felt her strong arm wrap around her. Warm, sated, and safe, she drifted to sleep.

She woke when Kit shifted beneath her. It was still dark out.

"Sorry, my arm is asleep," Kit said softly.

Clio sat up so Kit could recover her arm, but then she grew distracted by the way the moonlight was glinting off Kit's body, creating shadows in the curves and hollows of her solid form. She moved so she could get between Kit's legs and looked up at her, the question in her eyes. Kit gave a small grin, her eyes half-lidded.

Clio slid Kit's tight boxers off and inhaled the scent of her. Sliding her fingertip along Kit's length drew a deep sharp intake of breath from Kit, which in turn made her own center clench again. She knelt and twined her arms beneath Kit's legs, holding them in place as she lightly drew her tongue over Kit's clit. Kit moaned and swore as she crumpled the sheets in her fists. Clio kept going, drawing light circles around her clit, sometimes pressing harder, sometimes even lighter, until Kit was swearing in one long multisyllabic sound.

She pressed harder, sucking lightly, and Kit exploded, her body jerking as she yelled.

Once she'd settled, Clio rested her head on Kit's thigh and caressed her stomach in soft circles. Kit's skin twitched under her touch, making her smile.

"Come up here." Kit tugged gently on Clio's hair.

She scooted up and curled onto her side. Kit wrapped her arm around Clio and pulled her in close. She wanted to stay awake so she could remember how amazing it felt to be held that way, but sleep overtook her.

❖

"Unless that's a sex toy, please turn it off." Clio snuggled deeper under the blanket as Kit's phone vibrated again from somewhere on the floor.

"Fuck." Kit got caught tangled in the sheet as she was reaching for her jeans and crashed onto the floor. "Ow."

The buzzing stopped, and Clio cracked one eye open when Kit didn't get back into bed. "Everything okay?"

Kit's head popped up so Clio could see her. "I was supposed to meet Sian for a workout half an hour ago." She grinned and rested her chin on the bed. "Should I tell her why I'm late?"

Clio threw a pillow at her. "Don't tell me you're the kind to kiss and tell."

"Depends." Kit climbed back into bed like a panther. "If you tell me I'm better in bed than she is, then I'll keep it to myself so she doesn't feel bad. If you tell me I'm not as good..." She stopped and pretended to think. "Well, I can't imagine you saying that, so I probably won't tell her."

Clio laughed and curled against her again. "Comparing old lovers with new ones is never a sound idea."

"I'm going to interpret that as me being better." She kissed the top of Clio's head.

"Breakfast?"

Kit's stomach rumbled in response. "How about you let me make it?"

Clio yanked the covers off her. "Offer accepted. Get to it."

Kit shivered. "Can I at least borrow a robe? Or do I have to do it naked?"

"Are you really asking me that?" Clio climbed out of bed and took her robe off the back of the door. "It will suit you, I think."

Kit held up the short, red silk robe. "Yeah. Just my thing." She put it on and modeled it. "What do you think?"

Clio reached for it. "I think I prefer you naked."

Kit danced away and sang some demented version of "I Feel Pretty" down the hallway.

Clio stretched and relished the sore muscles and feel of swollen lips. She hadn't woken this way in so long. Thankfully, there didn't seem to be any weirdness between them either, which was always a concern the morning after. She put on a long, soft black robe and followed Kit's singing to the kitchen.

The eggs and scallions were already on the counter. Kit motioned with the chopping knife. "That is a hell of a view."

Clio nodded and sat at the breakfast bar. "The view of the bridge over the ocean calms me. Whenever I'm upset or stressed, I can close my eyes and listen to the waves hitting the shore and I feel better."

"Do you feel that way often?" Kit asked, not looking up from her chopping. "And don't think I didn't notice that you had an alternative robe you could have given me."

"But that one shows off your legs." Clio wiggled her eyebrows and got an eye roll in return. When she didn't answer Kit's question, Kit stopped chopping and motioned with the knife, prompting her to continue. "Out of all of my sisters, I think I'm the most emotional. I always have been. They used to tease me about it when we were kids. Things that bounced off them would send me into some kind of emotional tailspin. I learned to control it as I got older, but I still spin occasionally." She plucked a piece of avocado from the cutting board. "Maybe that's why I needed to cut myself off from humanity for a while. It all got to be too much. Global communication means global emotion."

Kit seemed to think about that while she chopped. "So why go on TV? Why not close yourself off in some library and read history texts for the next hundred years?"

"History texts?" Clio tried to snag another piece of avocado but got thwarted by the knife. "I said I wanted to feel less, not relive all the stuff I've already cried over."

"Okay, romance novels, then." Kit smirked. "I saw your bookshelf."

Clio flushed. "There's nothing like a good emotional romance novel to give you all the good feels."

"No judgment here." Kit tilted her head. "Or, at least not a lot."

She whisked the eggs into fluffiness and dropped in the chopped tomatoes, scallions, and avocado. Then she added spices from Clio's spice rack. "Why TV?"

"You really are relentless." Clio got up and took out plates, needing something to do. "Like I said, I wanted fun. After the pandemic, I'd had more than enough of people and their history for a while. I wanted to remind people that there's good out there, and to help them take their minds off the ugly stuff." There was more, but she wasn't ready to talk about that. Not yet.

"Well, I'm glad you're doing the show with me now. You can still do fun stuff without having to act like you don't have a brain in that beautiful head of yours."

Kit's back was to her, so she didn't see the way her words hit Clio like silk-covered bricks. "Is that how you saw me? As brainless?"

Kit's back stiffened but she didn't turn around. "I mean, come on. You never said a serious word on your show. You just had gods running around doing an obstacle course designed for kids. There was no point. Now you can do stuff like the chocolate place and the kids' camp, and it's still fun, but now it has a point. And you get to show people how awesome you are."

Clio sat still, trying to process. "I'm not hungry. I'm going to go shower."

Kit spun around, looking almost resigned. "I was hoping we'd do that together."

"I was hoping we might do a lot of things together. But knowing how little you value what I do and that you see me as brainless, makes it hard to want to do anything with you at all. And you know, pointing out people's flaws and all the bad stuff in the world doesn't make you better than me, or your job any more important. It makes it more depressing and gives people a bleak view of the only world they have to live in." Clio turned away and locked herself in the bathroom. She sat on the toilet and let the tears fall.

She heard Kit's footsteps go into and then leave the bedroom, and then the front door shut loudly. How had something with so much promise gone so wrong? She cried until she got hiccups and a headache. A hot shower helped ease some of the tension, but when she went into the kitchen and saw the omelet sitting there on a plate, she started to cry again.

She picked up the phone and left Eris a message. Her sister was rarely up this early, given the late nights she kept, but she needed to hear her voice. She sat in the armchair facing the sea and wrapped her arms around herself. How had it come to this? To having only one person in the world she felt like she could really call? At one time she might have called Sian, but now that she and Kit were friends, that was out of the question. She considered calling Boreas, but she didn't know him well enough to spill her heart. And how did you tell the wind you were lonely? What was lonelier than being the wind?

An idea struck and she picked up her phone. "Dad?"

❖

She breathed in deeply, savoring the scent of earthy incense and the feel of hot Mediterranean air. Below, Athens spread out in a solid display of red roofs and white buildings. Clio sat on the temple steps of the Acropolis bathed in a pale sherbet sunset and let the worry drift away into the marble under her feet.

"This what you needed?" Zeus asked as he lowered himself to the step beside her. He was eating an extra large Snickers bar, made especially for him by the company that celebrated the fact that one of the gods loved their product.

The temple had been emptied except for the priests and priestesses who now kept it running all year round. When she'd called Zeus and asked if they could go away, he'd called in a favor and had a Yama bring him to her place. They'd driven to the airfield and were airborne and on their way to Athens within two hours. She'd never been so grateful to leave California behind. She'd served the drinks and food herself, since she hadn't let Sian know she was leaving. She could stay behind and work out with her new bestie.

It was petulant, but she didn't care.

Now, sitting in a beautifully restored temple where the ancient Greek gods were being revered once again, her soul settled somewhat. "It is what I needed. Thank you."

He wrapped his massive arm around her. "I'm not always the greatest dad, but I do what I can."

On the flight over they'd talked about what had happened, and he'd offered to throw a lightning bolt in Kit's direction. She'd quickly declined the offer, but it had felt good to have someone on her side. "You've loved mortal women in the past. How did you do it?"

He stared out at the city below. "Not well."

"What do you mean?"

"You've heard the stories. I'm not exactly a one-woman god. Being with Ama has changed me, and I'm happier than I've ever been. But there's something about mortal women. They have such passion. Us gods get jaded. We get bored and we're always searching for something new. But mortal women can love with their whole hearts, for their whole lives. Spectacular, really." He looked at her apologetically. "But I always had the option, too. I'm sorry Aphrodite did what she did to you."

Clio hugged her knees to her chest. "Me too."

They were quiet for a while, listening to the music and laughter filtering up from the city. "You know, you're the most mortal of my children, you and your sisters."

"I've always thought so, but what do you mean?" It had been a long time, centuries, really, since she'd had a chance to sit and talk with her dad this way. It was comforting to have family to turn to. It occurred to her that Kit didn't have that luxury, and it made her ache for her. She was still mad at her though.

"You were born to walk among them. You've never lived apart. You know them inside and out. Your mother was practically pure emotion. As the goddess of memory, she's the one you're most like. History and memory go hand in hand. It's hard, I imagine." He grinned. "Not that I'd really know, not being one for emotion myself."

She laughed. "You've burnt things to the ground repeatedly because someone irked you. I once saw you zap a temple because the olives were the wrong shade of green. I'd call that emotion."

His laugh bounced off the thick stone walls around them. "Okay, sure. Maybe I am more emotional than I like to admit." He tapped her head. "Maybe there are things you don't want to admit, too."

"Subtlety has never been your strongest trait." She hugged her knees tighter.

"I'm just saying…" He held up his hand and little lightning bolts played between his fingers. "Since the Merge, and for a long while before, people have forgotten that I'm a god. And I was one of the originals. But I'd become a kind of administrator, a paper pusher who bullied the gods into toeing the line. I'm coming back into my own now, though, and I know how to watch over people. Especially my family. I let you live your lives and all of you figure things out on your own. But I know when you're struggling, and I pay attention, even if you don't know it." He held up a tiny lightning bolt that wriggled between his fingertips. "Like I said on the phone when we talked before, you're probably the most like me and your mother. You're not one to take criticism. You hurt deeply, but like your sisters, you don't lash out." He stood and gave her shoulder a squeeze. "I can't tell you what to do. You have to figure that out on your own. But what I can tell you is this. The muses don't just *inspire* beauty and creativity, any more than I'm just a guy with a good beard. You *are* beauty and creativity. You are the embodiment of all that is good in the world. Don't forget who you are." He threw a lightning bolt into the air that popped and flared. "Just like I know I was the original, and none are as good as me."

She laughed along with him and continued to smile after his laughter had faded. Zeus wasn't known for his wisdom any more than he was known for his fidelity, but what he'd said made sense. Now she just had to figure out who she wanted to be at this point in her existence. When she mulled over Kit's words, hurtful as they were, she had to admit that there was some truth to them. But did something have to be serious to have a point? Jumping on a trampoline didn't really have a point, but it was fun.

She got up and went into the temple, where a priestess met her and showed her to a room in the caves below. It was cozy and decorated just like her old room had been, with colorful blankets showing all kinds of mythological feats. A table was set with honeyed dates and wine, as well as a plate of souvlaki. Memories rushed in as she ate, and she relived much of her history with her sisters as they played in the hills above the temple of Delphi, where they often stole sweets when they thought no one was looking. Of course, someone always was, but no one was going to reprimand Zeus's special daughters.

She curled up on the bed and listened to the music coming from above. Maybe she should give up not only her show, but the whole celebrity lifestyle. She loved Greece. Maybe it was time to come back, to return to recording history and helping virtuous people find the paths that would help them help others.

As she drifted to sleep, the pang of not seeing Kit again brought tears to her eyes. Maybe it was better to let that part go too, before it crushed her entirely.

CHAPTER FIFTEEN

K it slammed her fists into the punching bag, throwing jabs and hooks until her shoulders burned with exertion.

"Okay! Enough!" Sian let go of the bag and shook out her arms and rolled her neck. "You're going to punch through that bag and hit me in the face."

The image of Clio in bed with Sian on top of her flashed in her mind, and she considered the option of hitting her in the face after all.

"Hey now." Sian backed up. "I've seen that look enough times to know you don't want to go there."

Kit blew out a frustrated breath and held her hands up in surrender. "Sorry." She flopped onto a workout mat and stared at the ceiling. "Eating moldy cheese with a toothpick would be more fun than trying to figure out women."

Sian sat on the mat next to her and started to stretch. "Truer words were never said. I take it you've pissed her off somehow?"

Kit turned to look at her. "Obviously. Are you in love with her?"

Sian continued to stretch and didn't make eye contact. "That would be stupid. I'm an employee, nothing more."

"That doesn't answer my question." Kit rolled up and started stretching too, before she began to stiffen up.

"Only an idiot wouldn't fall in love with Clio. And I'm not an idiot." She shook her head and stretched her triceps. "But she doesn't feel the same way, and it's not like there's any question of that. She wears her heart on her sleeve. If she felt the same, I'd already be on my knees proposing."

"Damn." Kit wasn't sure what to say. It wasn't like she could admit—

"I assume you slept with her and then you somehow fucked things up." Sian looked at her pointedly this time. "Did you hurt her?"

"Dude, you don't want to hear this." Kit rolled onto her back to stretch her quads. She'd kicked the hell out of the bag too.

"Probably not. But I do want to know she's okay and what to expect when we fly out tomorrow." She sat cross-legged and looked at Kit. "I like you, but she'll always come first for me. What happened?"

"I don't know. I heard her singing at this club, and then she sat with me and my friends, and then things just got out of hand, and we ended up at her place." She got it out in a rush, omitting details.

Sian waved her on. "And?"

"And things were great. In the morning I told her how much I was enjoying doing the show with her."

Sian's eyes narrowed. "She wouldn't get upset about that, and I have no question it was you who upset her. What else?"

Kit got up and headed toward the locker room. "I might have said she could stop doing that stupid show of hers and do something more important."

Sian slammed her locker shut and looked at Kit incredulously. "You're fucking kidding me? How would you have felt if she said something like that to you?"

"But my show is important. Hers is…dumb."

"Wow." Sian backed away with her towel and wash bag in hand. "I thought way more of you than you deserved. How judgmental and blind can you be?" She stomped away to the showers.

Kit got into the shower next to hers. "You think her show is worth watching?" she asked over the water.

"Yeah, I do. It's fun and allows me to chill out for a while. She's sweet and kind, and you don't get a lot of that on TV these days. Hell, or anywhere." Sian's water turned off. "And even if I didn't like it, I sure as hell wouldn't tell someone I cared about that what she was doing, the thing she cared about, wasn't worth my time." The shower curtain squealed back. "You're a dumb-ass."

By the time Kit got back to her locker, Sian was gone. She felt like a dumb-ass, but she didn't feel wrong. Maybe that made her more of a dumb-ass. What she did know was that she was sorry she'd hurt Clio, and that she needed to apologize. Again. Barb always said that an apology only meant anything if you actually changed your behavior after. If you kept doing things you had to apologize for, then you weren't really sorry.

She could apologize for hurting Clio and making her feel bad. That would be genuine and something she'd try hard not to do again. But she couldn't apologize for thinking that the show they were doing together was better than the one Clio had been doing before.

She finished getting ready, the release from the hard workout already fading in light of the thoughts constantly bumping around in her head.

When she got home, she put Buster in the car and took him to her favorite beach. They walked for miles, and he chased his ball and sniffed everything he could possibly sniff. She managed to keep him from rolling in some of those magnificent scents, fortunately. She chatted with a few other dog owners and sat on a rock while Buster played in the surf, barking at the small fish that were always in the shallow water. He caught one in his mouth, and she laughed at the horrified look on his face when it flapped and slapped at him. He dropped it and jumped back, barking at it for its impudence.

She took out her phone when it buzzed and read the text from Sian.

She took the plane to Athens. You're flying cattle tomorrow. Dumb-ass.

Clio had left the country? Christ, her last girlfriend had just gone back to her mom's place in the next county over. Yet another difference between them. Although, she supposed she too could book a flight at the last minute if she wanted to. She was being petty now. She was building up a great list of attributes.

She sent Clio a message.

Heard you're out of town. Still doing the interview tomorrow? I hope we can talk.

It was a shit text without emotion. She considered adding to it but wasn't sure what to say.

See you there.

No x's and o's, no smiley emoji. Buster came over and shook hard, spraying her with water and sand.

"At least I have you, buddy. And a job I'll love with or without her, right?" He barked at her. "Yeah, I'm not sure that's still the case either." She could still see the stricken look in Clio's eyes and the tears that had welled up. She should have gone to her right then, apologized, taken her back to bed and made amends. Repeatedly. Instead, she'd left and let the situation fester.

But what was the answer, really? Yeah, the sex had been mind-blowing. And it hadn't been just a physical release like she found with other people. She'd fallen asleep with Clio in her arms, and it had been fucking magical. She'd danced into the kitchen feeling like she belonged there, cooking a beautiful woman a beautiful breakfast. And then she'd opened her mouth and it had all gone to hell.

Because she'd been honest. She'd been true to herself and what she believed. But maybe her black-and-white system was crashing. Clio had brought color into her life, and maybe that was messing with her head. She couldn't imagine doing the show without Clio now, which was weird in its own way since she'd always preferred working alone.

What if Clio quit? What if Kit had really put her foot in it this time? She'd go back to doing her show her way. But deep down, it would feel empty. Less black-and-white and more of a smudge of gray.

She forced herself off the cold rock and called to Buster, who seemed to have finally worn himself out. He trotted along next to her and flopped into the back of her SUV with a groan. "Yeah, I know how you feel."

❖

"I'm getting tired of being pulled into these meetings, Jag." Kit hadn't had time for her morning coffee, thanks to the hangover that had made it hard to stumble out of bed.

Clio was attending via a Zoom call. She wore a loose-fitting gray top and gray trousers. There wasn't a speck of color on her, and it made the meeting feel even worse. They hadn't said a word to one another when Clio had come online, but the puffy bags under Clio's eyes were a clear indication she'd been crying. Kit wanted to wrap her arms around her and tell her everything would be okay, that they'd find a way to work through things. But she didn't quite believe it, so she couldn't. Plus, Clio was still in Athens.

"I know. I'm sorry," Jag said, looking at the others at the table. "It seems we have some conflicting information, and we need to get it right. Best to do that with everyone in the room so there are no miscommunications."

"Honestly, when you get this many producers on a show, there are bound to be teething issues." Clio's producer gave that irritating fake smile. "Merging shows like this hasn't been done before, so there's plenty to learn."

"I was told that the show went down well with viewers, and we were in the clear." Kit tilted back in her chair. "Clio was told something entirely different. Which is it?"

Jag raised his eyebrows at Clio's team and didn't say anything.

"Well, it's just that you're so different. And we thought that would be great. But, well..."

Clio shifted slightly so all eyes were on her. "I'm aware you don't like me," she said softly, her focus remaining on her hands. "I'm aware how people felt working on my show. And it's been made very clear to me lately how insipid and insignificant people really find my show." She brushed away a tear but still didn't make eye contact with anyone. "If you're trying to get me to leave the show, please just say so."

Kit blanched. "Clio, that's not what they're saying."

She finally looked up. "Maybe not about the show you and I are doing together, but definitely about the one that was mine." She looked at her agent, who had an ugly little smile on her face. "But you gave me that feedback because you want me to back out on my own, so you don't have to work with or for me anymore." She held up her hand when the agent started to half-heartedly deny it. "But I'm not contracted to you personally, and I'm fine with you releasing me as a client. And anyone else who doesn't want to be around me anymore can also find other work."

Her tone had become soft steel, and Kit's heart ached for her. It didn't help that she'd been part of the problem.

"Jag, what is the truth about the show, please?"

"As I told Kit. Reviews came in solid, although people felt bad that you were so distraught. Emotion sells, though, and the combination of you together has been seen as a good pairing."

"Are you firing me?" Clio's agent asked, rising to her feet. "After all I've done for you?"

Clio looked at her almost as though she was looking through her. "You were behind me when things were good, and then when things weren't so good, you lied to me and tried to make me feel bad about myself." Her voice stayed calm and even. "If you're wondering what it is to be non-virtuous, I'm pretty sure that's a good definition."

Clio's producer stood up too. "If that's how you feel about us, Clio, then it's best we part ways. You can tag along on Kit's show if they want you, and we'll stop wasting our time and cancel your contract."

Clio simply nodded and refocused on her hands.

"I'm going to sue for defamation." Her agent slung her bag over her arm, her eyes blazing with hurt ego.

"Oh please," Kit said, dropping her chair onto all four legs. "I have no doubt you've been called far worse than non-virtuous. Hell, I've silently called you worse in the last ten minutes. Want to hear those?"

She huffed and flounced out of the office, followed by Clio's producer.

"That's it, then." Clio sighed heavily and looked into the camera. "Kit, you have your show back. You can go back to your hard-hitting stories and leave the fluff out."

Jag looked at Kit with his eyebrows raised.

"Clio, please don't leave the show." She got up and moved closer to the laptop. "I'm so incredibly sorry I insulted you, and that I hurt your feelings. But I meant what I said. I think we're on to something, and just because your team is no longer involved doesn't mean you can't continue with me. I'm sure Jag would be happy to contract for you properly and to help you find a new agent." She looked at him for confirmation and he nodded.

"Clio, I know it's hard. But you bring something really special to the show. We both know that Kit is way too intense sometimes, and you're going to keep her from getting walloped by a god when she insults them one too many times."

Clio wiped away her tears and gave them a small smile. "So now I'm her immortal bodyguard?"

Kit grinned. "Surely there are worse things to be?"

Clio's smile faltered a little. "I'd like to think about it, if that's okay with you? I'll still meet you in Moscow as planned."

"Clio, I'm really sorry—"

She shook her head. "I'll see you there." She hit the button and the screen went blank.

"Want to tell me about it?"

Kit rubbed her temples. "You don't want to know."

"Probably not, but I can guess." He stood. "Come on. Looks like you need coffee to melt away the booze, and I'm hungry."

They left the office and walked to JT's. Kit automatically looked into the corner where Clio had been the last time she'd been there, but of course, the corner was empty.

"Food?" Jag asked, and she nodded. She sat at what she thought of as Clio's table while he went and ordered. He came back with huge mugs of coffee for them both.

"My husband won't let me have pancakes," he said when he sat down. "Something about my heart and cholesterol." He sipped his coffee and looked at her over the rim. "Spill."

She drew swirls in her coffee with a spoon. "Do you think I only see the dark side of things?"

"I think you're a pro who does her job damn well and with the passion it needs."

"I hear a but."

"But you carry that with you outside the job, too. You don't seem to relax and enjoy anything."

"Totally untrue." She held up her hand and ticked things down on her fingers. "I love the gym. I like going out with my friends every week and having a few drinks. I like dating women—"

He grunted.

"Okay, maybe dating isn't the right word but I'm trying to be politically correct. The point is, I do have a life outside work."

"And when you're at the gym, you go full force, right? You don't do yoga. And when you're out with your friends, I'd bet next month's wine selection that you talk about work." He waited and she frowned at him. "See? I'll grant that you enjoy the women you're with, but you never get serious with anyone."

"I don't have time to get serious with anyone. My job comes first. Why is that so bad?"

They leaned back to get out of the server's way when the pancakes were put in front of them. She dug in, knowing full well it was the perfect cure-all for her hangover.

"It's not bad. But life is about more than work, Kit. Or, it should be. Don't you want to love someone? Come home to someone other than Buster?"

She pointed her fork at him. "Leave my perfect child out of this. And loving someone can break you to pieces when they leave."

They ate in silence for a minute before he shook his head. "I'm going to be mean. You don't respond to subtlety." He sipped his coffee. "Your parents died in an accident, Kit. No kid should have to grow up without parents, and I know you were really close to them. But you're a fucking grown-up now. People lose people all the time, and they don't just throw up a wall and say, okay, no more people." He lifted his fork and flung a drop of syrup at her when she went to interrupt. "Life is literally what you make of it. If you want to stay single and alone all your life, fine. But if that's the case, decide it's what you really want. Childhood trauma doesn't have to define you."

She stared at him. "I can't believe you just played the dead parents' card."

He shrugged. "You're right that there's a lot of shit still happening out there. And yeah, it shouldn't be ignored. But Jesus, Kit. Life doesn't have to be so intense every minute of the day. And I have a feeling I know what you said to upset Clio. Probably something along the lines of how shit her old show was."

She flinched and stabbed at her pancake. "It was a compliment, in my own way."

"Your own way can be like using a lemon to keep a wound from getting infected." He pushed away his plate and patted his stomach. "This is going to come as a surprise to you, Kit." He leaned forward. "You're not always right, and people can enjoy the things you don't," he whispered as though it were the reveal of a big secret.

"She called me judgmental." Kit pushed her plate away and felt physically far better than she had when she'd woken up. Her mental state was another thing altogether.

"You know, if a three-thousand-year-old muse called me judgmental, I'd probably give it some serious thought." His expression left no doubt as to how serious he'd take it. "I have to get back to work. Do what you want, think what you want. But stop being a jackass to the one person who is willing to work with you."

"What do you mean the one person? I've always worked alone."

"And why is that?" He winked at her and left the café, whistling as he walked back in the direction of the office.

She stared unseeing out the window as she pondered what he'd said. It stung, but in the way that meant he was right, not in the way that meant she was being unfairly set upon. What about the thing about love? It was true that her grief for her parents had been underlined by the fact that she'd been put into foster homes. She'd gotten close to a few foster parents, but then they'd always moved her on when things had gotten crowded or when she'd punched another of the kids for being a bully. Love was temporary, a transient and unreliable emotion.

She thought of Clio's eyes and how defeated she'd looked. It made her stomach hurt. Clio, too, had endured her fill of love and loss. Their night together had been astounding, and she wanted a repeat. But if their hearts got involved, how would it end?

CHAPTER SIXTEEN

Clio filled herself with Zeus's energy as she hugged him hard. "Thanks for everything."

He turned her and led her into the temple. "Before you go, I wanted you to see something. Look there."

At the side of the temple was a new altar. Incense smoke curled up from the slab of marble. In the middle was a statue. She walked around it, her heart hammering in her chest. It was clearly Clio, who knelt with her hands outstretched. At her side was a guitar, and on her lap was a thick book with the Greek words for history and virtue, *historia* and *aretí*, inscribed across the pages.

"You've set up an altar to me in your own temple?" She looked up at him, and his eyes were shining with pride.

"The only one I'd ever allow in one of my temples." His laughter boomed through the hall. "Like I said, you're the best of both me and your mother. There's the temple to you and your sisters in Scotland, but I think one here in our ancient home is a good idea. The world needs virtue, Clio. It needs humans who reach out more and think of themselves less. Anyone who comes to my temple will be reminded of that by your altar."

Tears welled in her eyes, and she threw herself into his arms again. "It's beautiful. Thank you. I'll be sure to come often to see what offerings have been left and if I can help anyone."

He patted her back and playfully hurried her to the door. "Good, good. Now, get going. Go show those gods in Moscow how it's done."

She laughed and began the long walk down the stairs to the bottom of the acropolis, where her car waited to take her to the airport. It was a walk she'd done many, many times, but now, with her own little altar set up in the temple, it felt particularly special.

The drive to the airport was quick, and she waited in the sun for as long as she could before boarding to go to Moscow.

The plane felt so empty. The air steward was polite but distant, and she missed Sian's banter and sexy smile, as well as the way she always felt cared for with her. She missed Paul's steady presence, too, even though he'd only been on one trip with them. She felt a little bad for not missing Tamara at all. Even the thought of her fussing over her made her wince. But actually, would she even be around anymore? The rest of Clio's team were gone along with her old contract. That probably meant the stylist had gone too. So there was a silver lining after all.

What she missed most was Kit. Kit's grumpy, funny sarcasm. Her sexy body and understanding eyes. The spicy cologne she wore and the way she didn't care an iota about how she looked as long as she got her story. She missed staring into her eyes and the conversations, both serious and silly, that they'd had.

She missed the way Kit always seemed to know when Clio needed support. The way she stood beside her and took the lead if it looked like Clio was overwhelmed. And gods, did she miss the way Kit looked at her, her eyes full of desire. Those kisses that could melt obsidian back to lava had been haunting her dreams.

Picking up a folder, she decided to focus on the interview ahead. The deep sense of loneliness had abated a little thanks to her time in Athens, but there was no question she was still very much alone right now.

The four-hour flight went by quickly once she put on a movie and lost herself in the world of superheroes, and she was refreshed and ready when she disembarked at the Moscow airport. She pulled her jacket tighter around her to block the wind. There was a car waiting for her and the driver stood outside.

"Ms. Clio, nice to have you back." The driver tipped his hat to her. "I understand your co-workers have arrived at their terminal. Would you like to pick them up as well?"

For a brief second she considered saying no, but that wouldn't be right. "Yes, thank you."

They got in and he radioed ahead so they'd be brought down to the private exit area. Clio strained to see them, and at her first glimpse of Kit, her shoulders relaxed and her stomach flipped. The car slowed and the driver got out and opened the doors.

Kit ducked down and looked in, and then gave a wide smile when she saw Clio. "I wondered if we were being very classily kidnapped."

She got in beside Clio, and then Paul and Tamara got in as well. The driver loaded their many bags into the trunk, and Clio tried not to show her surprise that Tamara was still with them. She'd had a feeling that Paul would stick around, but Tamara hadn't ever seemed to like her. Odd.

"That was simply awful." Tamara ran her hands through her hair. "It smelled so bad."

Kit held Clio's hand. "You can't leave the show. I can't travel that way ever again. You've spoiled me and if I never have another kid kicking the back of my seat or another meal that tastes like the leftovers of the plane's tire, it will be too soon."

Clio laughed. "So I'm a bodyguard and your transportation. I'm not sure if it's getting better or worse." She turned to Paul, aware of how easy it would be to forget he was there. "Was your flight as bad as theirs?"

He held up his ever-present book. "When you can fall into the pages of one of these, the rest of the world goes away."

Clio handed Tamara and Paul a file each. "Tamara, I know you're behind the scenes, but you should have an idea what's going on just in case things go sideways. And, Paul, you're already familiar with what's been going on here, but just a refresher."

Kit looked up from her own file. "Why is Paul already familiar with the issues?"

As usual, she hadn't missed a thing. "Paul? I think it would be good for you to tell them, in case anyone recognizes you. Not that they would, but…well, it's a good idea anyway."

He tilted his head in acknowledgement. "My original name was Anulap. I'm what they currently call a pre-fader god. I chose to retire before belief in me died away to the point I disappeared along with the people who believed in me." He glanced between the mortals. "That is knowledge that shouldn't leave this car, if you don't mind."

"What region?" Kit asked.

"Ancient Micronesia. Knowledge and magic."

Kit sighed and closed her eyes. "Seems like you can't go anywhere now without bumping into an immortal."

"Which simply means more access to knowledge from areas you may not expect to find it." His tone was light, as always.

The car pulled up outside the hotel and they piled out.

"I can't believe we're staying at the Four Seasons. How many people could we help with this kind of money?"

Clio took Kit's hand, unable to stop herself. "It isn't just about the money. It's also about safety. The security here is second to none, and the camera crew will be staying here as well. As outsiders, we're perfect targets for kidnapping or worse."

Kit's shoulders dropped. "You're right. I'm sorry. I hadn't thought about that."

Clio poked her in the side. "How painful was that to say?"

Kit clutched at her chest. "So painful. I might die of shock."

They were all laughing as they entered the lavish hotel lobby, and they were quickly shown to their rooms, all on the same floor and side by side.

"To keep an eye on us?" Paul asked.

Clio looked around at the guards standing at various entrances. "Maybe a little. But also for our own safety. Our group stays together so we can keep an eye out for one another."

The hotel manager came up and shook their hands. "We have been briefed as to why you are here, and we've been given your schedule. We have two cars to take you and your crew to the interview site in the morning."

Their luggage had been brought up on trolleys behind them. The camera crew said they were heading out to take some footage.

"Let's meet up in the Bystro Restaurant for dinner at nine." Kit looked around the group. "Tomorrow could get crazy, so let's talk about exit plans and what's most important to capture if push comes to literal shove."

It was agreed, and Tamara insisted that she and Clio have some time before dinner to go over outfit choices. "I've brought quite a few to choose from. You should be as colorful as the Kremlin."

"I think you mean Basil's Cathedral," Paul said and gave a little smile. "The Kremlin is quite a plain concrete structure."

Tamara waved it away. "Whatever." She went into her room without another word.

"Maybe you can find something between Kremlin and Basilica." Kit leaned against the wall, as though waiting.

Clio leaned against the doorframe too. "I'm still upset with you."

Kit traced a line of paint on the doorframe. "Yeah. I'm beginning to understand why. I'm sorry, Clio. I never meant to hurt you."

Clio fought off the desire to drag Kit into her room. There was still too much to be said between them. "Thank you. Apology accepted." She hesitated, then kissed Kit's cheek, lingering for a moment. "See you at dinner."

She didn't miss the flicker of disappointment and desire in Kit's eyes, but she still went into her room and closed the door behind her.

An hour later, Tamara knocked on the door, calling from the hallway. "Yoo-hoo! Time for some fabulous wardrobe options!"

Clio closed her book, the first she'd picked up in a long time, and sighed. She opened the door, and Tamara flounced in with her arms full of clothing in every primary color and type of material under the sun. She started hanging things up wherever she could find some space so they could be seen, chattering away about how Clio was going to stand out like a flamingo among blackbirds.

"I'm not sure that's really the right idea for this segment, Tamara." Clio ran her fingers over a thick sweater with a massive cowl neck. It was fuchsia and had little bobbles hanging from the sleeves.

Tamara's exasperation was obvious when she looked at the ceiling and shook her head. "You know, Clio, the rest of the team are gone. I'm the only one left on your side. I'd think you'd be grateful that I stayed on to make you look fabulous. Can you trust me to do my job, please?"

Kit's words about Clio not standing up for herself came back to her, and she took Tamara's hand. "I know you're good at your job, honey. I'm really good at mine too, and I've been doing it for a lot longer than you have."

"What, like, two years?" Tamara scoffed, trying to pull her hand free, but Clio held on.

"No. For the last three thousand years, give or take. I've been dressing myself for best effect for a very long time. And I've even been doing my own makeup." She tugged her to the sofa. "Let me show you something." She pulled out her iPad and opened a specific photo album. "These are photos of me over the centuries. Well, most are paintings or drawings done before the camera was invented."

Tamara took the iPad begrudgingly but settled in and started really looking. Eventually she turned to Clio with tears in her eyes. "I'm sorry. I really do just want to help you look good. But some of the looks you've come up with…" She pulled up one particular photo. "This is stunning. You look incredible."

Clio took the iPad and set it aside. "I didn't show you this to make you feel bad. I showed it to you so you'd understand that I'm a partner in this, not someone who doesn't know what they're talking about. So instead of dressing me like a doll, maybe we could collaborate and talk it out?"

Tamara gave her a watery smile. "Okay."

"Before we go on," Clio handed her a tissue. "Why did you decide to stay with me?"

Tamara folded the tissue into tight little pieces. "It sounds stupid."

"Try me?"

"Being around you makes me feel like I could be a better person. Like, I like helping people, and not just because it makes me look good. I like seeing them smile. But when I'm not around you, that fades, and I don't want it to fade. I want to be a good person."

The tears flowed freely, and Clio pulled her into a tight hug. "Then we're stuck together, aren't we?" Clio's heart hurt from how lovely it was to hear someone say that about being around her. It was a far cry from everyone else who'd been working with her, and it showed that Tamara had a deeper sense of virtue than she let on. Being around Clio brought it out.

From that point on, they began to have fun. They discussed the political climate and what they'd likely be seeing tomorrow, and then talked through the emotions that each piece of clothing might bring out. It was fun, and more than that, Clio enjoyed giving Tamara an overview of the history that was coming into play in the present.

"I didn't know all that stuff," Tamara said. "I mean, I knew things were different here, but I didn't know how long it had been going on. You should talk about this stuff on the show! You make it so interesting." She winced when she realized what she said.

"It's okay. Maybe you're right. Maybe I should discuss more of the history and less of the fashion."

"Or both." They looked up when someone knocked. "Maybe you could find a way to put all of you out there." Tamara gave Clio a shy, genuine smile. "I think you're pretty great."

She opened the door to find Kit standing there, her hands shoved into her pockets. "Ready for dinner?"

Tamara looked her over and shook her head. "Oh no you don't. Did you find those clothes in a mechanic's pile of rags?" She moved forward, forcing Kit back, and looked over her shoulder at Clio. "Give us ten minutes and we'll meet you downstairs."

"It's just dinner. Really, it isn't—"

Clio heard Kit protesting as the door closed. She shook her head and dressed in something warm. It felt so good to have chatted with Tamara the way she had. Maybe this was the start of something new, a friendship she could count on later.

She headed downstairs and into the Bystro, where they served traditional Russian food. Paul and the rest of the crew were already there, and she joined them. The camera crew were discussing the architecture and history, and she joined in quickly. She was counting down the minutes, though, until Kit and Tamara showed up.

When they did, her throat went dry. Kit was in a black button-down shirt that looked like it had been made for her. Her black trousers hugged her just right and her shoes were so shiny they caught the light. She was a walking advertisement for lesbianism, and Clio very much wanted to buy in.

They sat down and Kit leaned over. "I'm going to dress this way every hour of the day if it gets you to look at me that way."

Clio sipped her drink. "That would be very distracting. You're adorable when you're rumpled, but this look is another thing altogether."

Kit harumphed. "No one has ever called me adorable. That isn't the look I'm going for."

"Then you should buy stock in that clothing company."

They ordered and the conversation was easy. Even Tamara joined in, asking genuine questions and taking their teasing in stride.

When they made it to dessert, Kit tapped the table. "Right, gang. Let's do a little planning for tomorrow."

One of the camera crew put a map on the table. "The main event is going on inside the Kremlin walls. They're expecting a huge crowd, and security will be tight. There are only two main entrance points." He circled them in pencil. "Here and here."

"And where are the press interviews being held?" Kit traced various buildings with her fingertip as though trying to memorize paths.

"Here, outside the Kremlin Palace."

Kit sat back. "I don't like this. If things go sideways, we'll be trapped."

Paul looked concerned as well. "I went for a wander today and listened to conversations in cafés and on the streets. People here are angry, and there's a heartbeat of violence beating beneath it all."

Clio took a deep breath. "That's why we're here, right? To find out what's going on. To hunt down the truth." She smiled when the others groaned at her including their show's title. "We've been granted fifteen minutes with the two gods who will be on hand after they've spoken with the government and the people. Kit and I have our questions in hand." She looked at Kit for confirmation, even though she knew Kit was always prepared when it came to work. "And we'll get through as many as we can as fast as we can."

"Sian is going to be with the plane, and the pilot has instructions to be ready to go at a moment's notice." Kit was still studying the map.

"She came with you?" Clio hadn't thought of that possibility.

"After calling me a bunch of names, and then more as she thought of them during the flight, she agreed it would be a good idea for us to have someone we trust on the ground and waiting." Kit's cheeks pinked a little.

That meant that Sian knew what had transpired between them. She wasn't ashamed of it, but she hoped that Sian wasn't hurt by it. If she'd flown all the way to Moscow stuck in economy with three hundred other people, she couldn't be that upset.

"One thing," Clio said softly, leaning forward and picking up the pencil. "I took a tour when it was built, and the czar at the time was so proud of it, he told me there were secret passageways. He even showed me one." She circled an area at the end of an ornate garden. "The St. Nicholas Tower has a secret door. Use your foot to push on the third brick up, fourth brick over. A door should slide open and take you into a tunnel that will lead you beyond the wall."

Kit took the pencil and drew a line. "That's good. It's almost a straight shot from the palace. If we get separated, try to get out via one of the regular entrances. If you can't, head for Clio's secret entrance." She grinned at some private thought and Clio kicked her under the table.

"Obviously, that entrance was built a very long time ago. I'm hoping it will still work."

"Well, if not, it still gives us a place out of the way of the main buildings to regroup." Paul was looking at the map intently. "There are likely several other ways out like this one."

"True, but don't waste time trying to find them unless you really have no choice." Kit folded the map over when a server came to clear the dishes. "And if worse comes to worst, make your way to the plane and we'll regroup there."

The jovial tone of the evening had turned somber, and Clio's nerves were on edge. "I think I'll get some sleep." Everyone else stood as well, and they made their way to their floor.

Clio and Kit were the last ones outside their room.

"I don't suppose you want a nightcap?" Kit asked, standing close, her eyes dark with desire.

Clio put her hand on Kit's chest, over her heart. "I want a lot more than that." When Kit bent to kiss her, she backed away a little. "But not here. We still need to talk, and I'm nervous about tomorrow. Maybe when we get back we can have that nightcap?"

Kit rested her head against the doorframe. "You've got me so turned on I can barely walk. I'm going to be a wet mess all night. Have pity on me."

Clio laughed and kissed her, slowly, letting her tongue slide over Kit's bottom lip. "I think you'll live. Good night."

Kit groaned and walked backward to her room. "Cruel, Clio. So cruel."

Clio laughed as she went into her room. Things were going to be okay. No matter what they decided to do about the attraction between them, it would work out for the best.

CHAPTER SEVENTEEN

Energy thrummed in the air like a bow pulled back, ready to fire. The streets were packed with people holding signs and chanting. They'd walked from their hotel to the Kremlin, and all along the way people had stopped them, wanting to say their piece in front of a camera. Most didn't speak English, but Paul had studied enough Russian to translate, and Clio too had a basic knowledge though she hadn't used it in many years.

Kit wanted to hold Clio's hand and lead her through the chaos. She'd nearly suggested that she and Tamara stay at the hotel, where they'd be safe. Then she'd mentally slapped herself upside the head. Clio was immortal and had lived through worse than a massive, angry protest. It was the humans she needed to worry about. But the part of her that had so desperately wanted to take Clio in her arms last night wouldn't back down. When Clio pressed close to her in the crowd, she looked over. "You okay?"

She gave her a shaky smile. "A bit bigger than the protest in Milwaukee, isn't it?"

Kit relented and took her hand. "Just a little. But you've been through bigger and worse, right?"

Clio's smile grew. "Yes, I have. I forget that sometimes." She squeezed Kit's hand and let go. "Let's keep going."

They shouldered their way through, and Kit kept looking behind them to make sure the group stayed together. They finally reached the press area in front of the Senate Building, where they could breathe more freely.

"So much anger," Paul said, gazing at the crowd held back with large metal barriers.

A siren sounded a short burst, and the crowd instantly went silent. The Muslim god, the Russian Orthodox god, and the president of Russia took to the stage.

"I bet the president uses that for every election for the rest of his life," Kit murmured.

The president spoke first. "My people of Russia, we are here to hear what you have to say. To help in all ways we can so our people can have the best life possible." He paused. "You have elected people to speak for you today, and we will hear what they have to say."

One by one, the elected people stepped forward, all of them bowing low to the gods and more than one looking like they might faint. Kit understood the feeling.

Most of the questions, though, were directed at the president. It wasn't surprising, given that most of Russia remained non-religious, even so long after the Soviet fall. Questions revolved around immigration, job loss, living wages, and energy resources. The president answered many questions but flinched and stepped back when the gods stepped forward.

The Muslim god spoke first, his dark eyes scanning the crowd. "You would turn away those in need? People who need kindness and care, not your slaps and disgust. Take those who need shelter and food and help them, and your reward will be great."

There was a murmur of discontent in the crowd, who clearly weren't impressed with a reward in the afterlife when they were suffering in this one.

"There is so much room in Russia," the Orthodox God said, his voice booming off the buildings. "This beautiful country can hold everyone. If we build more cities, there will be room to spread out. There will be more jobs. I invite your leaders to speak with me to discuss building cities beyond Moscow."

The murmurs in the crowd seemed a little more positive this time. Someone shouted a question from the crowd about energy resources and how they would help other cities when they couldn't even power Moscow. It wasn't a religious question, it was a practical question, and the gods waited for the president to answer.

"There is plenty of energy to go around," he said, waving his hands as though it were a silly question. "You pay for it like they do in other countries, and you receive energy."

"Not good," Clio said, her shoulders tense. "They pay almost three times what they pay in other countries and still have constant blackouts."

Anger vibrated through the crowd and questions were shouted by random people instead of the elected ones. Chanting began again, signs waved.

The Muslim god held up his hands. "Shouting does not give you answers." The crowd quieted. "Your president has not heard you. We do. We will find out why you do not have the resources you need, and we will find the people who will fix that for you. But if you do not listen to them, if you do not elect them, then we cannot help further."

The crowd erupted with fury. They didn't want to hear that they had to help themselves, and the promise that the gods would look into the matter sounded like more platitudes. The Russian people were done with platitudes.

Suddenly, machine gun fire split the air, and Kit grabbed Clio's hand and pulled her to the ground. Bottles were flung over the crowd, burning rags stuffed into the ends. Within minutes, the air was full of smoke and screams. Kit's eyes burned as she and the crew pressed against the wall as the crowd surged forward, over the barriers. The gods left the stage and moved into the crowd, pushing people aside like water. One grabbed someone holding a machine gun and yanked it away from him, then bent the gun like it was a straw. He threw the man through the air, and he hit the wall with a sickening thud. The other god had grown impossibly huge, and he gathered a group of people in his hands and lifted them away from the burning bottles and smoke to set them on top of a building.

The president scurried away, escorted by his security team.

More gunfire went off, and smoke began to rise from a building, flames licking at the windows. "We need to get out of here." Kit took Clio's hand as well as Tamara's. "You guys ready?"

They nodded, and although the cameraman kept shooting, the rest of the team looked as shaken as Kit felt. "Keep the map in mind. I'm going to head for the exit, but if we can't get there, I'll turn for the other escape route."

Clio tugged on Kit's hand. "Look. The exit is blocked."

It wasn't just blocked. Someone had dumped burning material over the gates and wall, creating a blaze of fire that kept people from being able to leave. "Okay. Straight to plan B. Let's go."

They set off, shouldering their way through the screaming frenzy. Kit kept a tight grip on Clio and Tamara, pulling them through any time they got stuck. Acrid smoke burned her eyes and lungs, and the screams around them deafened her. She heard Clio calling her and looked back.

Clio's eyes were wide, and she pointed to the small tower on their left. A group of school children, presumably brought to see the gods, were screaming as flames kept them backed against a wall. Kit looked for the gods, but they were still in the worst of the riot.

She looked at Clio, who nodded resolutely. She pulled the long silk scarf from around her neck and tore it in half.

Kit turned to Paul and put Tamara's hand in his. "Get to the exit!" He nodded and started away with her. "You guys too!" she yelled at the camera crew. Then she took the piece of scarf Clio held out to her and tied it around her face the way Clio had. Together they ran to the children. The teacher was yelling something to them in Russian, but they couldn't get close enough to hear it clearly.

Clio ripped off her thick jacket and threw it over the smallest area of flames, right near the wall. Kit did the same and leapt over the jackets to the little group. One by one, she picked up a child and passed it to Clio, who set the child by the wall behind her. The smoke grew thicker, and the children were coughing and crying. Finally, Kit grabbed the teacher and thrust her forward just as the coats caught fire and went up in a blaze.

"Hold hands!" Kit yelled and made the gesture so they understood. They did it quickly, and Kit took hold of the one in the front and led, and Clio stayed at the back. Their teacher, coughing and retching, stumbled alongside.

The garden area was almost empty, and the worst of the smoke was gone. The door Clio had told them would be there was open, and Kit went straight in without hesitating, the little hand in hers squeezing tightly. The tunnel wasn't more than twenty feet long, and they were quickly beyond the wall once more.

The teacher dropped to her knees and the children gathered around her, all crying. The street was mostly empty, with the worst of the violence happening on the other side.

"They're safe. We need to get out of here. We'll be targets the moment they see us." Kit's throat burned and she wanted water. It was only then that she noticed the camera crew behind them, also soot covered. Paul and Tamara waited close by.

"The car isn't here. Gods know where it is. We'll need to walk away from the city so we can get a taxi." Paul waved in a direction. "That's our best bet."

They moved quickly, staying to side streets. Behind them there was still the sound of burning buildings and fire engines, screams and gunfire. They entered a large, deserted square and stopped to look around. There didn't appear to be anyone there, let alone a taxi. Thanks to their jackets having burned up earlier, Kit and Clio were both shivering.

"You need help." A man came out of the shadows, his gray hair and grizzled face making him look ancient.

"We need to get to the airport." Kit didn't mince words.

"Come." He waved them forward and went back into the alley.

Kit hesitated and looked at Clio and Paul, the two immortals who might have a better idea of what the hell to do.

"He's okay," Clio said. "I can feel his heart."

It was a weird thing to hear, but it was good enough. Kit led the way down the alley, which opened into a parking lot in the back. The man threw her a set of car keys. "Take that one. It has a sticker on it. My friend at the airport will get it back to me."

Clio kissed his cheek and cupped his face in her hands. "May the gods bless you. You're a vision of virtue."

His eyes narrowed and he cupped her face in his hands in return. "I need no blessings. Your beauty is enough." He waved. "Go, before they close the roads and you can't leave."

They wedged themselves into the car, practically sitting on top of one another, and Paul drove because he was the one who had been in this part of the country last, and he seemed to have a good sense of direction.

The drive was tense, and police cars in long lines raced toward the city in the opposite direction. Tamara cried softly against Kit's shoulder, but other than that, there was no sound in the car.

"Finally," Clio said, the relief clear in her voice. Paul sped through to the private entry section, spoke with the guard at the gate, and then drove all the way onto the tarmac. They tumbled from the car and onto the waiting plane. The camera guys, however, stayed behind.

"We're out of the worst of it now. We want to get some footage of the aftermath once things have settled. We promise we'll be okay. We won't leave the airport until we know it's safe."

Kit nodded. They were as dedicated to their job as she was to hers, and she understood. "Take care of yourselves."

She got on board and sat down as the plane engine kicked in. Everyone else was already strapped in.

"We shouldn't be flying, but it can't be helped. There's a storm, but the pilot thinks the worst of it will be gone by the time we get to it." Sian's face was pale. She unlocked the stairway and shoved it away, then closed and airlocked the door before she sat down and strapped in too. From where she was sitting, she threw light jackets to Kit and Clio. "Sorry, it's all we have on board, but it's better than nothing."

They were taxiing within minutes and then were airborne. Kit looked out the window. "Jesus." Moscow burned below them, the fires creating an eerie glow in the plane until they'd left the blazing city behind.

An hour into the flight, she felt like she could finally breathe. Sian had passed out bottles of water, and they'd taken turns going to the bathroom to wash off the worst of the dirt. Sian also handed out food, and everyone seemed to take comfort in eating something hot.

"That was awful," Tamara said. "I love you, Clio, but I'm resigning as your stylist. I don't want to go places like that ever again. I much preferred your nice, safe studio."

Clio closed her eyes. "Me too." She opened her eyes and looked at Kit. "But you know something? I expected the gods to disappear when the violence kicked off. But instead, they went straight into the chaos."

Kit nodded. "Yeah, I was thinking about that. Has it ever happened before, that you know of? Where gods got so directly involved like that?"

Clio shook her head. "Not that I can remember, and my memory is pretty good. I think it's a really important turning point. They tried to provide some answers, and that didn't go very well, granted. But instead of turning away and leaving the people to their stupidity, they actually tried to get in there and help."

Kit yawned loudly. "It will be interesting to see what the guys got on camera and how the rest of the world views what happened. Will the other gods be okay with these gods getting their hands dirty like this? And if they are, will they be expected to do the same from now on?" Kit couldn't process all the possible implications. "This could change the game."

A massive bump of turbulence had them all grabbing their armrests, and Kit's stomach lurched. "Fuck. I hate flying." The plane jerked like an overstuffed washing machine.

Sian came in fast. "Buckle in." She quickly took their food and drinks away, throwing them in a trash bag that she then chucked in the back with one hand, as she was holding onto a seat back with the other.

The pilot's voice came over the intercom. "We're in for it, folks. Hold on. This is going to get ugly."

The plane slammed up and down. Something in the rear cabin fell from a shelf and broke. Tamara was crying so hard she was gasping for air. Paul had his eyes closed and was mouthing a prayer of some sort.

Clio's eyes were wide with fear, and her gaze never left Kit's face. Kit tried to smile, but the plane slammed upward, and she grimaced as her dinner threatened to come up again.

Bang.

The plane jerked upright at an unnatural angle, then went sideways. The pilot's voice came on. "Brace for impact."

They assumed the brace position as the plane plummeted from the sky. Kit stretched out her leg so her foot touched Clio's. If she was about to die, then she wanted to be touching the woman who'd stolen her heart.

CHAPTER EIGHTEEN

It was cold. So, so cold. Clio wanted to pull the blanket up and snuggle down, but it didn't feel like there was one. She'd never been so cold. And there was pain, too. It slowly sifted into her consciousness like icing sugar, little flakes of throbbing until they created a mound. She groaned and shifted, her body protesting with every infinitesimal move.

She finally got her eyes open, but she couldn't figure out what she was seeing. Metal, twisted and dark. White. Lots of white. She shivered and forced herself up. Panic soared through her, making her heart race. Twisted chunks of the plane were scattered around her, some already covered in the thickly falling snow. It was completely and utterly silent.

She struggled to her knees and saw the blood staining the snow where she'd been lying. It seemed it was just cuts to her face and one to her calf. She turned, searching the snow, her soul already crying. There were several other mounds of clothing, also quickly becoming snow covered.

On her hands and knees, she crawled to the closest one and gave a sob when she saw Tamara, her head at an unnatural angle, her eyes open to the sky. Clio closed them, her hand shaking so hard she could barely do so. She crawled on and let out a cry of relief when she saw Paul turn his head to look at her. She helped him sit up.

"The others?" he asked, his voice like gravel.

"Still looking." She needed to find Kit, but her body turned to molasses at the thought she might not have survived.

Paul got to his feet and helped Clio to hers, and they went in separate directions.

Clio saw Kit's jacket and dropped to her knees beside her. She was breathing but unconscious. "Kit? Kit, please wake up." She wanted to cradle her but didn't want to move her in case there were injuries she couldn't see.

Paul knelt next to her in the snow, followed by Sian, who was bleeding with a massive cut to her head.

"She's breathing but not responding to me." Clio smoothed the hair back from Kit's face.

"Look." Sian brushed away the snow next to Kit and revealed a pool of blood beneath her thigh. A chunk of metal stuck out. "We need to get that wrapped before she bleeds out."

Clio went to take off her jacket, but Sian stopped her.

"There were blankets on board. You're going to need all the warmth you can get." She and Paul went to search the wreckage.

"Kit? Please don't leave me. We have so much to talk about. So much we still need to do together." Clio's tears fell on Kit's cheeks so they looked like they were both crying.

Paul and Sian came back carrying blankets and a first aid bag.

"We'll need to move her. It's best if she's not awake for this anyway." Paul took a tourniquet from the medical bag, and Clio and Sian moved to support Kit's leg as he quickly tied off the area just above where the metal had gone into her leg.

Kit didn't so much as stir.

"Anyone have any idea where we are? My phone doesn't have any signal." Sian held up her phone.

Clio and Paul checked theirs, and they had no signal either.

"If I had to guess, I'd say we're in Greenland, given the trajectory we were on. And if the pilot wasn't off course because of the storm, we shouldn't be too far from the lower coasts, where most of the population is." Paul stood and moved in a slow circle as he scanned the horizon. "But if we were off course, we could be farther up and inland."

"We need to get Kit out of the snow." Clio was doing everything she could to stay calm. Searching her memory for what to do in this kind of emergency was helping. "The cold might keep her from bleeding too quickly, which is good, but it will also make her hypothermic, which is bad."

Sian started back toward the plane. "I have an idea," she called over her shoulder. She returned with a huge stiff bag. "Inflatable slide from the plane in case of a water landing. We'll use it as a sled." She opened it and it automatically inflated a giant orange sled for Kit.

They maneuvered Kit onto it, and then stood looking around.

"I can't tell which way is which in this snow," Clio said. "We might have to choose a direction and cross our fingers." She looked at Tamara's snow-covered body, and then at the pilot's, who was still in the smashed cockpit. "We have to leave them, don't we?"

Paul put his hand on her shoulder. "We can send someone to recover them after we've found help."

Clio shivered so hard it hurt. "We'd better start walking."

Paul and Sian went to the front of the makeshift sled and pulled it using the rope along the side. Clio walked behind to make sure Kit didn't slide off or end up in a position that could further hurt her. The snow came down heavier, coating her. Clio's whole body felt frozen, and the only sound was of their footsteps and the static sound of the snow falling on itself.

They'd been walking for at least an hour when Clio spotted something to their left. "Look!"

They turned and headed toward it. It wasn't much more than a big box with a pipe leading from the inside to show it had a fireplace. They carried Kit inside because the slide wouldn't fit through the narrow door, and they placed her on a long, padded bench that ran the length of one wall.

There was an old fireplace with a small bit of kindling and a few logs stacked beside it. On the end was a countertop that had a sink and electric kettle, but when Paul tried it, there was no power. "Probably needs a generator."

Sian rubbed her arms. "What is this?"

"A fishing shack, if I'm not mistaken. They're dotted all over the ice here but they're not in use until January." Paul gave them a wry smile. "I told you having a god of knowledge would be useful."

"So." Sian looked at them expectantly. "Are you going to call for help?"

They looked at her blankly until Clio realized what she meant. "You mean because we're immortal and should be able to contact the other gods."

Sian shrugged. "Isn't that how it works?"

Paul sat down on a stool next to Kit. "I'm a pre-fader. My abilities in that realm have long since gone."

Clio ran her hands through her hair. "My sisters can sometimes feel when I'm unhappy, and they give me a call. But I don't have a telepathic link with them." She knelt in front of the fire and smiled when she saw the flint. "There's a chance that if I pray to my father, he might hear my voice. But I'm one in a million praying to him. He probably won't hear me." He'd said, though, that he always kept an eye on his children. Hopefully this would be one of those times.

"Fantastic. I'm in a plane wreck with not one, but two immortals, and neither one can get us help." Sian sat down on the bench alongside the other wall and put her head in her hands.

Clio managed to get a spark and the fire started, providing a sense of calm. She picked up the medical bag and sat next to Sian. "Let me clean up your head."

Sian didn't say anything, she just sat still and let Clio clean up the dried blood on her face. The wound in Sian's scalp wasn't too bad, it had just bled a lot. She cleaned it and put a Steri-Strip across it to keep it from opening up again.

"Your turn." Sian took the bag from her. "Don't think we didn't notice the blood on your jeans."

Clio lifted her leg and shivered when Sian's cold hand touched her skin.

"Sorry." She felt along the gash that was bigger than the one on Sian's head. "I think you've got a piece of metal in there, Clio. I should get it out."

Clio nodded and gripped the edge of the seat, but she couldn't help but cry out when Sian pulled the metal sliver from her leg. It started bleeding again, and Sian quickly applied pressure. Once she'd wrapped it, they sat silently together. As Clio stared at Kit, willing her to wake up, silently begging her to give her that maddeningly sexy smile, she began to cry. Sian pulled her close and Clio let go, allowing all the emotions of the last day pour out of her. Poor Tamara, who had just opened up to her. And she hadn't even learned the pilot's name. Sian held her and kissed the top of her head, telling her everything was going to be okay, and she hung on, needing Sian's optimism and sweet, solid strength.

"One little plane crash and you make your move. Bastard. You could have waited till I was actually dead." Kit's voice sounded like sandpaper.

Clio gasped and dropped to Kit's side. She put her palm over Kit's forehead. "I don't know if you're talking to me or Sian."

"Sian. I already know I can rock your world better than she did." Kit's smile quickly became a grimace. "I feel like shit."

"Falling from the sky will do that to you. I mean, not to the rest of us. We're way tougher than you." Sian's smile was tender as she looked at the bandage on Kit's leg.

"Fuck off." Kit's eyes fluttered closed, and she drifted off again.

"It's good that she woke up," Paul said. "But we shouldn't leave that tourniquet on much longer, and I'm worried about the metal in her leg."

Clio moved away from Kit's side and knelt in front of the fire. If ever there was a time for her to be able to reach her sisters or parents, this was it. *Dad, Zeus, if you can hear me, I need you. We need you. We're somewhere in Greenland and Kit is hurt. If you can find us, please come.*

She didn't know what else to say. She sent a similar mental message to her sisters, even though she knew full well it didn't work that way. But lately Eris had said she had a feeling when Clio needed her. And she really needed her now.

They were careful about how much firewood they burned, and when night fell it was pitch-black inside. They used their phone flashlights when they needed to move around, but decided they'd conserve energy for as long as they could. No one said it, but they all knew their situation was dire. Greenland was an ice sheet, with the only populations on the coasts. "I wonder if the pilot got off a mayday call before we went down," Clio said to no one in particular.

"If he did, then hopefully we'll have people searching for us once the storm lifts." Sian's voice floated out of the darkness.

"The snow will have covered our tracks from the wreck site," Paul said. "We'll have to be vigilant about listening for searchers, as we may have to wave them down."

Clio had slid onto the bench Kit was lying on. She curled up against her, sharing her body warmth. The temperature had dropped drastically. Sian and Paul lay next to one another on the opposite bench.

Morning came, and the others looked as tired and stiff as Clio felt. Every muscle in her body hurt, and the wound in her calf was swollen and red. The two windows were covered in snow, so Sian opened the door to look outside. Snow blew in and she quickly shut it again.

"No rescue today, then." She lit the fire and the little hut warmed quickly.

Paul had found a book on fishing and sat propped against the wall as he read.

Sian sat beside Clio at Kit's feet. "Clio, I need to tell you something."

She looked into Sian's eyes and knew what was coming. "Okay?"

"I love you. I've been in love with you for a long time." She took a deep breath and stared at the floor. "I know you don't feel the same way, and it sucks, but it is what it is. But if we don't get help, and things get even worse, I need you to know." She held Clio's hand in hers. "I will always be here for you. No matter what you need or who you're with, I'll be here."

Clio held Sian's hand to her face. "Thank you," she whispered. "And I do love you, Sian. You've been there for me when no one else has, and you've been someone I could always count on to make me feel better."

Sian's smile was sad. "But you're not in love with me."

Clio wouldn't lie to her. She couldn't. "No. I'm sorry."

Sian nodded and sighed deeply. "Still. I mean it. If you need me, I'm here."

The creak of the hut under the still falling snow was often the only sound for the rest of the day. Conversation took too much energy, and there was no food in the little hut. They brought in snow and melted it in front of the fire, so they had something to drink, and sipping water had never felt so good. They managed to dribble some into Kit's mouth as well.

It was just getting dark again when Kit's eyes opened. "Still stuck in paradise, huh?" She clutched at Clio's hand, the tremor belying her joking façade.

"Afraid so." Clio held a cup to her mouth. "Can you drink?"

Kit tried to raise herself up on her elbows but groaned in pain and sank back again. "I think something is broken in there."

Clio's heart lurched. She'd been worried about internal injuries but there was nothing she could do. "We're just waiting for it to stop snowing before we make another plan."

Kit sipped the water and it seemed to take all her energy. She lay back and closed her eyes once again.

Although she shouldn't have had any more tears, they continued to fall. She looked up when there was a scraping sound. Paul had moved the heavy metal cover over the ice hole, and he held up the broken fishing reel he'd found in the cupboard. "I think we need to try for dinner."

Clio had learned to fish when she was young, and she'd done her share of gutting and cleaning fish over the centuries, though she'd never liked it. But her stomach rumbled, and she knew the others must be as hungry.

They waited in near darkness as Paul fished, and when he gave a shout they looked on as he pulled up a large halibut. He and Clio took it outside to gut it while Sian built up the fire and kept an eye on Kit.

It wasn't long before the little hut was filled with the scent of freshly cooked fish, and they all ate quickly.

"I prefer it with herbs and a sauce, but that was damn good." Sian licked her fingers. "Too bad Kit wasn't awake to get some."

"I've set some aside for her." Paul tapped a little cloth wrapped around some leftover halibut.

There wasn't much else to say or do. They turned off the one phone light and curled up as they had the night before.

Clio woke to a strange noise. A kind of huffing, snuffling sound.

"Polar bear," Paul whispered. "It must have been attracted by the fish we gutted."

"I didn't even think about that," she whispered back.

"Will it try to get in?" Sian's tone was more worried than it had been this whole time.

"Hopefully not. We cleaned well enough to get the smell out."

They sat in the pitch-black and listened to the sounds of the bear outside as it ate and searched for more. It bumped against the door several times and Clio's heart thumped so hard she put her hand to her chest to keep it in place. She'd protect Kit with her life, even if it meant going up against a polar bear.

After an eternity, the huffing sounds faded. The bear had left.

"Fucking hell." Sian's voice was breathy. "I don't think I've ever been that scared."

"That's saying something, given that we're here after being in a plane wreck." Clio tried to keep her tone light.

None of them slept well. Clio lay awake listening to Kit's breathing, which seemed to be getting more labored, and she heard the others tossing and turning. By morning, she couldn't remember having been more exhausted in her life.

Sian opened the door and sunlight beamed into the little hut. "I'm going to go out and look for help. Or at least figure out where we are in relation to…well, something else."

Paul stood and zipped his coat. "I'll go with you. We'll walk opposite directions for thirty minutes each and then come back here."

Sian nodded and looked at Clio. "You'll be okay?"

Clio sat on the stool beside Kit, holding her hand. How difficult must it be for Sian to see? Still, she couldn't bring herself to let go. "We'll be fine. Just be careful. Watch out for bears."

Paul pulled his scarf around his ears. "If you see one, freeze. Stand straight and hold still, so you look like neither prey nor a threat. They're the biggest bears on earth, so best if you can avoid it altogether."

Sian stared at him for a moment. "Great. Fantastic advice." She turned to the door. "Fucking perfect."

Clio couldn't help but smile. It was no wonder she and Kit had become friends. They were very much alike. She tucked the blanket tighter around Kit and was startled when Kit's hand tugged at the blanket.

"If you wrap me up any tighter, I'm going to transform into a butterfly. And I really like being a moth." Her eyes opened and were instantly filled with pain.

"I'm pretty sure that's not how it works, but I'll go with it and argue with you later." Clio put her hand on Kit's forehead. "You're burning up."

Kit took Clio's hand from her forehead and kissed it with dry, papery lips. "I need to tell you something."

It sounded awfully like the conversation with Sian. "Don't. Save your strength."

She shook her head. "Listen, okay? Things are pretty shit right now, and if I don't make it, I need you to know some stuff."

Clio didn't say it would be okay, didn't tell her not to think that way. Historically, more than ninety percent of people survived plane crashes. But that meant there were about ten percent who didn't. "I'm listening."

"In the short time I've known you, you've made me a better person." She winced. "God, that sounds so cheesy. But it's true. I've always believed there were only two sides to a coin. But you've shown me there are a lot of coins with different sides. And to be honest, you've shown me that there's some stuff I'm not crazy about when it comes to my behavior. You've made me want to be the kind of woman who deserves you." She took a shuddery breath and her eyes closed. "And I want you. Not just because you're hot and a goddess in bed, but because you're kind, and sweet." Her head rolled to the side. "Like a marshmallow that goes on hot chocolate," she mumbled as she drifted off again.

Tears rolled down Clio's cheeks. "You're amazing, Kit. You're sexy, and infuriatingly stubborn. You're straightforward and you're all about helping people. You've helped me see that I've lost some of who I am, and I need to find my way back." She pressed Kit's limp hand to her cheek, covering it with tears. "Please don't leave me before we have the chance to see what we are together. Please fight to stay." She rested her head against Kit's shoulder and sobbed when there was no response.

CHAPTER NINETEEN

Frigid wind whipped into the hut as Sian and Paul came in, shaking snow from their coats.

"The drifts are hip high in places. I couldn't see anything but white. I couldn't even see the wreck site." Sian looked at Paul, who silently nodded agreement.

"I say we try again in a few hours, going the opposite direction. Maybe we'll get lucky." Sian hung her coat over the fireplace. "Anything with the patient?"

"She has a fever. She woke up again briefly." Clio didn't share what Kit had said. It was personal, between them, and she held the words to her like a safety blanket.

Sian dug in the medical kit. "Let's get some painkillers in her to see if we can fight the fever."

Paul held her back. "Aspirin could make the bleeding worse. We shouldn't give her anything unless we absolutely have to."

Sian sighed. "Okay. Makes sense. I just feel so helpless."

"We all do." Clio left Kit's side and knelt in front of the fireplace once again. She bowed her head and sent out prayers once more. But had anyone heard? Would anyone come? In that moment, she realized how Kit had felt when she'd lost her parents. Sending thoughts into the void, even knowing the gods were out there, felt like screaming into a vacuum. Faith meant believing you were heard, even if you didn't hear the answer. But when you were by the bedside of a dying loved one, what good was faith when you needed help?

Behind her, she heard the metal lid being removed from the ice. She turned to see Paul setting up the fishing line again. "This time we'll take the fish well away from the hut to clean it," he said and gave a small, gentle smile.

Sian sat with Kit while Clio sat beside Paul. She was so very grateful they'd survived the crash.

"It doesn't get any easier, does it?" Paul said in his quiet, even way.

"What doesn't?" Clio asked.

"Loving humans. Seeing how fragile they are and feeling their pain." He played with the fishing line. "We're lucky to get to be around them, and yet they break our hearts century after century."

Clio looked at Sian and Kit, women she loved in different ways. She swallowed at the admission, even if she'd only made it to herself. "So true."

"It's easy to get lost in this new world too, isn't it?" His smile was sad. "Of all the changes over the years, this century has been the most difficult for me. The world is connected by an unseen net, but that same net seems to keep us in a panic, like fish trapped by a fisherman. Only there's no fisherman, not really. The companies set things up for people to use, and people use them. But the companies don't care that the people are growing more depressed, more lonely, than ever before. And the people feel like they *should* feel connected because of all the people in their same net. But they don't."

Clio pondered that as she stared at the patterns in the ice. "It's not just humans feeling that way though, is it?"

He glanced sideways at her. "Is it not?"

She smiled a little at his game. "I've fallen into that same trap. It's my own doing, because I couldn't stand the messiness of human life anymore. Like Moscow. They never learn from history. No matter what text it's in or how it's taught, they don't *learn*. It's just violence and rage, year after year." She wiped away tears. "I don't want to keep writing down all the ways they kill each other. Maybe I have stuck my head in the sand, and maybe I am lonely. But I think I have good reason."

She looked up to find Sian watching her thoughtfully, but she looked away, unable to keep eye contact when she'd made herself so transparent.

"On your show, you tell people to look for the beauty. You say that perception is reality. Does that not apply to the way you think as well?" he asked. There was a tug on the line, and he pulled, gently, winding it in. The tug sharpened, and the old fishing line snapped, sending Paul sprawling backward. He held up the rod. "That was the only fishing line we had. Maybe we can unravel one of the blankets and weigh it down with something."

He started doing just that and looked at Clio. "So? Why does that not apply to you?"

"Because I know better," she whispered. "I know that life is awful for so many people. I remember it all."

"So everything you say on your show is a lie?" Sian was hunched over her knees. "You tell people to think about things in a way that even you can't?"

Clio frowned. "It's not that. It's just that I have way more understanding of the world, of humans."

"Ah, but us poor little humans with our simple minds can believe what you tell us, even if it's a lie." Sian stood and pulled her coat on roughly. "I'm going to walk in the other direction."

"Sian, please don't go." Clio held out her hand to stop her.

Sian took Clio's hand in hers and her expression softened. "You're remarkable, Clio, and I can't imagine what you've endured over the years. But for all that you tell Kit you want to show the world light and fun, it seems to me all you can see around you is the dark." She kissed her hand. "And you deserve better than that, especially from yourself." She let go of Clio's hand and opened the door. "I'll be back in thirty minutes."

Paul stood and let the soppy mess of string drop to the floor with the rod. "This isn't going to work. I'll go the other direction."

They went out, once again leaving Clio alone with her thoughts.

Kit shifted and moaned. Her skin was hot and damp, and her hair was stuck to her head.

"You knew there could be light," Clio said softly, stroking her head. "That's why you were so focused on the dark. You wanted to show people it could be better, that light was possible if only we fixed things." She gave a half-laugh, half-sob. "And I was so determined to ignore the dark because I couldn't find the light." She bent her head to Kit's chest and cried. "Please don't go."

❖

Kit opened her eyes and blinked several times until things came into focus. The first thing she saw was Clio, head bent, shoulders heaving with sobs. She wanted to tell her it would be okay, but when she went to speak, she couldn't. And the angle was wrong. She tilted her head trying to figure out what was off.

Shit. She was looking down at Clio. And, next to Clio, her own fucking body. *Am I dead?* Could she panic as a ghost? Because it sure as hell felt like she was panicking, even though she couldn't feel her heart beating or her pulse racing. She looked closer and saw that her chest was still rising and falling. At least that was something. But what the hell was she supposed to do now? Just float there until her body gave up? Watch as Clio sobbed her poor heart out, with no one there to comfort her? Where the hell was Sian? And Paul? Why had they left her alone?

She managed to float down so it was like she was sitting on the bench opposite her body. Surely it couldn't get any more surreal. Clio was pleading with her not to leave. She was telling her about the things she wanted them to do together and how she needed her to show her how to be real again.

I'm right here, baby. She reached out but her hand went right through Clio's arm. She shivered like she could feel it though.

She sat there, watching, wondering how she could get back into her body, although it looked pretty wrecked at the moment.

A figure in a black robe appeared next to her on the bench and she would have jumped out of her skin, if she'd had any. "Fuck me backwards!" she said out loud. "Hey, I can talk."

"Of course you can," the figure in the black robe said. "Good for you."

Kit took in the scythe and the black bag in the figure's hand. It was a Yama, a death worker there to take her soul. "Oh no you don't. I'm not one of yours. Not yet. I belong right over there, with my body and the woman I adore."

The figure flung her hood back. "Oh, it's you again. Hello."

Kit breathed a sigh of relief. "Soc, right? There's been a big mistake. I'm not going yet. And don't you work Mexico?"

"The Greenland Yama is on vacation, and I offered to take her place. Hardly anyone dies up here because it's so sparsely populated. It gives me time to read. But then I got the call about two souls and I went and got them, and then there was a message to hang around for an incoming, too." She seemed to take in the scene around them. "Oh! Oh, wow. I found you. People are looking all over for you guys. Well, for Clio, really, but you by proxy."

"I wouldn't really say you found us as much as you came to take my soul, but whatever." Kit pointed to her body. "I'm still breathing over there."

Soc nodded, her brow furrowed. "Yeah, but not for much longer, or I wouldn't be here. We need to get you help, fast." She bit her lip. "I'm not authorized to take you into the Deadlands though, and we don't have medicine anyway. Because, you know, it's mostly for dead people or people who don't die, ever." She stood and hooked her scythe over her shoulder. "I'm going for the boss. Try to keep your body alive."

She disappeared before Kit could ask exactly how she was supposed to do that. Kit sighed and put her ghostly head in her hands. *I wish you could hear me, Clio.* She looked up when Paul came in, shaking off the snow.

"Nothing." He frowned. "Sian isn't back? I'm already five minutes late because I got caught in deep snow."

Clio stood. "She's fine though, right?"

Paul put his jacket back on. "I'll follow her tracks." He was gone in an instant.

Clio sank to her knees, her arms wrapped around herself. She looked at the ceiling. "Dad, sisters, anyone. Please, please find a way to hear me. I need you. Kit needs you." She bent double, crying even harder.

"Gods, I hate it when beautiful women cry." Dani appeared beside Kit, looking like her usual self.

"I'm so glad you don't have your skull face on. I don't think I could deal with that."

Dani smiled. "I can understand that." She looked around the little hut. "Soc tells me you're in Greenland. I've got help coming your way. I'd take you myself through the Deadlands, but your body doesn't have much time, and I haven't needed any underworld roads through Greenland, so I don't have a lot of options."

"Can you talk to Clio? Tell her I'm okay?"

Dani shook her head. "I'm not actually with you. I'm too far away to be there physically, and I'm still dealing with the fallout in Mexico. I'm projecting myself to you, which I can do because you're a soul nearly in my realm. I can't do it with the living from this far away."

"You understand how weird that is, right?" She looked down at Clio. "I want her to know it'll be okay."

Dani put her hand on Kit's shoulder, which felt real enough. "Kit, we don't know that. You've been gravely injured, and your body is giving out." She raised her head. "Your help is only about fifteen minutes away. I think you'll make it. Soc is going to come keep you company, and now I can tell Clio's father and sisters where she is. They could hear her calling but couldn't figure out where she was. Be prepared for a family visit at the hospital." She grinned. "Good luck."

Left to her own thoughts, Kit couldn't help but wonder again what purpose the gods served. If even the goddess of Death couldn't help keep her alive, what was the point? But then, she argued with herself, it wasn't Death's job to keep people alive, was it? Rather the opposite. It was kind of her to send help at all, in that case.

Paul came in again. "I followed her tracks as far as I could, but the light is fading, and I don't have much power left in my phone. I didn't want to get stuck out there in the dark."

"Where could she have gone?"

He shook his head. "She loves you very much, and I think she's become rather attached to our sarcastic friend there, too. She doesn't strike me as the type to give up, even if it's foolish."

Clio went to the door and looked out at the dim landscape. "She's out there in the dark, alone. Maybe I should go after her."

He took her hand. "Clio, we're immortal, but we can still suffer. You could still lose fingers and toes to frostbite. You could still get hypothermia."

"But she's even more prone to those things." Clio hugged herself at the open door. "Sian, what have you done?"

Kit jumped again when Soc appeared next to her, this time in jeans and a simple T-shirt with the Grateful Dead logo on it.

"Boss said I should come hang out with you and let people know where you are if they can't find you. But they're nearly here."

"Hey, can you tell Clio what's going on?"

Soc nodded and disappeared from beside her, then reappeared beside Clio.

Clio jumped up, her expression one of fury. "No! No, Soc. You can't take her. I won't let you!" She stood between Soc and Kit's body, as though she'd physically take on the Yama if it came to it.

Kit loved her even more.

"Whoa, girl. I was here for her, yeah, but then I realized who it was, and we had a chat, and I got Dani, and now help is like, minutes away."

Clio blinked, looking startled, and then she threw herself into Soc's arms. "Thank you."

"No problem. It was her idea to tell you, so you'd stop freaking out. But the boss says we're not allowed to tell you it's all going to be okay, because it might not be. She's in pretty bad shape."

Clio blanched. "She's not in her body?"

"Oh. Sorry. I didn't think about that. No, she's over there." She pointed to where Kit sat on the bench. "Look, the boss said I had to keep her company, so I'm going to go hang out with her. She's between places, so I can't be with both of you. But you guys should probably get everything ready to go."

Soc did her disappearing act and came to Kit's side.

"Soc, how far can I go from my body without breaking the cable, so to speak?" Kit asked.

"Pretty far, I think. I mean, this doesn't happen often so I'm not an expert. Why?"

"Sian went out to look for help and didn't come back. I want to go out and see if we can find her. Will you help me?"

Soc's eyes went misty for a second. "Sure. Your rescue team is just about here, but I can get you back to your body even if it's moving. Let's go."

Soc took her hand, and they went straight through the roof of the hut.

"I'd rather not do that again." Kit shuddered at the strangeness of the feeling, like her body was made of Jell-O and something had just passed through it.

"Let's hope you don't have to. Come on." Together they floated through the air, searching the blank white landscape below.

They followed the two sets of footprints, which became one where Paul had turned back. Sian had gone far beyond her thirty-minute walk and Kit grew worried.

"There," Soc said, pointing.

They landed beside Sian's inert body where she lay in the snow. She wasn't even shivering.

"That doesn't look good," Kit said. "But you didn't come for her?"

Once again Soc's eyes went misty. "She's not close yet, but help is going the other way. I'll be back. Stay with her."

Soc disappeared and Kit squatted beside Sian's body. "Hey, buddy. You'd better hang in there. Clio can't lose us both, and she has enough on her plate worrying about me. You'd better be there to serve us drinks when we're back on that plane." She had no idea if Sian could hear her or not, but she couldn't just sit there and stare at her like some creepy snow ghost.

The sound of snow crunching made her look up. A god riding a reindeer was a new one. But there was no question he was a god, although he was even bigger than the others she'd come into contact with. The reindeer came to a halt next to Sian's body and he jumped off.

"Hey there, little human. Let's get you warm." He dragged a blanket from the reindeer's back and wrapped Sian like a burrito, handling her like she was an infant.

"I'm so going to give you shit about this when I see you again," Kit said. "Little human."

The god looked right at her. "Sorry, I didn't see you there. Didn't mean to be rude. You're welcome to ride with us. Don't think the reindeer will notice." He climbed back on and tucked Sian against his chest.

Soc floated next to Kit. "I'm not sure why you'd want to ride, but go for it. He'll take you back to your body anyway."

Kit wondered if it might be her only chance. If she died, she doubted her afterlife would include reindeer rides. If she lived, it looked like it might be a while before she was back on her feet, let alone riding a reindeer while seated behind a god. She floated down and sat back-to-back with the god, on the reindeer's behind. She couldn't feel it, but it was a cool thing to do anyway.

As they galloped through the snow, she looked up at the sky. Sheets of green and blue danced through the black sky, casting slices of gem-like shadows across the white landscape below, a magnificent display that would have brought tears to her eyes, if she were in an actual body. She so wanted to be sharing this with Clio. She watched the heavenly ballet, mesmerized by the beauty, until it faded away.

"Here we go," the god said as they pulled up behind another sled being pulled by eight reindeer with huge antlers. Clio, Paul, and Kit's body were buried under heavy blankets, and a woman guided the sled with expert hands. They cleared a rise and city lights became visible. They took the sled right up to the back of a hospital, where hospital staff came running out almost right away.

Kit's body was placed on a stretcher and rushed inside, as was Sian's. Clio cried out when she saw Sian unconscious as well, and Paul held her tightly as they watched the gurneys disappear down a corridor they weren't allowed into. Clio was safe, and Kit figuratively breathed a sigh of relief. She decided she missed being able to sigh for real. The god and the woman who'd been driving the sled put their arms around Clio and Paul, making a strange and striking foursome.

Things were getting a little blurry again. "What's going on?" she asked.

"Your body is in trouble." Soc took her hand. "You should get back into it so you have a fighting chance."

Soc led her down the hallway and into a surgical room where her body was already hooked up to tubes and bags and things that were beeping. Her leg was lifted, the piece of metal sticking out at a bad angle.

"Yikes. Maybe I should stay up here till all that's done."

"If you do, you won't go back in." Soc shrugged apologetically. "It's your choice, though. You can choose not to go back in, and your body will give up. Then I'll take you on to the afterlife of your choice."

Kit thought of Clio, and how badly she wanted to hold her again. "No way." She floated down to her body just as there was a flurry of action and they put paddles on her chest. She pushed downward and gasped when the electric shock made her body bounce like rubber.

"She's back with us," she heard someone say.

Back. She let her soul go quiet, knowing she'd be with Clio again soon.

Chapter Twenty

Clio rested her head on Eris's shoulder. They'd been there for hours, and after she'd been given antibiotics and stitches for her calf wound, she'd sat with Eris and Prometheus in the waiting room.

Having a god ask the doctors and nurses questions turned out to be a good thing. Clio and Paul looked far too mortal to be intimidating, but Prometheus, at nearly nine feet tall, never got no for an answer. So they knew Kit had gone into surgery and was in critical condition. Sian was suffering from hypothermia but was expected to fully recover once they'd brought her body back to temperature and stabilized her. They said Clio could see her soon.

"I don't know what I would have done if you hadn't made it on time." The thought kept going through Clio's mind, how close she'd come to losing both Kit and Sian in one night.

"It sounds like she wasn't about to leave you without a fight," Eris said. "This is the one we talked about on the phone, right?"

Clio nodded. "Kit is incredible, Eris. She makes me want to throttle her and jump her bones at the same time."

"That can be a sexy combination." Eris grinned. "But I don't think we're thinking the same thing."

Clio rolled her eyes, comforted by her sister's usual relaxed, blasé manner. "No, probably not."

"And the other one? Who is she to you?" Eris asked.

"She's quite attractive, as humans go," Prometheus said. "Quite a lot of muscle."

"Yeah?" Eris said, her eyebrow raising suggestively. "Do tell."

"You're not her type, sorry." Clio shook her head at the twinge of jealousy. "She's been my lover off and on for several years and she works for me, in a way. Always casual. She's also truly wonderful."

"But you're in love with the sarcastic hot one, not the hot worker one?" Prometheus said.

"Right."

Eris looked surprised. "In love again, eh? That's got to be tough."

Clio rested her head on Eris's shoulder again. "It is. But it's worth it. She's worth it."

The doctor hovered outside the waiting room door, looking like a rabbit. Some people weren't relaxed around the gods yet. "You can see Sian, Ms. Ardalides."

She got up and followed him down the hall, and he motioned her into a room. "She's had a mild sedative. She kept trying to get up to go find you and Ms. Kalloway, and short of tying her down, we had no other option than to sedate her."

Clio smiled and kissed Sian's forehead. "What were you thinking, going so far out there?"

"I don't think you're supposed to reprimand someone in a hospital bed. There are rules." Sian smiled at her sleepily. "Is Kit okay?"

"She's in surgery. We'll see."

Sian nodded, her eyes drifting shut. "I just wanted to save you."

"Oh, Sian. What would I have done if I'd have lost you too?"

"I dreamt I was saved by a god. But knowing you, it wasn't a dream, was it?"

Clio shook her head, unsure if Sian had heard her question and was ignoring it or was just too out of it to follow the conversation. "My uncle Prometheus and my sister Eris came for us. It was Uncle Prom who found you in the snow."

Sian's eyes flew open. "The Titan god?"

"Yeah. It's going to be intense when my dad gets here. Zeus has never forgiven Prometheus for helping the humans be more independent. And Prometheus has never forgiven Zeus for chaining him to a rock and letting an eagle eat his liver over and over again. Family dynamics are complicated. Too bad you're going to miss it."

Sian mumbled something, but Clio didn't catch it. She sat down beside Sian's bed and held her hand. What was it that made you fall in love with someone, she wondered, not for the first time in her long life. Sian was a perfect partner. Sexy, intelligent, caring. And as much as Clio cared for her, she'd never once thought she was in love with her. But then Kit had come into her life, and it was ungrounded electricity between them. Her attraction was almost painful, and Kit had broken open Clio's shell of fear and confusion, for it to spill into the open to be dealt with, one way or another.

Was it fair to Sian, though? Was it cruel to keep her in her life knowing that she was in love with Clio, when Clio was unquestionably in love with Kit? Her heart ached at the thought of separating herself from Sian, but she'd had to do it in the past when humans became too attached to the muse at their side.

And then there was the rest of her life to look at. When she got home, when Kit was safe and on the mend, what did she want from her life? Going back to the way it had been didn't feel right.

"Hey," Eris shout-whispered from the hallway.

Clio got up and went to her.

"Dad is in the waiting room freaking everyone out. Come show him you're okay before everyone goes running for the hills."

She followed Eris back to the waiting room, where Zeus and Prometheus stood glaring at one another. She went straight to her dad and hugged him tightly and relaxed into his strong hug in return.

"You had us so worried." He held her at arm's length. "You're okay?"

She nodded. "You heard me call to you?"

"I could hear you, but I couldn't get a read on exactly where you were. All that damn ice and snow can blind even a god. And when Eris called to say she could feel that you needed us, I knew you were in real trouble. But honestly, we were looking in the wrong place. We thought you were in the middle of the Moscow mess. I was so worried you were hurt."

"But I'm immortal. I needed you for Kit, not for myself."

He tilted his head side to side. "Well, see, that's the thing. You're not aging anymore, and you won't technically die. But unlike the other immortals, I'm pretty sure you and your sisters could be killed."

She stared at him open-mouthed. "Well, that's new news. You might have mentioned that a few centuries ago. Do my sisters know that?"

"Didn't really seem necessary to tell you before. You've all been pretty careful creatures." He laughed. "Anyway. I'm glad you're safe and the mortals you care about are too." He leaned down and gave her a conspiratorial grin. "Is this the one who drove you to the temple in Greece? It's always the one who drives you craziest that makes you love them the most."

"That's a healthy outlook, Dad." Eris, muse of love, clearly wasn't impressed.

"Okay, I'm going to head back to HQ. If you need me, call." He glared at Prometheus, who glared back. "Thank you for saving my daughter and her friends."

The words sounded far more "fuck off" than "thank you," but then, that was their relationship.

Clio hugged him and waved as he left, shooting a lightning bolt into the sky, and holding onto it as he disappeared from sight. Prometheus smiled down at Clio. "Now that you're safe and sound, I'm going to head home. Eris can get hold of me if you need me again."

She gave him a tight hug. "Thank you, Uncle. I owe you dinner one night."

"You never owe me anything. You know I'd do anything for you and your sisters."

"Could I go with you?" Paul asked. "If you don't mind, Clio, I'd very much like to go home, and now that your sister is with you, you'll be okay, yes?"

Prometheus looked surprised.

"Anulap is a pre-fader Micronesian god," Clio explained, and Prometheus smiled.

"By all means, little god! I'd be happy to have the company." After giving Clio a hug, they went out the back door and jumped on the sled with the reindeer, waving as they drove off into the night.

Eris wrapped her arm around Clio's shoulders. "Come on. Let's go get something to eat in that crime lab they call the cafeteria, where we won't be able to pronounce any of the names of things."

They went to the cafeteria and got hot food, though Clio couldn't tell what it was. The coffee was good, though and she had several cups.

The doctor came to their table. "Ms. Kalloway is out of surgery and is currently stable. She sustained massive blood loss. The tourniquet on her leg kept her from bleeding out, but it may have done some nerve damage. It's too early to tell. The wound also got infected from the metal, which was causing her fever. She has two broken ribs, one of which was close to puncturing her lung." He looked at the chart in his hands. "Recovery is going to be difficult, but with luck and help, she'll get there."

Clio thanked him and he hurried away. Religion was minimal in Greenland, so they'd likely had little to do with the Mcrgc. No wonder they were all jittery.

After they'd finished eating, they found their way to Kit's recovery room. Eris put her arm around Clio when her breath caught, and she had to lean against the wall to stay upright. She'd been with Kit throughout the crisis but seeing her in bed with tubes and wires everywhere, and her leg held by a contraption, made her weak.

Only then did it really hit her. "She was dying, Eris. A Yama came for her."

"That's how we found you." Eris sounded confused.

"But she was *dying*. I was so close to losing her. If it hadn't been Soc who'd come for her, if it had been another Yama who didn't know us…"

"But it was Soc, and we did find you." Eris's tone was firm. "Focus on what is, not what might have been. History is about what happened, not what didn't."

Clio made her way to the chair next to Kit's bed and slid her hand into Kit's cold one. "That's not true. History is also about what was averted."

"Okay, well, Kit's death was averted. So there." Eris smiled and stretched her legs out in front of her in the other chair.

Eris turned on the TV and eventually found an English station with old sitcoms on. They watched in silence until Eris finally clicked it off. "Gods, that's mind-numbing stuff. TV is the one thing humans shouldn't have invented."

Clio looked at her pointedly.

"Sorry." Eris leaned her head back on the chair. "You know how much I like movies. And I know a lot of the gods had fun on your show."

She focused on the beeping of Kit's monitor. "I really did think I was doing something good, E. And when they merged my show with Kit's, it felt like a gut punch. But the interviews we did together were good, and I was starting to see what the producers imagined. But after Moscow…" She shuddered. "I've been on the sidelines of so many wars and battles, and I simply don't want to do it anymore. I know that now. I hope Kit will forgive me, but I simply can't do it to my soul."

Eris picked up a straw from a tray and began to tie it in knots. "I get it, and I bet Kit will too, if she's as great as you say she is." She pointed the knotted straw at Clio. "So what do you want to do next?"

Clio searched Kit's gaunt face for an answer, but none was forthcoming. "I don't know yet. But I do know that I want Kit in my life, whatever it is I do."

Eris slapped her hands to her knees and stood. "That's a good start. Sometimes just knowing what you don't want can take you to what you do." She stretched and yawned. "I'm going to the hotel to get some sleep. You should come too. Kit probably won't wake till morning, and you know Sian will be fine."

Clio was torn. She was exhausted, cold, and sore. A hot shower sounded divine. But what if Kit woke up, alone?

"Okay, decision made." Eris came around and pulled her up. "You look like you're headed to the underworld yourself and not even Hades would find you attractive right now. You can't take care of her if you're half dead yourself. You can come back first thing in the morning."

Clio leaned down and kissed Kit's forehead. "I'll see you in the morning," she whispered.

They took a taxi for the three-minute ride to the hotel, given that it was well below freezing and they'd both had enough of the cold.

"There are only two hotels in Tasiilaq. One is for the adventure traveler, and one is for the comfort traveler. You can guess which one I picked."

Clio just nodded, grateful that Eris had taken charge. She was too tired to care. "Hey, did you know we can be killed?" she asked.

Eris rolled her eyes. "Yeah, I heard Dad tell you. Nice of him to mention it three thousand years later, huh?" She shrugged. "Knowing you could die is a mortal thing. Probably better not to mention it to our sisters."

Clio wasn't sure about that. "Shouldn't we all know so we can be more careful?" She pictured the flames pouring from the building, the children screaming as they were surrounded by smoke and fire.

"Would you do anything differently?"

Clio followed her up to their room, barely noticing what the hotel looked like. "No, probably not."

"Then live in the moment, sis."

"I'm the muse of history. Living in the moment isn't really my thing." The metaphorical and cliché lightbulb went off in her mind. "And that's what I've been trying to do."

Eris flopped into bed after shucking her clothes onto the floor. "There she is."

Clio lay staring at the ceiling, desperate to sleep but her racing mind wouldn't allow it. She'd gone so far from where she'd begun. No wonder she felt so rootless lately. She turned onto her side and remembered the feel of Kit's hands on her body, the way her lips felt as they made their way over her neck. And she thought of Kit's words in the hut when she wasn't sure if she was going to survive. Had they been true? Was it emotion brought on by the possibility of death? Would she still feel the same once she woke? Or was Clio about to get her heart broken yet again?

CHAPTER TWENTY-ONE

The moment Kit woke she wanted to go back to sleep. Her body hurt in a way she'd never known before. It even hurt to breathe. And she couldn't move right. Slowly, she managed to crack open grit-filled eyes and blearily look around. *All hospitals look the same.* It was a mundane thought, but it was true. Always some pastel color meant to soothe and calm, no matter the chaos within. She felt anything but soothed as she took in the tubes attached to her hands and touched the breathing thing in her nose that started to irritate her the moment she became aware of it.

She followed the line of the metal holding her leg steady and winced. Yeah, that part of her hurt most.

"Well, hello there." A woman in a white lab coat walked in holding a file. "You're awake. That's probably unpleasant."

A doctor with a sense of humor was always better than one who took things too seriously. "If you could hit me in the head with a mallet and knock me back out, that would be great."

"We have far superior methods to a mallet these days." The doctor shined a light in her eyes and listened to her chest. "But for a plane crash victim, I'd say you look better than most."

"The people who were with me?" she asked. She'd seen Clio when she was in her surreal out-of-body state, so she knew she was okay. But she couldn't bring herself to say Sian's name.

"You're the worst of it. Sian is making a nuisance of herself, and we'll need to discharge her if only to give our nurses a break. Clio and her sister went to a hotel for the night, but I'm expecting them to return any moment. Thankfully, the gods left before the staff all quit."

Kit closed her eyes, already tired out from the conversation. "Thanks." She realized there was at least one name missing and opened her eyes again. "Tamara? The pilot?" She didn't remember seeing them when she was in the hut.

"I'm sorry, they didn't make it. A team has gone out today to retrieve their bodies from the wreck site, if they can be found. There's been a lot of snow, and they might have to stay out there until spring when it thaws." The doctor looked genuinely apologetic.

Kit didn't have a reply, and the doctor squeezed her good foot in sympathy. "As far as your own injuries, you got to us just in time. Your rib was about to puncture your lung and your leg was already infected thanks to the compound fracture. We got the metal out and have tried our best to repair the tendon, and we've reset the broken tibia, but it's going to take some serious rehab to get your leg back to normal. Your ribs should heal up in about six weeks or so." She pressed a button on the machine with a small bag attached to it. "The morphine will help you feel less like you've been in a plane crash."

Kit thanked her and promised to hit the call button if she needed anything, and then she was left alone with her thoughts.

Moscow had been terrifying. The memory of all those children, trapped behind a wall of flames, would stay with her forever. As would the image of the god flinging that first gunman through the air like a toy. It was easy to forget that the gods were gods, sometimes, with all the talking and interviews and such. But that one moment was a reminder that they were, in fact, very different from the people they watched over.

She let her head push into the thick pillow as thoughts flitted through her head. She'd become a journalist so she could make a difference. She wanted to show people what was going on in the world so that change could happen. After her parents had died and the Merge had taken place, that desire had become entangled with her anger and pain.

Clio had shown her how lost in that anger she'd become. It had been her only path for so long, she didn't even realize she was on it.

She heard a sound and opened her eyes. Clio stood in the doorway smiling at her, tears slipping down her cheeks.

"Hey. I hope you don't mind that I didn't dress up for you." Kit lifted one hand and let it fall back to the bed. "I didn't have a thing to wear."

Clio moved to her side and pressed her soft, warm lips to Kit's forehead. "I've never been so glad to hear you awake."

"I feel like I should be insulted but I'm too tired to figure out why." Kit looked over Clio's shoulder. "You must be her sister?"

"Eris. Nice to meet you, in a way. It would have been better at a nightclub or family dinner night but saving you from death works too." She grinned.

Kit liked her right away. "If it's okay, I'd like to stay very far away from your family dinner nights. You all terrify me."

Eris scoffed. "I've seen your show. We're the ones terrified of you." She looked at Clio. "I'll go get us that black gasoline they call coffee."

Clio sat at Kit's side. "How are you feeling?"

Kit closed her eyes. "I'm glad you're here. The pain meds are super-duper, so I won't be much of a conversationalist." She formed the word again, liking the way it felt in her mouth. "Con-ver-sayyy-sion-alll-ist."

Clio laughed. "Now that I know you'll be okay, I guess I'll head back to California."

Kit's eyes snapped open, and her heart raced. "You're leaving me here?"

"No." Clio's eyes sparkled. "I just wanted to see your reaction to make sure you want me to stay."

"At least I'm in the right place for a heart attack." Kit turned her hand over for Clio to take it. "Clio, I'm sorry for ever diminishing what you do for a living. When I was dead—"

"So you really were a soul outside your body?" Clio asked. "Soc said you were between worlds, but I didn't want to believe it."

Kit grunted. "Weirdest thing ever, and I don't recommend the experience. Two stars, seriously. Seeing your body down there and knowing you're about to die isn't at all what it's like in the movies."

She squeezed Clio's hand. "We'll get back to that later. When I was above my body and watching you kneel there next to me, begging me not to leave you…" She swallowed hard, tears welling in her eyes. "Damn. I couldn't get to you. I couldn't hold you and tell you it was going to be okay. I had the goddess of death standing there telling me that she couldn't tell you it would be okay and that there was a good possibility I wasn't going to make it. I was going to lose you."

Clio's shoulders shook as she cried. "But you didn't. You're here."

Kit held her hand a little tighter. "I love you, Clio. We haven't known one another for very long, and we might very well kill each other one day after we've survived this. But I love you."

Clio cried harder and leaned over to kiss her, her tears dropping onto Kit's cheeks. "I love you too. When I thought I was going to lose you I couldn't imagine how I'd keep going. You're such a good, beautiful person, inside and out. I've always been a muse, but since we met, I think you've become mine."

Kit struggled to keep her eyes open, but one thought kept bouncing through her head. *She loves me.*

Kit had no idea how much time had passed when she came to again. The sound of voices talking quietly was soothing, and she let herself listen without opening her eyes.

"That's so crazy. I have to admit that I'm glad I didn't have some soul eater come for me."

It was Sian's voice, sounding strong and calm as ever.

"They don't eat souls. They take them to their proper afterlife. But I get your point."

Clio, sounding more relaxed and upbeat.

"Want me to arrange for a new plane?"

That was the sister. Kit could picture the tall, suave-looking butch with dark black hair. Eris, was it?

"As much as I hate to admit that I'll be a little freaked out about flying again, taking a boat all the way to San Francisco seems pretty silly. And Kit can't travel on a regular commercial plane with her leg the way it is. So I think the answer has to be yes."

"Do I get a say in this?" Kit asked. Her throat was sore and dry. She squinted and looked for water.

Clio was up in an instant and holding a cup with a straw for her. "You're the invalid. I don't think you get a say."

Kit drank gratefully and let her head flop back. "I think an insanely long cruise sounds perfectly romantic."

"Romance is the very first thing I think of when I look at you," Sian said, nodding seriously. "Nothing like a gaunt, bruised and broken up woman to say let's jump in bed and do the dirty."

Eris laughed out loud and slapped Sian on the back. "When you're back in California, we're going to have so much fun."

Clio frowned. "Why does everyone keep trying to take Sian away?"

Sian's smile faltered a little. "No one will take me away. Promise."

Clio gave her a small, sad look of understanding. "I was teasing. But I'm glad you're sticking around."

There was an undercurrent between them that Kit didn't fully understand, but she had a feeling she knew what it revolved around. She made eye contact with Sian, who looked away. So she'd told Clio how she felt. Given their experience, it made sense that she'd opened up, but Kit couldn't help but wonder how Clio felt. Had it changed her feelings toward Kit at all? No. She'd told her she loved her, and Clio was nothing if not completely honest. Still, she felt bad for Sian. Watching the woman you loved love someone else had to be the worst. Thankfully, she didn't have to be the one to do it.

The doctor came in and went straight to the TV remote. "It turns out we have heroes in our midst."

The news came on, and although the newscaster was speaking Greenlandic, the video didn't need translation.

It was the riot in Moscow. The camera crew had gotten phenomenal footage of the gods wading into the crowd, trying to save people. But the camera lingered longest on Kit and Clio as they rescued the children. Flames painted the scene in an eerie, horror movie kind of scenario as the children cried. Then they were holding hands, through the tunnel, and out the other side. The camera had never stopped rolling.

Pictures of Clio and Kit taken from their press photos for their shows came up on screen, identifying them, along with a picture of Clio's plane. The doctor turned the TV off when it went to a commercial.

"They're saying you're missing, and it's being presumed that your plane went down, and the search is on although there isn't much hope for your survival, given the pilot's emergency message saying the plane was going down. I hope you don't mind, I called the authorities and let them know what happened. And saving the children was quite the feat," the doctor said. "Some of our staff want your autographs."

Kit and Clio looked at one another. "We did it because it had to be done," Kit said. "Any of you would have done the same."

Sian was staring at the floor, her shoulders rigid. "But no one else did, did they?" She looked up at both of them. "No one stopped to help you. I had no idea you were in the middle of it like that."

"And then you get in a plane crash." Eris laughed. "You survive a riot in the middle of Moscow only to fall into the snow in Greenland."

Kit began to laugh too, and then held her ribs. "We're fucking invincible!"

"Please don't say that. We still have to take a plane to get back home. I'd rather not test that theory." Clio thanked the doctor for showing them the footage. "How soon can we move Kit, so we can all head home?"

"You can leave tomorrow if you have the right transport. You don't want to move that leg around too much. I'll get your discharge papers ready." She left with a lingering look at Eris, who winked at her.

"Must you ply your trade here?" Clio asked. "It's unseemly."

"When love is in the air, love does as love will," Eris said and gave a little half smirk.

"If that's love, I've been in it *a lot*." Sian leaned over to look out the door at the doctor's butt.

"Anyway." Clio rolled her eyes. "Can you two see about getting us a ride home?"

They stood and Eris saluted. "Yes, boss. We'll get right on it."

It was blessedly quiet when they left, and Kit focused on Clio. "Is everything okay?"

"Honestly?" Clio rested her chin on the railing of Kit's bed. "I'm exhausted and I want to be home in my own bed." She threaded her fingers through Kit's. "I wondered if you'd be willing to come stay at my place while you recover? We can go get Buster and bring him over."

Kit didn't like the sound of it being temporary, but it was too soon to talk about moving in together on a more permanent basis. "I'd like that. You'll have to take care of my every need until I can walk again."

Clio leaned closer. "Oh, I'll be taking care of your needs, don't you worry."

Even in her drugged, battered state, Kit's clit twitched at the promise in Clio's voice. "Now?"

Clio leaned back, laughing. "No, not now. You'll jerk your leg, and the doctor will tell me off and then you'll be stuck here for goodness knows how long. You'll just have to wait until you're in my bed."

Kit yawned. "I'll keep asking until you give in." Her eyes closed even though she didn't want them to. She wanted to stay awake and talk to Clio. Her body had other plans though, and as she drifted to sleep, she heard Clio whisper, "I love you."

CHAPTER TWENTY-TWO

Thankfully, the flight home was calm. There was no turbulence, and with Sian and Eris aboard, there was plenty of banter and laughter to keep them all distracted. Still, Clio breathed a sigh of relief when the plane landed, and they were headed toward the terminal. Kit, too, looked relieved and let go of her death grip on Clio's hand.

Sian had wanted to work as the steward, as she always did, but Clio had insisted that she rest and relax. The doctor had reassured them that Sian was in the clear, but she still looked tired. Plus, the plane had been borrowed from an eccentric millionaire who was living on the topmost coast of the populated section of Greenland. Few people knew he was there, but after a few phone calls, Sian had found him and begged the use of his plane. His only condition was that he be allowed to visit Clio in San Francisco one day so he could learn more about the 1400s in Italy. Why, Clio had no idea, but whatever worked.

They brought a special wheelchair for Kit, one that kept her leg elevated. The moment they were in the terminal, their phones started pinging and vibrating, and then the ringing began.

Clio simply turned hers off. The producers had been notified they were still alive, and her family knew as well. There was no one she needed to talk to right away. Kit, on the other hand, had her friends, and she called Barb while they made their way to the van that would take them to Clio's place. Barb could be heard even though Kit didn't have it on speaker, and her love and worry made Clio smile. It was good that Kit had such close friends who'd become her family.

Barb promised to swing by Kit's place and get Buster, then bring him over to Clio's. When she hung up, Kit texted Barb Clio's address.

The sliding doors opened as they left the terminal, and they were greeted by a barrage of questions and cameras. The press was out in full, and there were so many questions Clio couldn't make them out even if she wanted to answer them. She looked at Sian and Eris, her heart pounding in panic. "Protect Kit's leg!"

They moved to either side of Kit's wheelchair like bodyguards and kept the press from moving too close. They stayed in place while they loaded Kit into the van, and then Clio got in beside her. Sian and Eris got in and slammed the van door shut behind them. They pulled away, reporters still shouting questions at the moving vehicle.

"Jesus." Kit sounded shaky. "What the hell was that?"

"Unexpected, I'd say." Sian, too, looked shaken. "I guess there's no question that word got out about Moscow and the plane crash."

Clio took out her phone. "I need to make sure my place isn't buried in them." She called her housekeeper, who informed her that there were a few reporters hanging around outside the gate, but not too many. Clio told her that they'd be there in about an hour, and she promised to have things ready.

Sian, Eris, and Kit were all on their phones, too. Kit held hers away from her mouth. "Jag wants to know if he can come see us."

Clio nodded, already tired out. "Of course. Maybe tomorrow, though? I think we could both use an early night."

Kit agreed and set a time with Jag for the following day. By the time they made it to Clio's house, Sian looked wiped out too. Eris, per usual, looked like she was enjoying a regular day out.

The gate opened when the van pulled up, and the few reporters there rushed forward, shouting questions as though someone would pop out to answer them. Fortunately, they seemed to know better than to try to go beyond the gate and onto the property.

They managed to get Kit into the house, though it was a little bumpier than it should have been. Clio sent a text to Jag to ask him to have someone come fit the house for the wheelchair the next day, and he replied to say he'd take care of it. She was a little bothered that with her own agent gone, she had no one to ask for things like this. But then, there was a time she'd done these things on her own. It was a sobering thought, and another example of how she'd forgotten to live like a regular person.

When Kit was settled on the sofa with pillows under her leg, Clio turned to the other two. "Are you going to stay the night?" In one sense, she was hoping they'd say yes, since it would be easier to move Kit around with someone else there. But in another sense, she wanted some alone time with Kit, away from Sian's contemplative gaze and Eris's amused one.

"I called a service on our way here," Sian said. "They're sending over a nurse to help out. I figured they could stay in your guest room since Kit won't be able to get up the couple of stairs to it."

Kit's eyebrow twitched but she didn't say anything. She didn't need to.

"Not that she'd be sleeping in the guest room." Sian sighed and rubbed at her eyes. "Anyway, you'll have help. So I'll be on my way. I've already called for an Uber."

Eris looked between them like she was watching a play unfold in front of her. Clio kicked her shin.

"Ow! Just for that, I'm leaving too." She hugged Clio tightly. "I'm going to work. But call me if you need me for anything at all. I'll send someone over." She grinned when Clio punched her arm. She put her hand on Sian's shoulder and guided her to the front door. "Now, my lovelorn friend, I have a suggestion for you—"

The door closed behind them so Clio didn't have to hear just what her suggestion might entail, though it would likely include getting on top of someone to get from under someone else. She'd heard that advice before.

She went back to the living room to find Kit sound asleep. There were deep bags under her eyes and her forehead was furrowed in pain. In the kitchen, Clio found that the housekeeper had left a note to say there was a meal ready to go in the fridge, she just had to heat it up. She'd also baked Clio's favorite, maple and pecan cookies, which were in a tin by the toaster.

Clio bent and rested her forehead on her arms on the counter. The last few days had been harrowing in so many ways. All she wanted was to curl up and sleep for hours. With that in mind, she poured a glass of water and got out Kit's pain pills, then joined her on the sofa. She curled up on Kit's good side, and fell asleep.

The buzzer at the front gate woke her, and she looked around the dark room, confused for a moment.

"Hey," Kit said, sounding like she'd just woken too.

"Hey," Clio said, shifting and forcing her aching body upright. "That's probably the service Sian called to help us out." She realized then that she did have someone she could call, just the way that Kit had someone. But it might not be fair to ask Sian for help anymore.

She looked at the camera and saw two cars waiting. One large guy leaned out, hitting the buzzer. She hit the open key and watched the cars come in. The press seemed to have given up, which gave her some little peace.

She opened the front door to a big man dressed all in white. She liked him right away.

"Hi, I'm Troy. Looks like I woke you. Sorry about that, but it sounded like you might need some help over here." He looked over her shoulder. "Everything okay?"

Confused, she looked behind her and realized she hadn't turned on any lights at all. "Oh, sorry. Yeah, we fell asleep on the couch. Come on in."

Behind him was Barb, along with a tall, dapper-looking man who was holding a huge dog straining at his leash.

Barb came up and hugged her hard. "We thought the worst," she whispered, her tears wetting Clio's neck. "I'm so glad you made it back. I thought I'd lost her."

Clio returned her hug. "You nearly did. She's in the living room. Go on in."

Barb rushed in, leaving Clio to smile at the other man. "Hi. I'm guessing this is Buster?"

He held out his hand. "I'm Abel, Kit's extraordinary dog sitter and personal chef when she can't be bothered to cook for herself." He leaned in and gave her a half hug. "I was also worried I'd just inherited an extremely large child who eats his way through life." His joke was tempered by the serious look in his eyes.

"Well, I'm afraid you'll have to adopt your own. Kit will be glad to see this one. And you, I imagine." Clio waved them in and gave Buster's big head a cuddle. He sniffed her like a vacuum, and then tugged his way into the house.

Clio heard them all talking and leaned against the front door for one last moment of quiet. Waking with Kit on the couch would be much better down the road. When she got back to the living room, she found that Troy had already maneuvered Kit into her wheelchair and was taking her to the bathroom. Buster was at their side, sniffing suspiciously at the metal and the cast on Kit's leg.

Barb was sitting on the couch with her head in her hands, her shoulders moving a little as she cried. Abel stood in front of the window looking out at the sea. It was the most people Clio'd had in her home in years, but she was too exhausted to properly play hostess.

Abel turned. "How can we help? Or do you just want us to go away?"

She sat down next to Barb and put her arm around her. "My housekeeper very kindly left some food in the fridge to be heated up for dinner. Would you mind taking care of it, and then we can all eat together, if you'll stay?"

He nodded and headed off toward the kitchen without another word.

Barb wiped her eyes on her shirt. "I'm sorry. You've been through enough without having me fall apart on you. I'm just so relieved. What happened?"

Clio slowly shook her head. "Why don't we tell you that story together over dinner? What's most important for you to know is that she's okay. She needs physical therapy once she heals, but she's going to be fine. She's staying here with me, and Troy is going to be staying on site to help too."

Barb's sigh of relief went with her shoulders releasing. "I'm going to call the others. They made me promise."

Clio squeezed her shoulder and went into the kitchen to give her some privacy. She sat at the breakfast bar and watched as Abel chopped up the ingredients for a salad. He seemed to understand her desire for quiet, and he simply hummed softly.

"I'm glad you're here," she finally said. "It's good for Kit to see how much she's loved."

"Did she doubt it?" he asked, looking surprised.

She startled. "No, I don't think she did. I suppose I'm projecting." She gave him a wry smile.

He gave her a sympathetic look. "Well, now you know you're loved too. Barb talked about how lovely you were all the way here, and she said that Kit looked at you the way she's never looked at anyone before."

"It's true," Barb said as she came in looking much better. "Like she wanted to rip your clothes off and worship you at the same time."

Clio flushed. "That makes me very lucky."

They looked at her expectantly, waiting for more.

"I'll let Kit tell you," she said. "She may not want you to know how madly in love we are."

Abel laughed and Barb held her hands under her chin. "It's about time," she said.

"About time for what?" Kit asked as Troy wheeled her into the room. "And why was I abandoned out there?"

Clio's heart ached at how good it felt to have Kit there with her. "Did you want us to come to the bathroom with you?"

"No, I don't play those kinds of games, thank you very much." She nodded thanks to Troy when he parked her beside Clio so she could take her hand. "About time for what?"

"About time you've fallen madly in love with someone other than your dog." Abel threw her a carrot disc, which she caught and bit into.

Buster had his big head on Kit's good leg, and he was groaning under the rigorous scratching she was giving him behind his ears. She smiled at Clio. "You've already told them?"

"No. I said they had to wait for you to tell them that I'm the best thing ever to happen to you."

Conversation continued for the next few hours as Clio and Kit took turns telling them all about Moscow and the crash after. They were all enthralled when Kit shared her out-of-body experience, including her discussion with Dani. Troy fit right in, and Clio enjoyed the feeling of having a friendship group like she hadn't had in a long time.

Soon, they were both yawning almost non-stop.

"Okay, we get the hint," Abel said, standing. "We'll go. Do you want me to leave Buster, or should I take him?"

Kit looked to Clio, the question in her eyes.

"I think he'd love it here, and he can keep an eye on Kit. I'll walk him on the beach every day, which will be good for me." The look of gratitude in Kit's eyes made her want to say it all over again.

"Okay, I'll put all his things by the front door." He leaned down and hugged Kit gently. "I'll take care of your mail and plants."

"I don't have any plants." Kit hugged him back, her eyes closed.

"I know, but it sounded less sad than just taking care of your mail." He backed up so Barb could take his place.

"Trish and Jim want to see you when you're ready, okay?" She too hugged Kit gently, but for a long while.

"Tell them to give me a couple of days, okay?" Kit looked at Clio and smiled. "We want to spend some time together without fires or riots."

The two of them left. Troy came in from the bedroom that Clio had indicated they'd be sharing. "I've gone ahead and fixed up the bed so it should be comfortable for Kit, and you'll be sleeping on her other side, Clio, so you won't have to worry about bumping her."

Together they got Kit undressed and into loose boxers and a T-shirt. Clio's breath hitched at the deep bruising around Kit's ribs. She'd have to use the arnica salve she still had in her medicine chest, a gift from her sister who was interested in all that stuff.

Once they were in bed with only a side light on, Clio lay on her side looking at Kit beside her. "You okay?"

Kit sighed. "This is going to take some getting used to. I hate being unable to even dress myself. And going to the bathroom with someone isn't a whole lot of fun."

Clio gently stroked her arm. "Once your ribs are better and we can let your leg down, it will be easier. Just try to be patient and let me take care of you."

"I'd feel a lot better if you'd kiss me."

Clio leaned over and kissed her softly, lingering, teasing. "Like that?"

"You're evil," Kit murmured against her lips, reaching up for more. "Don't make me beg."

"I won't, not yet." Clio kissed her again and then snuggled against her side. "Sleep well." She listened as Kit's breathing settled into a steady, even rhythm. She kept her hand on Kit's hip, needing the connection. They were home, and they had yet to talk about any kind of future between them. But for now, she was there beside her, and it was enough.

CHAPTER TWENTY-THREE

K it groaned as the world slowly came to her. Everything hurt. She finally got her eyes open and found that she was alone in the big bed. A note was on Clio's pillow.

Press the buzzer on your nightstand, sleepyhead, and we'll come running. It was signed with a heart.

She pressed the little white remote and listened as footsteps quickly sounded in the hallway. The door cracked open, and Clio came in looking like a spring morning, her pale green, deep V-neck sweater and skinny jeans showing off every curve.

"We wanted you to wake up on your own. How are you feeling?" She sat on the edge of the bed and caressed Kit's face.

"Keep doing that and I'll be fine." She closed her eyes and sank into Clio's touch. "I think you took me outside in my sleep and let a bus drag me down a gravel road."

"Oh, good. I thought you'd be feeling rough after yesterday. Glad to hear I was wrong." Clio's lips touched hers softly.

"What time is it?" Kit asked.

"Eleven."

"No wonder I need to pee so bad. And I'm starving."

Clio got off the bed. "I'll get Troy to help you with the one thing, and I'll take care of the other."

Clio seemed back to her effervescent self, and it made Kit smile, as did Buster when he put his big head on the bed for a good morning kiss. Troy came in, all business, and helped her perform her morning ablutions. Brushing her teeth while sitting down felt like the weirdest thing in the world.

He wheeled her into the kitchen, where breakfast was already waiting. She grinned. "Pancakes with maple syrup."

Clio tapped the little dishes. "And chopped strawberries and bananas, if you want them."

Kit dug in, barely taking time to breathe she was so ravenous. When she finished, she found them watching her, both looking amused. Buster, lying at her feet, sighed deeply when he didn't get a treat.

"Want some more?" Clio asked, taking her plate.

"No, thanks. Lunch will be in an hour or so, right?" Kit tried to smile past the pain.

Troy brought over a glass of water and some pills. "This will take the edge off. Want a shower?"

She grimaced. "I like you, Troy. And I'm really glad you're here. But the thought of showering with you makes me a very sad puppy."

He managed to look offended. "I'll have you know that lots of women have wanted to shower with me over the years." He motioned at Clio. "I've got a special chair we'll put in the shower. It'll keep your leg up after we put the protector on, and you can sit there and water yourself down all you like."

Kit looked at Clio and could almost read her thoughts. "I could probably still use help, though."

He raised his hands. "That's up to you guys. I'll go get it set up."

He left and Clio came over, her hips swaying seductively. "Are you asking me for help getting wet?"

Kit moaned and closed her eyes. "You're so evil. I thought muses were kind. You're just mean." She opened her eyes again. "And yes, that's what I'm asking."

Clio laughed and wheeled Kit to the bathroom. She helped her undress and wrapped her in a towel, and then Troy came in and lifted her onto the shower seat, making sure her leg was where it needed to be.

"All yours. Give me a shout when you need me."

Clio got the water up to temperature and then quirked her eyebrow. "Are you keeping the towel on? I think showers work better when you're naked."

Kit hesitated and was horrified when tears filled her eyes. "Shit."

Clio dropped the shower head and knelt beside her. "What's wrong, babe?"

"This isn't how it's supposed to be. It should be sexy, and hot. It should be dirty, and I should be all over you like butter on toast. Instead..." She motioned at her broken, bruised body. "I'm sitting here unable to do anything other than think about how it still hurts to move."

Clio gently wiped away Kit's tears. "Believe me, as soon as you get the cast off, it's going to be dirty and all those other things. But for now, you'll have to accept that I'm in love with you, and that means I get to take care of you when you're hurting." She kissed Kit's cheeks. "Let me?"

Kit nodded. "I'm sorry. You can have Troy do it, if you want. He's probably seen more bodies than we have combined."

"Are you kidding?" Clio picked up the water again. "I can tease you without mercy. I'm not giving that up."

It was one of the best showers of Kit's life. Clio washed her hair, taking her time and massaging her scalp. Then she soaped her up, lingering over her nipples and pussy until Kit begged her to stop. By the end of it, she felt wonderfully clean and delightfully dirty. Clio got her dressed and then called in Troy.

They went into the living room. It was gray and cold outside, and Clio took Buster out for a short walk. By the time she got back, Kit was nearly asleep again. "Is it almost time for lunch?"

As though summoned by her question, someone rang the buzzer at the gate.

"It's Jag." Clio opened the gate and went to meet him at the door.

Although Kit liked Jag, she found that she wasn't looking forward to seeing him. The last thing she wanted to think about was work. But then, she wouldn't be working for a while. What did that mean for their show? She heard Clio greet him, and then Buster led the way as they came into the living room.

He leaned down and hugged her, making her grunt a little when he pushed on her ribs.

"Sorry." He sat on the couch opposite her. "At first, all we knew was that Moscow had gone insane. Then there was the footage of you helping those kids. Then nothing. We couldn't get any information on whether your plane had taken off or not. And then there was something about a mayday from your pilot…"

He was rambling, and his eyes were glassy. Clio came and sat next to him and held his hand.

"We thought we'd lost you both." He accepted the glass of water Troy handed him.

"But you didn't. We're still here."

He nodded and seemed to steady himself. "It sounds like you had a hell of a trip. That footage from Moscow was something else." He looked between Kit and Clio. "Is it okay to talk work for a second?" They nodded and he kept on. "The segment showing the gods getting involved in the chaos has exploded. I've heard they're calling big meetings at the Afterlife compound to discuss what happened and if it has any effect on how the gods are going to operate from here forward." He sipped his water, his gaze on Kit. "And then the footage of you two saving that group of kids? Jesus. The networks are bidding for your show. *Everyone* wants you. Obviously, I've said the show is on hiatus until you're back on your feet, but when you come back, you can name your price and whatever interviews you want to do." He leaned forward. "I've even got you access into the Afterlife compound for some of their meetings."

Logically, Kit should be ecstatic. This kind of thing could make someone's career. But it felt empty. "And all we had to do was nearly die."

Clio's expression suggested she, too, wasn't sure how to receive the news.

Jag frowned at them. "I thought this was what you wanted? I thought we'd be celebrating."

Kit rested her head against her fist. "Babe?"

Jag blinked. "Babe? Are you together?" When they smiled at each other, he shrugged. "Even better, really. The fact that you're a couple after the rough start you had and the tragedy you went through will drive viewers wild."

Clio bit her lip. "I think we have some things to talk about."

Kit breathed a sigh of relief. It was good they were on the same page.

He looked between them, and then his expression cleared. He reached out and took Kit's hand. "I don't care what decision you make, as long as it makes you happy. You deserve that."

Kit squeezed his hand. "Don't get all soppy on me. There's been enough tears over the last few days."

He stood and wiped his hands on his thighs. "Okay. You have some time. You know I'll be getting calls for your decision, but I'll put them off as long as I can to give you time to figure out what you want to do." He gave Buster a rub. "But I wanted to say this, Kit." He looked down at her seriously. "You wanted to do a show that made a difference. You wanted to get people and gods to pay attention. You've done that, and you should be damn proud of what you accomplished." He waved his hands like he was waving away emotion. "Okay, I'm gone. Call me if you need me."

He left after they promised to call, and when Clio came back, Kit held out her hand. She took it and sat on the couch beside her wheelchair.

"Babe?" Kit asked softly.

"What is it?"

"I'm still hungry and Jag didn't bring food." She kissed Clio's hand, and her heart leapt at Clio's laugh.

"I had hoped he'd bring something. People always seem to do that. Throughout history, people have brought over food in times of trouble." Clio reached for her phone and read the text. "Fortunately, you have friends who are desperate to help out. Abel will be here any minute with supplies."

Kit's stomach rumbled in response, making them laugh. "Seriously, though, it sounds like we need to talk about career things."

Clio stood. "I agree. But let's do it after Abel is gone, so we can talk uninterrupted, okay?"

Kit couldn't help it. Her eyes drifted shut. "That sounds perfect. God, I feel like I'm ninety. I can't seem to stay awake."

"It's the body's way of helping you heal. Take a nap. I'll wake you again for food." Clio moved Kit's chair to the window, where the weak sun was filtering through the clouds.

Kit drifted off, but her dreams were quickly filled with the weightless terror of falling from the sky, with flames and screams, and the knowledge that death was coming for her. She woke with sweat on her forehead and her hands shaking. Clio knelt beside her, humming softly and stroking her hand.

Kit took a shuddery breath. "Guess that's going to happen for a while, huh?"

Her eyes were soft and sympathetic. "For all of us, I think." She waited until Kit's breathing had settled. "If you're ready, Abel has cooked something that smells divine. And I would know."

Kit rolled her eyes and nodded, but she wasn't quite ready to talk yet. She used the short distance to the kitchen to ground herself, and when Abel looked up, she hoped she didn't still look spooked. The flash of sympathy in his eyes told her she'd failed.

He didn't falter though. "Are you ready? I've made your all-time favorite." He brought a casserole dish to the table and uncovered it with a flourish.

"Mac and cheese. You're the best." She leaned over it and inhaled. "You've put truffles in it, too. And there's garlic bread."

"That's quite the upgrade to the traditional." Clio handed Abel the serving spoon. "And we're incredibly grateful."

Troy sat at the table with them, but he ate a salad, claiming he had to keep away from the big carbs so he could keep carting Kit around.

Abel paused over his bread. "I don't imagine you've had time to watch TV?" They shook their heads and continued to eat. "You guys are all over it. Every talk show, every news channel. They're saying Moscow changed everything."

Neither Kit nor Clio responded, and Abel whistled. "Well, that says something, doesn't it? Kit, you've never had nothing to say in all the time I've known you. What's going on?"

When Clio didn't say anything, Kit knew she had to. "The networks are in a bidding war for our show." It sounded so simplistic, put that way. Why did it feel the very opposite of simple?

"And you're not going bat-shit crazy happy over that because?" Kit looked at Clio. "I don't know, really. Do you?"

Clio finished her last bite of macaroni. "That was delicious, Abel. Thank you so much. And to your question, I'm not sure either. We're going to try to figure it out together."

Abel grinned as he looked between them. "I've been telling Kit for years that she needs to find a good woman. Trust her to go beyond that and find not just a good one, but a muse. Only you, Kit." He stood and began clearing the plates. "I've got this. You go relax."

Clio made them coffee and they relaxed by the windows overlooking the ocean. Troy, as usual, made himself scarce when they didn't need him. Abel came in wiping his hands on a dishtowel. "Now. I have a problem I need to discuss with you. I mean, it will be less of a discussion and more of a this is how things are going to work." He glanced at Clio. "If it's okay with you."

"Here we go," Kit said, smiling at him. "Lay it on us."

"You pay me to watch over Buster when you're gone. Now you're home, which means you're no longer paying me to watch him, and I no longer get to cook for you. But you can't really look after him either, because you're being all lazy in that wheelchair."

Clio went to object, but he held up his hand to stop her.

"Yes, I'm aware you can take care of him. But you have to take care of her, and that's where all your attention should be, from morning till night. Poor Buster will waste away from neglect."

They all looked at Buster, who was lying on his back on the sofa, his belly in the air. He was snoring in a patch of sunshine.

"Neglected indeed. He looks miserable." Kit sighed and shook her head. "Poor thing."

"Exactly." Abel crossed his arms. "And I understand you like to cook, Clio, but if you go back to what I was saying—"

"My attention should be fully focused on the lazy patient. I understand."

He nodded emphatically. "I'm glad you're paying attention. So, I'll be here by lunch time each day, and I'll leave after dinner. I'll handle poor, neglected Buster, and I'll make your meals because you're too lazy and too focused to do so on your own. And you'll pay me, obviously."

"Obviously." Kit looked at Clio semi-seriously. "I don't see that we have a choice. Do you?"

Clio frowned and leaned forward like she was thinking. "I have a problem with what you'll be doing to the climate with all that driving. I'm afraid I'd have to insist that you stay here some nights. I have another guest room."

He shrugged. "I can live with that, if I must. I don't see how getting to wake up to this gorgeous view and being able to walk Buster on that beautiful beach will do me any good, but if you insist, then so be it." He finally broke into a big grin. "I'll bring my stuff tomorrow." He kissed them both on the cheek and then left, singing a show tune on his way out.

Clio laughed and sipped the last of her coffee. "I take it he doesn't have a day job?"

Kit took Clio's free hand in hers, needing to feel the softness of it. "He's some kind of finance guru. He's a private contractor for huge companies. He can work from anywhere, and I don't know why I pay him. He doesn't need the money."

"Ah, now I understand."

They sat quietly for a while before Clio said, "Want to talk it out?"

Kit turned her wheelchair so she could look at her more directly. "I'm so weirdly confused. I don't really know what's bothering me. Does that make sense?"

Clio turned her coffee cup around and around in her hands. "I understand completely. To be honest, I'm pretty lost myself."

"Will you talk me through it?" Kit asked.

Clio stared out the window, her gaze unfocused. "I think, before you, I was running away. Not just from the ugliness in the world, but from my role in it. I was pretending…I don't know. That I was normal, maybe. That I could be something other than the muse of history and virtue. But then there was you." She glanced at Kit and away again. "You made me look at myself, and I have to admit, I don't like what I saw. Working with you hurt a little bit. It brought me closer to the person I used to be, and it scared me."

"And are you still scared?"

"A little, yes. But now I'm scared for a different reason." She finally looked squarely at Kit. "I had time after the crash to think a lot. And I don't think I want to continue with the show, Kit. I'm really glad that we inadvertently made a change, and that something big might come from it. And I had so much fun with you on the easier segments." She lifted Kit's hand and kissed her knuckles. "But it isn't who I am. My old show isn't who I am either. I think it's time for me to get back to who I was born to be."

Kit's heart sank and her stomach turned. "Are you leaving to work at Afterlife, then?"

Clio laughed. "Gods, no. It's way too serious over there. I'm still me, after all."

Kit let out a whoosh of air. "I can live with that."

"Want to talk me through what you're feeling?" Clio asked. "Your turn."

Kit gathered her thoughts, trying to sift through them. "A while back, my friends asked me what I would do if I had to retrain in a new profession, and I couldn't think of a single thing I'd want to do other than be an investigative journalist. I love it. And I have to admit, I loved it even more when I started doing it with you. I love uncovering the truth of things." She rested her head against the back of her wheelchair. "Did I tell you I saw the northern lights?" Clio shook her head. "I was a soul, sitting on the butt of a reindeer as we raced to the hospital to keep Sian from dying. And the sky lit up in this incredible curtain of dancing light." Kit's eyes watered at the memory. "It was so beautiful, Clio. And I realized how focused I've been on the bad stuff, just like you've always said. Doing the show with you made me start to see that, but dying?" She shook her head. "I'm not sure I want to go out there and face more Moscows. But I don't want to give up on what I love doing either."

They sat silently together for long while, and Kit assumed Clio was as lost in her thoughts as she was. Troy came in to give her some pills and take her to the bathroom, for which she was grateful. When she came back, Clio had lit the fire and turned on the TV.

"I find that when decisions seem overwhelming, it's good to let the subconscious puzzle things out. Distraction can be invaluable. So," she held up two movies, "romantic comedy or animated film?"

Kit winced. "Those are my options?"

"Animated film it is." Clio kissed her nose playfully. "Come on, Buster. You'll love this one."

Troy helped Kit onto the sofa and found a way to prop up her leg, then excused himself to go read a book. Clio curled up on Kit's good side, her head resting on her shoulder. Firelight threw shadows over them, and somehow Kit knew that whatever happened, they'd be okay.

CHAPTER TWENTY-FOUR

Energy suffused her, and Clio knew without a doubt she was on the right track. The plan had come to her in the night, and she'd begun to put it into motion the moment she'd gotten up.

"How is my celebrity sister?" Calliope asked when she answered the phone. "Are you okay?"

"Better than okay." Clio studied the list of things in front of her. "I want your help on a new project."

"I'm not going on TV. I've already told you that."

Clio huffed. "I'm not asking. I have something really specific in mind. Are you still in contact with Ukko?"

Calliope hesitated. "I am. Why?"

"I could use a contact over there. I promise it's not for anything you'd find untoward. In fact, I think you'll be proud of me. But I want to keep it a secret for now."

"Okay. I'll trust you." Calliope still sounded uncertain. "I'll email you his contact details. Can I help in any other way?"

Clio studied her list. "You can, but not just yet. I'll let you know. And thanks." She hung up, excitement building. She hadn't felt this way in far, far too long.

Kit's buzzer went off, and Clio practically skipped to the bedroom. "Sleepyhead. We're taking a field trip today." She tugged the covers off, making Kit groan.

"So, so evil." She accepted Clio's kiss with a smile.

"I'm going to make breakfast." She met with Troy in the hallway and gave him a spontaneous hug. "We're going out today."

"Do you need me?"

She thought about where they were going, and how. "No, I can take care of things. Meet you back here around four?"

"Perfect." He whistled as he went into Kit's room to start her day.

Clio sang as she made omelets for the three of them and was happy to see Kit looking flushed and happy. Troy showed her how to work the special van to get Kit in and out, and then they were off.

"Are you going to tell me where we're headed?" Kit asked.

"No. I want it to be a surprise." She turned and headed toward the bridge, but then took a small side road that led beneath it.

Kit paled slightly when the side of the bridge disappeared, and a road appeared ahead of them. A Yama stood off to the side and waved. Clio stopped and the Yama got in the back.

"Good to see you both not dead," Soc said, thumping Kit's shoulder lightly.

"I hope you don't mind me saying this, but I'd really hoped not to see the underworld again until I was actually dead. Again." Kit held onto the door handle.

"I'm sorry, babe. I wasn't thinking. This is just the fastest way to get you where I want to take you, and the easiest given your leg." Clio's heart sank. How selfish of her not to consider Kit's recent brush with death.

"Dude." Soc leaned forward from the back seat. "If anything, this should totally calm you down about the whole death thing. Look how normal all this is. Nothing scary. Just a lot of houses and streets."

Kit's grip slowly relaxed. "You're right. I hadn't thought of it that way."

Soc tapped Clio's shoulder. "Take the next left."

Clio did as she was told and became more excited the closer they got. The road lined with palm trees ended and turned into one lined with fields. Clio stopped so Soc could get out. "Thank you again for this, Soc. I'll text you when we're on our way back." She glanced at Kit. "Maybe. Or maybe we'll take a road trip."

Soc rolled her eyes. "Kit's way tougher than that. She can handle the land of the dead. See you in a few."

Clio pulled onto the road and grinned. "Look."

Kit leaned forward. "Is that Mount Rushmore?"

"It is!" Clio laughed. "That's why we took the Deadlands roads. Time and space work differently down there, and their roads can get you all over the place in the blink of an eye." She narrowed her eyes, looking for markers. "Now, where is it..." She saw the old rock formation and turned onto a barely visible dirt road. She took it slow so as not to jostle Kit's leg, and the road smoothed out when they entered a dark tunnel with a steep grade. "Almost there."

The tunnel finally opened into a cavern, and a single light lit up a huge metal door. Clio took out a big key and held it up. "I've never shown anyone, in three thousand years, what I'm about to show you."

She got out and lowered Kit's chair to the ground, then she unlocked the huge door and pushed it open. She flipped on the lights and wheeled Kit inside.

"What the hell?" Kit whispered as she looked around. She took over wheeling her chair herself. "What is this place?"

Clio looked over the huge room lined with floor to ceiling shelves that were neatly stacked with books of all shapes and sizes. "Do you remember when I told you that I was responsible for making sure people wrote down history to the best of their abilities? And that if there was no one to do it, then I did?"

Kit looked at her, wide-eyed. "You wrote all of these?"

Clio laughed. "No. Many of them are the ones other people throughout history wrote, which I oversaw, and then rehomed once the authors had passed. Others, I wrote." She went to the far wall. "And yet others, I saved." She ran her fingertips over the ancient tomes. "These I managed to save from the Library of Alexandria just before it burned."

Kit gasped and wheeled herself over. "You're kidding. Those texts were assumed destroyed."

Clio sighed, remembering that night. "I know. I found out the library was going to be sacked and made it just in time to save many of the books, although I couldn't save them all and it broke my heart. I've kept them hidden all these years to make sure nothing happened to them. But last night I got to thinking. Having them back here, behind Abraham Lincoln's nose, isn't doing the world any good. And with the way things have changed, it's time to bring history out into the open again so people can learn from it."

Kit seemed to be taking it all in. "How'd you even get it here?"

"I had it in an ancient underground temple in Greece that's been forgotten, but with climate change I started to worry about fires or damage from the heat in general. So I had this built. No one would ever know it was here, and it was safe from all kinds of threats. I had a couple of pre-fader gods help because I knew they'd never say anything." She touched a book. "But it's time. I want to start a new library, one where people can go to learn." She turned to Kit. "And I'm going to record all the events happening around us. I'm going to talk to people living through them, and I'm going to be the muse of history, just as I was meant to be."

Kit's gaze traveled over the books. "There must be a million or more books here. Where are you going to put them?"

"That's the next step. But first, I want to show you something that means a lot to me." She pulled a thick, worn book from a high shelf. "This is a book of transcribed letters from various people over the years. Letters from Cleopatra to Antony, from Catherine to King Henry VIII, and others from a farm wife to her daughter living in the next village over." She stroked the hard cover and then handed it gently to Kit. "I completed it in the late seventeen hundreds."

Kit carefully opened it and traced her fingertip over the writing. "This is amazing, Clio."

Clio smiled and wandered past the shelves while Kit read, and her shoulders relaxed. Breathing was easier, another good sign she was doing what she needed to. She went back to Kit and touched her shoulder.

"We should head out." She put the book back on the shelf.

"Are you going to let me in on the next part of the plan? Or are you going to keep that a secret too?" Kit asked as they loaded her back into the van.

"For now, I'm keeping it a surprise. I might have to go away for a couple of days." They got back on the road, and she could tell that Kit was deep in thought. "Anything you want to talk about?"

"I'm not sure." Kit leaned her head against the glass. "You've suddenly got this plan, and I feel like I'm treading water, unsure which shore is closer and not going either direction."

"But you don't need to know yet, do you?" Clio turned onto the road leading back to where they'd enter the Deadlands. "You can't work for a long while yet, so you have time to figure it out."

Kit's shoulders were hunched. "And what if while I'm over here trying to work things out, you leave me behind?"

Clio's heart hurt for her. That was the injured child buried deep inside Kit, the one who'd been left behind when her parents had died. Some wounds left scars that continued to ache. "I'm not leaving you anywhere. Not in a snow drift at a plane crash, not at a hospital on a fjord in Greenland, and definitely not now that you've realized I'm the best thing since the wheel and we're all comfy in my house." She ran her hand over Kit's good leg. "And believe me, I'm going to show you just how much I mean that as soon as we don't have to worry about your leg."

Kit finally smiled. "You're weirdly rational for someone who loves to wear really bright colors."

Clio laughed. "I'm not sure what the correlation is between those things, but I guess I'll take it as a compliment."

The doorway opened into the Deadlands, and Soc once again jumped in the back seat.

"I take it you can't drive through here unless you work here? Or you're dead?" Kit asked.

"That's right. You have to have a Yama with you to go through, and really, if you're alive, you shouldn't be spending much time down here. I'm bending the rules pretty hard by letting you guys do this but Clio sounded so excited, I couldn't say no." She reached forward and pinched Kit's cheek, earning her a swat. "And I've become really fond of you, meat bag."

Kit grimaced. "Gross."

They were back out the other gateway in no time, and Soc waved them off again. Once they were back on the road, Clio saw Kit's shoulders ease. She wouldn't make use of those roads again, but it might throw a small wrench in her plans. They stopped at Kit's place so she could gather more clothes and some books she wanted for while Clio was away. Kit gave instructions by phone from the van while Clio packed, and they got more of Buster's toys, too. Clio couldn't help but look around, wanting an even better sense of Kit through the space that was hers alone. Mismatched pillows sat on an old, well-worn couch. It was tidy, but not overly so. Much like Kit. The thought made her smile.

"Can we stop at Violet's for lunch? I'm craving their big ass cookie."

"Is the cookie your lunch? Or will it be dessert?" Clio wheeled her out and stopped when Kit looked over her shoulder. "Is everything okay?"

"Yeah, it's fine. I just…" Kit swallowed hard. "I love this house. But I love your house. And I just feel like I don't know where the hell I'm supposed to be. I hate feeling out of control."

Clio turned toward her and cupped her cheeks. "I know it must be hard for you to be so dependent on people right now. But you have to remember that it's temporary. It will suck for a while, but you'll be back on your feet and running into danger soon enough." She kissed her lightly, lingering. "And you have other things to look forward to, too."

Kit shivered slightly. "That makes it better for sure."

Clio started the car and headed toward Violet's. "Then I'll just have to do it more often."

Over a light lunch at Violet's, Clio checked her email several times, earning her a disgruntled look from Kit. A few people came over and asked for autographs, and although they were respectful, Clio was reminded of the reporters who'd been at the airport and her house, and she couldn't help looking over her shoulder every so often.

"You know," Kit said, "it's weird how we're both completely fine in front of the camera, but when the questions are aimed at us, we freak out and want to hide."

Clio speared a French fry. "So true."

They made it back to the house without any incidents, and Kit wanted to take a nap, so Clio got her settled in bed and then went to make a list of all she'd need to do. Calliope had sent her Ukko's contact details, and she sent off an email asking him to meet with her in two days' time. Then she settled on the couch with a cup of hot tea and a laptop and started her search.

The buzzer broke her concentration some time later, and she saw Abel's car at the gate. She buzzed him in and met him at the door. "We need to get you your own set of keys." She kissed his cheek and took a bag of groceries from him.

"I agree completely."

Buster came bounding from Kit's room and leapt on Abel, his big head nearly at the height of Abel's face.

"How's our patient today?" He began putting things away after he'd given Buster a good rub down.

"Napping at the minute. We went to South Dakota for a little sight-seeing this morning and it tired her out." She grinned when he looked up at her from the fridge as though trying to figure out if she was kidding.

"Dating an immortal must be mind-boggling." He shook his head and put a bottle of wine in the fridge. "I'm taking Buster for a walk, then I'll make dinner."

While he was gone, Clio heard Kit buzz from the bedroom. "Hey, you're awake."

Kit rubbed her eyes, making her look utterly adorable in true gentle butch fashion. "I missed you when I woke up without you beside me."

"Sorry, I got caught up in some research." She helped Kit into her chair and then into the bathroom. "Need me to stay to help?"

Kit threw a hand towel at her. "That is most definitely not how we're starting this relationship. Troy taught me how to swing myself over, thanks. I'll call when I'm done."

Clio stood outside the door. "I was a nurse in World War Two, you know. I've seen worse," she said so Kit could hear her.

"And if I was a soldier in need, I'd be happy to have you wipe my butt. But let's not go down the role-play road just yet. Okay, I'm done."

Clio opened the door, and Kit wheeled herself out. "Abel is here. He's walking Buster and then he'll cook dinner."

They went into the living room and Clio quickly closed her laptop.

"If I were an insecure person, that would freak me out." Kit crossed her arms.

"If you were an insecure person, you probably wouldn't be with someone like me." Clio leaned down and kissed her. "I told you, I want this to be a surprise."

Kit held her hands. "But why?" She looked serious as her gaze swept Clio's face. "I feel like there's something you're not saying."

Clio sat down but didn't let go of Kit's hand. "Truth? I need to do this on my own." Embarrassment made her stomach turn a little. "I need to prove to myself that I'm still capable of doing things on my own, that I can handle things that really matter. I want to be able to make this incredibly spontaneous dream of mine work out by doing what I need to do." She bit her lip. "I don't want you to feel left out, but I need to do this first part on my own. Is that okay?"

Kit kissed Clio's hand. "Of course it's okay. I respect that, and I understand. Promise me that you'll let me help when the time comes though, okay?"

"I promise." Clio rested her head on Kit's shoulder. It felt amazing to have someone there beside her, someone who wanted to plan and play with her. But it was true. She needed to prove that she could still be the person she'd once been, but maybe even a better version.

CHAPTER TWENTY-FIVE

K it threw her book on the floor and instantly regretted it, since she wouldn't be able to reach it when she wanted to read again. Buster sighed, clearly unimpressed with her minimalist temper tantrum. "You know, if you were a better dog, you'd pick that up for me." He rolled over so his back was to her. "Butthead."

Clio had been gone for exactly sixteen hours and twenty-four minutes. And every one of those hours and minutes had gone by as quickly as a snail high on pot. Even when she'd been in one of her few long-term relationships, she'd valued her alone time and had rarely pined after a lover who wasn't home.

Now, all she could think about was Clio. Where was she? Who was she with? What was she setting up? She missed her kisses, the way she smiled, the way she laughed. She even missed the way she snored, those tiny little snores that sounded more like a rabbit snoring than a person. It was adorable.

"Hey, grump." Abel popped his head in. "Jag has just pulled up at the gate."

"Thank god, someone to talk to," she said, turning her wheelchair around.

"Kiss my lily-white perfect ass," Abel sang as he headed to the door.

In truth, he'd been a saint. Kit had been pissy and irritable and yet he'd still managed to make her laugh, and Troy had joined them for several rounds of poker the night before. It had helped take her mind off the fact that she missed Clio so much, until she went to bed alone.

"Hey there," Jag said and set a bag in front of her on the table. "I brought Devil's Teeth."

Kit grabbed the bag of artisan pastries and stuck her face in it, inhaling. "I knew there was a reason I liked you."

Abel grabbed the bag from Kit's hands and pulled out a cinnamon roll. "Thank you," he said around a mouthful as he handed the bag back to her and left the room.

"He's like a bloodhound." Kit rummaged through the bag. "Donut muffin. Now you're my second favorite human being. Clio being first, obviously."

"Obviously." He looked on, amused. "If I'd known that was all it'd take, I'd have brought them to you every day." He pulled out a muffin for himself. "I got a whole bunch of things so whoever was here could have something."

"That was very kind of you." Kit took another huge bite.

Jag daintily pulled off the wrapper from his. "So, I was wondering if you two had discussed anything about your careers? And by proxy, mine?"

Crap. Clio hadn't told him yet. "Kind of. But not really."

"I'll take the kind of, right now. If you don't mind." He raised his eyebrows and nibbled on his muffin.

Kit thought quickly. Was it her place to tell him that Clio was done with the show? She looked at him, his eyes hopeful, and knew she had to. "We had a talk the other night. Heart-to-heart kind of stuff. Jag, she doesn't want to do the show anymore. She said it's just not who she is or what she wants."

His shoulders sagged and he set the muffin down. "I see. And you?"

"Honestly?"

"Always."

She took the last bite of her donut and then tossed the bag to Troy when he looked in on her. He looked in the bag, saluted, and left with it.

"Honestly, I'm a little lost."

He settled back on the sofa. "Talk to me."

She told him much of what she'd told Clio, and it was easier this time around. "So, I don't know. I could go back to doing what I've always done, but somehow, it doesn't feel right. But what do I do if I'm not who I was?" She picked at the crumbs on her shirt and held them out for Buster, who was sitting beside her patiently. "When you literally come face-to-face with Death, you kind of look at life differently."

He tilted his head. "Not something I want to find out myself, I can tell you that." He smiled when Buster came over and put his head on Jag's lap. "You know, it's okay to have a career change. Lots of people do it."

"But that's the thing. I don't know what I'd do. It's not like I've got some hidden talent I can suddenly explore. I'm not a woodworker in my off hours. I'm not about to go run my own gym, because then I'd probably never have time to work out. And that's it. That's all there is to me. Investigative journalism and the gym. And dog mom."

"And girlfriend to an immortal. Don't forget that little nugget."

Kit gave him a big grin. "Yeah. I like that one."

"And Clio? What about her path?"

She shook her head. "She wants to surprise me. I know it has to do with books, but other than that, I'm in the dark." She could still smell all those old books in that huge bespoke cavern. How many gods had hidey holes all over the world?

"Okay. Well, at least I have some idea where your heads are at, and when I stall the other networks, I can bluff a little better." He squeezed Kit's shoulder. "Keep me in the loop, okay? And you know, sometimes you just have to shift perspective. You don't always have to become something else altogether."

She grabbed his hand. "Jag, thanks. For everything you've done. You've been an amazing producer, but an even better friend."

His eyes got glassy, and he turned away. "Yeah, yeah. Eat your muffins. Talk to you later."

Kit sat there for a long time, staring out at the waves as she mulled over her options. Jag's comment about shifting perspective made her start thinking down a new path. Maybe he was right. Maybe there was a way to bring a few of her passions together after all.

❖

Clio sat across from Ukko at a café. She'd only met him a few times over the centuries, as they rarely had need of muses in Finland, and the old Finnish Pagan gods had taken care of their creative believers well.

"I always forget how much you look like my father," Clio said.

He stroked his neatly trimmed white beard that was flecked through with little lightning bolts, as was his slicked-back white hair. "I saw Zeus on a Zoom call the other day. I don't think you're giving me a compliment."

She giggled a little. "He's really taken to sweatpants. I didn't mean any disrespect."

His smile was that of the old gods. It was distant, like he was there, but also somewhere else. "I'm only teasing. And I'm as fond of my plaid shirts as he is of his sweatpants." He tugged on the red-and-black flannel shirt that suited his rugged looks perfectly. "Now tell me what brings you from California to Finland."

Clio detailed her plan and answered his questions about why without a problem. She'd thought it all through.

He settled back, his hands folded over his stomach. His eyes moved as though he was looking at something she couldn't see. She'd seen it with plenty of other gods. He was looking over his territory.

"Hailuoto."

She did a mental scan. "I can't place it."

"It's an island. The museum there has been empty for a long time. There are less than nine hundred people who live there. The building would be perfect, and we can renovate it to make sure it protects everything inside."

She leapt from her seat and hugged him but jumped back when she got a little zap.

He shrugged. "Sorry. One of the problems with being me."

She took out her big notebook and they started sketching out plans, and he promised to have the workers in place by the end of the week. It was getting dark early, and the cold would set in, but they'd do what they could before they had to stop working.

"You're certain this is the place?" he asked as they got up to leave.

"Completely. It's perfect." Clio couldn't wait to get home to tell Kit.

"Very well, little sister. I'll let you know how things are going."

She refrained from hugging him again and watched as he walked off down the street, his axe over his shoulder. If it weren't for the lightning in his hair, he would have been any other taller-than-average lumberjack. It still amazed her how easily the gods fit into the world.

She pulled up Google maps and checked the drive time. It would take nine hours to go see the building that would become her project for some time to come, and that was simply too far. She needed to get home, so she headed to the airport. She'd bought a new private plane, one that was even nicer than her last one. She was going to be doing a lot of traveling if her plan worked out, and the chances of being in two plane crashes in one century were slim. Whenever she got nervous, she leaned on the statistics and historical probabilities.

By the time she got back to San Francisco, she was exhausted. It was a long journey for a short trip, and she wanted to crawl into bed. When she opened the door, she was greeted by a huge pile of fur, and it warmed her. She snuggled into his neck and hugged him tight, then let him go and followed him to Kit, who was sitting in the living room clearly waiting for her.

"Yikes, babe. You look wiped out." Concern was instantly etched into Kit's expression.

Clio yawned so hard her jaw hurt. "I have a ton to tell you, but I don't think I can stay awake for one more minute." She went to Kit and kissed her, then rested her head on her shoulder. Kit's scent filled her senses, and she felt her entire body relax. "I don't suppose you want to nap with me?"

Kit pulled back and grinned. "If I ever say no to that, take me to a doctor and have my head examined."

They went into the cool, dark bedroom and Clio shucked her clothes off and to the floor. She crawled into bed and then realized Kit was still waiting in her chair, looking chagrined.

"I'm so sorry." She climbed back out and helped maneuver Kit into the bed.

"Babe, you're naked and helping me into bed. Believe me, I'm the one who's sorry." Kit's hand caressed the side of Clio's breast. "I'm not sure I can wait much longer."

Clio snuggled down beside her, the feeling of home suffusing her. "When I wake up, you're on." She settled in against Kit, and the last thought she had as she fell asleep was how nice it was to have someone to come home to again.

That tickles. She shifted under the caress as she slowly came to. Fingertips slid up her thigh, along her waist, and over the side of her breast, making her shiver. Then the touch moved over her nipple, and she moaned softly, turning into the sweet feeling.

Her eyes fluttered open, and she found Kit's gaze following the line of her fingertips, her expression almost feral.

She looked into Clio's eyes. "I'm going to need you to make this happen, because I'm going insane and if I don't have you right this fucking instant, I'll explode."

Clio shifted so Kit could get to more of her. "We can't have that."

Kit pinched and tugged at her nipple and Clio gasped at how good it felt.

"Straddle me." Kit's voice was husky with need.

Clio did so carefully, and it put her breasts at perfect height for Kit's mouth. She didn't need encouragement. She quickly took one of Clio's nipples in her mouth and sucked, while her other hand caressed and squeezed Clio's other breast. She pushed against Kit's lower stomach, needing pressure on her aching clit.

Kit shifted and slid her hands lower. One gripped Clio's hip, the other slid between her thighs.

"God, yes. Please," she whispered.

Kit didn't say anything. Her grip on Clio's hip tightened, and she thrust two fingers into her, quickly adding a third when Clio ground down on her hand. "Ride me, baby. Take what you need."

Clio moaned and pushed hard against Kit's strong hand, grinding her clit against the heel of her palm. Kit let go of her hip and wrapped her arm around Clio's waist, holding her closer as Clio moved faster.

"Yesss…" Kit hissed, her eyes a storm of lust.

Clio's orgasm crashed through her, and she arched, throwing her head back and crying out. Kit pushed deep and held on as Clio shook, and she only let go when her body went limp.

"Much better." Kit helped her slide off and against her side once more. "I needed that."

"I think you'll find I needed it more." Clio grinned, her head pillowed against Kit's chest.

"I hope you don't mind me waking you, but I couldn't help myself. Not to mention I'm starving." Kit gently traced swirls on Clio's back. "But I'll gladly starve to death to keep you naked beside me."

"Death isn't conducive to further orgasms, so I'm going to veto that idea." Clio stood and stretched, very much liking the way Kit perused her body. "I'll go see if Abel has left anything for us. If not, I'll whip something up." She put on a robe, a silk one she'd bought that made her feel sexy.

While she was reheating the curry that Abel had left in the fridge with instructions, Troy wheeled Kit into the kitchen. "If you guys can get along without me for the night, I'd like to head on home."

Kit smiled at him. "You know, I think I've got this pretty well down now. And Clio can help me with most everything. At this point, all I need your help with is getting in and out of the shower." She looked at Clio, who nodded her agreement.

He looked a little disappointed. "I agree, but I'll be sorry not to be hanging out here. You're the easiest client I've had in ages, and not a lot of people get to say they've stayed in one of the immortal's houses." He laughed when Clio rolled her eyes. "Why don't we set a time for me to come help with the shower each day, and if you need to change it, just give me a shout." He paused. "And if anything goes sideways or you need more help, I can come back."

Clio asked if he wanted to have dinner with them, but he declined, saying he'd like to get home to his girlfriend. It hadn't occurred to her that he had one, since he'd been spending so much time with them. She felt a little guilty for not having asked more about him, but then, he'd kept to himself quite a bit. Some people liked their privacy and keeping their work and home lives private. In fact, that was something she needed to think about for herself.

Clio dished up their meals, and they sat in the living room.

"The doc called yesterday and said I could probably start using crutches next week. You don't know how excited I'll be to get out of the chair." Kit ate like she hadn't eaten in years.

"I can imagine."

Kit paused in wolfing down her food. "Are you okay? You seem a little distant."

Clio shook her head and squeezed Kit's thigh. "I'm sorry. I've got this new project on my mind. I wanted to keep it a surprise, but I don't think I can. I want to share it with you."

Kit motioned with her fork. "I'm here and I'm all ears. Bring it."

"I bought a building in Finland." She laughed when Kit looked baffled. "I'm having it redesigned, and I'm going to move all the books from Mount Rushmore to this little island in Finland." She went and got her laptop. She opened the maps app and showed Kit where it was. "I'm going to call it New Alexandria, and it will be a library that people can use to learn about history. They won't be able to remove the books from the library, and some of the books might need to be chained because they're so old, and we won't want them moved around the library, let alone taken out or stolen. But I want to hold lectures and have students come in. I want people to have genuine information at their fingertips. Maybe it will help people learn for the future." She wiped away the tears that were forming. "You've shown me that I can't just give up on them."

"Clio, that's amazing." Kit zoomed in on the little island, her meal seemingly forgotten. "There's not a lot there, babe. And if the waters rise with climate change, it could cause you problems, couldn't it? Wasn't the whole point to keep that from being an issue?"

Clio jumped up again and got the plans that she and Ukko had sketched out. "You're absolutely right, and Ukko and I considered that."

"Ukko?" Kit asked, her focus on the plans.

"He's the old pagan Finnish god of thunder and lightning. A Finnish Zeus, kind of. But more polished."

"Of course." Kit pointed to the sketch. "What's this?"

"It's a sea wall. We're going to fortify the library, like a castle or a fort. The wall will keep out any potential flooding, and the building itself is going to be refitted so it's climate-controlled."

Kit sat back. "Why Finland? Out of all the places in the world?"

Clio felt the heat rise in her cheeks. "The first reason is that it's incredibly peaceful. No wars, no big political upheavals, and it's incredibly green. They try to keep everything sustainable."

"I feel like that's more than one reason but go on."

"The second reason is you." Clio took her hand. "I asked what you most wanted to see, and you said you wanted to go to Finland to see the northern lights, and to pet a reindeer, and to go dog sledding."

Kit's expression softened. "That's really sweet, babe. But it's a pretty huge decision to make based on that. And I got to do both after the crash."

Clio shook her head. "You got to see the northern lights, but you couldn't pet the reindeer because you didn't have a body. And I think you'll appreciate doing both when you're physically in the world. Not to mention the dog sledding, which you'll love." She squeezed Kit's hand. "Besides, I'm probably going to be spending a lot of time there, and I'm hoping you'll come too. This way, you can see the lights often, and we can even get you your own reindeer herd, if you want one." She bit her lip. "I've heard you talk about your time in Minnesota. I know you miss the open spaces and lakes. This way, you can have a skiff of your own so you can sail, and there won't be any buildings that make it hard for you to breathe."

Kit's eyes welled up. "That's got to be the most romantic thing anyone in history has done for anyone else." She kissed Clio's hand and held it to her cheek. "Thank you. I'd love to be there with you as often as you want me."

They spent the next couple of hours discussing the plans for the library, making notes, and googling anything they weren't sure of. Clio loved every second of doing something so exciting with someone she loved. When they both grew eye-sore from the computer, Clio turned on a movie and they cuddled up on the couch.

It was halfway through when Kit hit pause. "I've had a thought."

Clio reached over and turned on the lamp. "Tell me."

"Jag came by while you were gone. He wanted to know if we had anything to tell him, and of course I said we didn't. But I did tell him you weren't interested in doing the show anymore."

"How did he take it?" She hated the idea of upsetting him.

"As well as can be expected." Kit turned to her as best she could with her leg still raised. "But he said something that got me thinking, and now that I know your plan, I have an even better idea. What if we did a show based on history?"

Clio laughed half-heartedly. "I wish something like that would interest people, but history is never very popular."

"I disagree. I mean, there's the History Channel. And you'd put a whole different spin on it. You could talk about what you saw firsthand. You could talk politics, and architecture, and sociology, and fashion. Anything. You could even talk about conversations *you* had with people. You'd bring it to life by using the books in the library to broach the topics."

Clio turned toward her and sat cross-legged on the sofa. "And you could do interviews…" Thoughts tumbled forward so fast she couldn't keep up. "You could talk to the gods of the places I'll be talking about from the library. You could ask them questions about the time period, and why they think certain things happened."

"And why they didn't step in." Kit grinned. "That's what people always want to know."

"We can use the contacts we've both made over the years, and I'll call in favors from Afterlife. Not many gods are willing to say no to a muse. We're too well liked." She batted her eyelashes, making Kit laugh. "You've done it. You've taken what I started, and you've made it so much better." She threw herself forward into Kit's arms. "I love it! Call Jag right now."

Despite the time, Kit made the call and gave Jag a rundown of their idea. He was on board almost instantly, after a few logistics questions, and said he'd put the word out in the morning. Given their popularity because of Moscow and the crash, he didn't think he'd have any problem selling their new show idea.

"He sounds as excited as we are," Kit said, pulling Clio against her. "Who knew? When we met, I thought you'd be the death of my patience. Now you're the start of my whole new life."

Clio sighed happily. "When Aphrodite cursed me so I'd only ever fall in love with mortals, she had no idea what a gift it would be." She tilted her head and kissed Kit's cheek. "I don't want you to interview her for the show. It will make her crazy to be excluded."

"Remind me not to get on your bad side."

Clio stood, stripped off her top, and let it drop to the floor. "How about you come get on my good side?"

CHAPTER TWENTY-SIX

The weeks flew by as Kit and Clio coordinated the new project. Kit finally got onto crutches, and then got her cast off, for which she was eternally grateful. She kept up with her physio so she could be back to fighting fit as soon as possible. Clio was making trips from Mount Rushmore to the new library facility in Finland, which had been built with speed and precision. She had various gods helping with the move now that it no longer had to be kept a secret, and Kit couldn't wait to visit the facility herself. With her leg finally on the mend, she just had to get up the nerve to get back on a plane.

While Clio was busy with the actual move, Kit took care of the show details. She and Jag had met with the major network who'd picked up their show, and they'd discussed programming and possible segments, but Kit wouldn't confirm anything without including Clio, because it was Clio who would be choosing the topics based on what she wanted to show people from the library. Kit had never wanted to be part of a team but dammed if she wasn't loving the cooperative venture being formed. The new network people were considerate, they listened well, and any suggestions they offered made sense. Kit knew Clio would like them as much as she did.

The phone rang and she reached over to grab it. On the beach far below, she could see Abel and Buster playing ball, and she wished she could be down there with them. She wasn't up to taking the zillion steps down yet, but it wouldn't be long.

"Hey, babe. How's the frigid north?"

Clio sighed. "I've hit the weirdest roadblock."

Kit sat down, still watching Abel and Buster. "What's wrong?"

"I met with the Finnish parliament today. Because of the nature of our new show, they wanted to understand what our parameters are."

"That sounds reasonable." She shook her head. Buster had launched himself into a wave and then run onto the beach, where he proceeded to roll in the sand and turn himself into a sand monster.

"It would be if they hadn't then decided that because you were doing the interviews, there was no need for other sectors' gods to be in the library. They want access restricted to mortals."

Kit frowned. "But why?"

"They basically said that the materials shouldn't be tampered with by immortals. That they're too important, and they don't want any immortal to be able to skew things in the library. I'll be the only one allowed because of the nature of who and what I am." She sounded defeated and tired. "What if I'm not up to this, Kit? Was it a bad idea?"

Then and there, Kit decided she needed to face her fear of flying. Clio shouldn't be there facing this alone. "You're more than up to it, babe. You've been through way worse, and you haven't backed down." She hesitated, but they were beyond tiptoeing around each other. "Do you think maybe they have a point?"

There was silence for so long, Kit wondered how much she'd pissed her off.

"*Of course* they have a point. But I don't have to like it. I didn't want the materials to be off limits to anyone. Even the gods should be able to look up historical events and remind themselves what their followers have been through. I mean, I know they're supposed to be all-knowing, but I can tell you that even gods forget things. And to say that they're not allowed into the library because they might tamper with historical accuracy is incredibly insulting to beings who are supposed to be above that kind of thing."

"What about if you accompanied the gods? Only let in one or two at a time so you can personally keep an eye on them?" Kit nearly laughed at the idea of gods being babysat by a muse. Would that, too, be insulting?

"You're a genius. I have to go. I'll call you soon."

Kit smiled and put the phone down. She had some plans to make.

❖

"You said I'd be proud of you, and you were absolutely right," Calliope said. "I think what you're doing is truly remarkable. And I had no idea you had this kind of treasure trove stored so safely."

Clio had always appreciated Calliope's level-headedness. She was the first born and most responsible of all the sisters. She'd left Afterlife to get back to doing what she loved, but she remained on retainer for those who needed assistance with legal questions. "So you'll help?"

"Absolutely. We'll draw up a contract and a schedule, and that way the Finnish government will know which gods will be in place on which days, and you'll swear an oath to oversee the gods while they're in the library. Any immortal who goes into the library will also have to swear not to tamper with any of the books so that they shed a different light on historical events. That should make Parliament happy."

Clio crossed the issue off her rather long list of things yet to do. "Thanks so much. I wanted to ask your opinion on one other thing."

"Okay?"

She hesitated, wondering if she was getting in over her head, but plunged forward anyway. "I want to contact various religious heads and ask for copies of their texts. Anything and everything they might have. Even pre-fader gods. I want to put out a huge call for books to add to the library." She waited. Would Calliope say she was being overzealous?

"Wow. That's a big ask. It's a lot of knowledge to be stored all in one place."

Clio played with a fork. The tiny house she'd rented came fully furnished, fortunately. "I know. I'm thinking I'd ask for copies, not necessarily originals." A new thought occurred to her, as was constantly happening while the project took shape. "In fact, we could have a transcription room, like they did when only monks knew how to read and write. Scholars could come in and dedicate themselves to making both print and digital copies. That way the information is stored in two places, so if anything went horribly wrong like it did in Egypt, we'd have backup copies."

"You're talking about potentially centuries' worth of work," Calliope said. "But I think scholars would come from all over the globe for the chance to do it."

Clio practically bounced in her seat. "You think it's a good idea?"

"I think it's such a good idea that I'll help you get the word out. I'll get Meg to use the Afterlife newsletter to let the different sectors know what you're doing and what you want. We'll also have Selene mention it on her show. Maybe the gods she's talking to will start conversations about ancient texts that you can then use for your show as well."

Clio wanted to cry and celebrate at the same time. "Thank you so much, Callie." She took a deep breath and closed her eyes to calm herself. "To be honest, I wasn't sure I could pull any of this off. It seemed like a great idea, but it's been so much work. I can barely stay on my feet long enough at the end of the day to make it to bed." She didn't say that more than once she'd thought about quitting or asking someone else to take charge. When those thoughts had taken over, she'd shoved them aside. She wanted Kit and her sisters to be proud of her. But she also needed to be proud of herself.

"Clio, we've always believed in you. Every one of us has lost our way at some point through the years. And I'm not sure you even lost your way so much as you took a different path for a little while." Her tone was kind and gentle, just like she was. "And I have to admit I'm glad to see you back to doing what you love."

"And still doing a TV show, which I also love."

Calliope laughed. "Still an extrovert. Nothing wrong with that, sis." There was the noise of instruments tuning in the background. Calliope was working at the ACA with her music students today.

"I'd better get going. I'll let you know what responses I get, and if you need anything else from me, just give me a shout. If you need me to come speak to the Finnish parliament myself, I'll gladly come over. I haven't been up that way in a long time."

"I expect you to be at the grand opening." Clio looked outside and saw that it was pitch-black outside. She'd need to get back to California often enough that she didn't miss the sunshine. "I can't wait to see you."

The call ended and Clio sat back. Her body ached and she was utterly exhausted, but it was coming together beautifully. Now all she needed was Kit at her side.

❖

The Dancing Bobcat was full. Rainbow streamers hung on the wall behind the small stage, and a dance floor took up most of the space in front of it. Comfortable chairs were placed off to one side, while tables with people eating a late dinner sat off to the other. As one of only five places available on the island to eat and drink, it wasn't surprising it was full. What was surprising, however, was how many were turned toward the stage, waiting.

News had flown across the island about the new library going up on the main road, and with the trucks and building happening, everyone on the island had an opinion about what to expect. What was also well known was that Clio was at the helm, and any time she went to get groceries, or for coffee, or even just took a walk, the locals stopped her to chat. People were friendly and respectful, and she had several wonderful debates over a pint of beer. More and more, she'd been welcomed as part of the community.

She held her guitar and closed her eyes. She began to sing about love and all the ways it changed you. She sang of new beginnings and of the feeling of wanting to find home in the person who had given her a way to see the world afresh. Emotion poured from her soul and into her fingers as she strummed, and she let it fill her voice so it could touch everyone in the room. Images of Kit, her smile, her body, her laughter, stayed in her mind's eye as she sang, and when it was over, it was like she'd been filled with passion even as she gave it away.

She opened her eyes to find the crowd staring at her, silently. And then they burst into applause, many wiping tears from their eyes. But her gaze fell on one person in particular, who wasn't clapping. She was staring at Clio and allowing the tears to stream down her cheeks unchecked.

Kit got up slowly and made her way to the stage, never taking her eyes off Clio even as she skirted people calling for an encore. Clio set down her guitar and sat on the edge of the stage, and when Kit got to her, she wrapped her arms around Clio and pulled her down into the most intense, passionate kiss Clio had ever had in all her existence.

It took a few minutes before she became aware of the catcalls and whistling around them. She leaned back and smiled at Kit. "What a wonderful surprise."

Kit rested her forehead against Clio's. "I couldn't wait another second. I hope it's okay."

Clio took her hand and guided her onto the stage. Another stool was set up beside her. "It's more than okay. I've missed you so much. Stay beside me?"

Kit nodded, and Clio picked up her guitar. The world felt new, and she couldn't wait to experience every day with Kit as they changed it in their own small way.

"I think it's time for you to strut your stuff," Clio said, striking up a dance song. The dance floor was soon full of people, and she laughed and sang for ages. Kit sang alongside her, and though her voice wasn't amazing, her pure enjoyment of singing her heart out, was.

By the time they left, it was cold and black outside. They walked arm in arm back to the little house Clio had rented, their breath puffing ahead of them.

"Were you okay on the flight over?" Clio asked. "I can't believe you flew without me."

Kit pulled her closer. "I won't say I didn't freak out once or twice, but Sian kept me calm."

"Sian flew commercial again?" After Sian had left the day they'd brought Kit home, Clio hadn't heard from her. She'd contacted her to say she'd be doing a lot of traveling, but Sian's response had been distant. She'd said she needed some time, so she'd be doing other work for a while. It had hurt, but Clio understood. She could only hope that Sian came back to her one day.

"She did. She was going to come with me tonight, but she was too tired. At least, that's what she said." Kit squeezed her arm. "Any regrets?"

Clio frowned. "About?"

"About not choosing Sian when she told you she loved you."

Clio blanched. "You heard?"

"No. I wasn't out of my body for that part. But she told me a long time ago when we were at the gym, and when I saw how she was acting around you after the crash, I knew she'd confessed."

Clio sighed and her breath curled into the air. "No regrets. I told you how I felt about her from the start, and that hasn't changed. I'm sorry it hurt her though."

"Based on the love bite on her neck, I'm going to say she's getting over you." Kit grinned.

Relieved, Clio opened the door to the little house and sighed happily when they were met with a wall of heat. "I'll be glad to see her tomorrow. I've missed her."

Kit hung her jacket on the wall and then pulled Clio to her. "Just so long as you remember whose bed you're supposed to be in." She kissed her possessively. "I don't intend to share."

Clio's knees went weak at the blatant desire in Kit's eyes. "Then you'd better show me what I'm in for by tying my life to yours."

As she led Kit to the bedroom, she wondered how she'd lost the sense of passion and awe that Kit infused her with. There was so much to be seen in the world. So much to be done. And she'd do it all with Kit at her side.

EPILOGUE

T his is insanity." Kit dodged a ball. Every inch of grass seemed to be covered with picnic blankets, students fooling around, kids playing games, and families feasting on lavish spreads pulled out of beautifully wrought baskets.

"It's so much like it has been for centuries." Clio had spent several Vappu spring festivals in the Nordic countries, and May first was always a little chaotic. It was a genuine celebration of rebirth, of the sun returning to a place that had been in darkness for months on end. It felt fitting for Clio to hold the grand opening of New Alexandria on a day of new beginnings.

The abandoned museum had been re-created beautifully. The simplicity of the structure overall remained, but now it was four stories high and twice as long. There was room to expand around it as well, which was fortunate given the number of texts being received from different religious sectors daily.

Calliope and her girlfriend, Jordan, were sitting on a picnic blanket a little out of the way. Clio flared her dress out around her as she sat down beside them. Kit pushed it out of the way so she could sit closer to her, earning her a mock glare. "Just because you're still a wrinkled mess doesn't mean I have to be one."

"I love you too," Kit said, getting a laugh from Callie and Jordan.

"It's really something, Clio," Jordan said, munching on cheese and crackers, before feeding a cracker to Buster as well. "I love the comfy chairs all over the place so people can relax as well as study."

Clio pointed to the end of the building. "That bit isn't done yet, but it'll be temporary scholar housing for those who need to stay on site longer for their research." Also in that section of the building would be the chariot clock from the art gallery in Santa Fe. Kit had bought it and said it was unimaginable that the new library wouldn't have a representation of Clio in it. In turn, Clio had placed Kit's trophy from the Archimedes camp beside it. They'd built the place together, and it should have elements of them both inside. But explaining that to the others would have felt like oversharing.

"How long is your list of people who want to study the original texts from the old Library of Alexandria?" Calliope rested against Jordan, looking calm and happy.

Kit laughed. "Really, really long. You should have heard Clio having a shouting match with some god who was pissed off they were on the same list as regular people."

Clio looked up when a shadow fell over her, and she jumped to her feet. "You made it!"

Eris swung her around. "Are you kidding? After all the hoopla we went through together, I wasn't about to miss it." She slapped Kit on the back. "Good to see you alive and kicking."

Kit rubbed at her shoulder. "Ow. Don't you immortal folk know your own strength?"

Eris looked around. "Well, if you can't take it, I bet I know another woman around here who could…"

Clio followed her gaze and warmed when she saw Sian standing off to the side, talking to a woman with auburn hair that sparkled in the sunlight. Sian, as though she knew she was being watched, looked up and smiled.

It had taken a few months before Sian had started traveling with them again, and for the most part, the sadness had gone from her smile, and she joked and laughed with them like she always had. Every once in a while, though, Clio caught Sian watching her out of the corner of her eye. But she couldn't do anything about that. Eventually, Sian's heart would heal, and she'd find someone who could return all she had to give.

"So," Eris said, joining Clio on the blanket, "when do you start filming?"

"Not for another month," Kit said, pulling Clio over so that her back rested against Kit's chest. "We need to allow people to get in there and start using it, and Clio needs time to decide what era of history she wants to start with so we know which gods to line up."

"Sensible," Eris said, frowning at a piece of blue cheese that she quickly set back down.

"Jordan and I were wondering if you wanted to join us in Scotland before you go back to California," Calliope said. "We could go over some of those textual contracts, and Kit could go to the adventure park with Jordan. She's installing new spelunking areas."

"Yes!" Kit said, making Clio pull her head away from the loud exclamation. "Sorry, babe. But I'm absolutely in. Can Abel and Buster come too? Neither one of them likes to be left home alone anymore, and our new house here isn't going to be ready for another month yet."

"Of course they can. Eris? Would you like to join us too?" Calli asked.

"Nah, but thanks. I've got to get back. I promised Hades I'd watch Cerberus while he's on vacation in Russia next month." Eris tucked her arms under her head and stared at the sky. "And I've got the club to run."

Clio took in Eris's relaxed posture but also saw the tension in her jaw and shoulders. Hopefully one day, Eris would find her path again, the way Clio and Calliope had. For now, all Clio could do was be there when Eris decided she needed to talk.

"I was hoping Dani would be here," Clio said. "I haven't had a chance to thank her for helping us in Greenland."

Kit shuddered against her back. "No offense, but I'll be glad not to see Dani again for a really long time. I'm sure she's nice enough, but I'm all about doing my living and socializing up here, with people who are about creating stuff while alive."

Jordan leaned forward and fist-bumped her in agreement, making the others laugh.

"You'll both come around eventually." Clio turned her head and kissed Kit's cheek. "We're all super lovable in our own ways."

"There's the optimist I love," Kit said, kissing her neck.

Conversation flowed, along with wine, and there was plenty of laughter and lighthearted banter. It seemed not very long ago that Clio had been snubbed by workmates, gone home to an empty house, and wondered why she was so alone on a planet of billions.

Now, sitting here with her sisters and the woman she'd love to the end of her lifetime, she knew she'd never lose her way again. She was the muse of history, and she now had her special library dedicated to preserving history in all its forms. She was the muse of virtue, and the woman she loved was the very vision of virtue. She closed her eyes and tilted her face to the warm spring sunshine. It was astounding that after three thousand years, she could still change, still grow, still love with all her heart.

About the Author

Brey Willows is a longtime editor and writer. When she's not running a social enterprise working with marginalized communities on writing projects, she's editing other people's writing or doing her own. She lives in the middle of England with her partner and fellow author and spends entirely too much time exploring castles and ancient ruins while bemoaning the rain.

Books Available from Bold Strokes Books

A Good Chance by Ali Vali. Harry, Desi, and Desi's sister Rachel are so close to getting everything they've ever wanted, but Desi's ex-husband is coming back to get his revenge and rip apart their chance at happiness. (978-1-63679-023-7)

A Perfect Fifth by Jaycie Morrison. Streetwise pianist Zara Keller and Lady Jillian Stansfield couldn't be more different; yet their connection brings a new awareness of who they are and what they truly want in their lives—including each other. (978-1-63679-132-6)

Catching Feelings by Ana Hartnett Reichardt. Andrea Foster expected to catch a lot of pitches from the Alder Lion's star pitcher, Maya, but she didn't expect to catch feelings. (978-1-63679-227-9)

Defiant Hearts by Lee Lynch. In these stories, you'll find your lovers, friends, and lesbians you wish you knew—maybe even yourself. (978-1-63679-237-8)

Love and Duty by Catherine Young. All Princess Roseli wants is to marry her three lovers, but with war looming, she must instead marry Princess Lucia to establish a military alliance between their planets. (978-1-63679-256-9)

Murder at Union Station by David S. Pederson. Private Detective Mason Adler struggles to determine who killed a woman found in a trunk without getting himself killed in the process. (978-1-63679-269-9)

Serendipity by Kris Bryant. Serendipity brings jingle writer Annie Foster and celebrity pop star Bristol Baines together, and their undeniable attraction keeps them close, but will their different paths drive them apart? (978-1-63679-224-8)

The Haunted Heart by Jane Kolven. A ghost, a ring, and a quest to find a missing psychic—it's a spell for love. (978-1-63679-245-3)

The Rules of Forever by Nan Campbell. After reconnecting at their high school reunion, Cara and Lauren agree to embark on a textbook definition friends-with-benefits relationship, but trying to keep it uncomplicated is harder than it seems. (978-1-63679-248-4)

Vision of Virtue by Brey Willows. When virtue and desire come together, be prepared for sparks in this next installment of the Memory's Muses series. (978-1-63679-118-0)

Cherry on Top by Georgia Beers. A chance meeting leaves Cherry and Ellis longing for a different life, but when Ellis's search for truth crashes into Cherry's insta-filter world, do they have any hope at all of a happily ever after? (978-1-63679-158-6)

Love and Other Rare Birds by Angie Williams. Ornithologist Dr. Jamie Martin and park ranger Rowan Fleming are searching the Alaskan wilderness for a bird thought to be extinct and they're about to discover opposites really do attract. (978-1-63679-108-1)

Parallel Paradise by Mayapee Chowdhury. When their love affair is put to the test by the homophobia of their family, community, and culture, Bindi and Rimli will need to fight for a chance at love. (978-1-63679-204-0)

Perfectly Matched by Toni Logan. A beautiful Cupid named Hannah, a runaway arrow, and just seventy-two hours to fix a mishap that could be the best mistake she has ever made. (978-1-63679-120-3)

Royal Exposé by Jenny Frame. When they're grouped together for a class assignment, Poppy's enthusiasm for life and love may just save Casey's soul, but will she ever forgive Casey for using her to expose royal secrets? (978-1-63679-165-4)

Slow Burn by Missouri Vaun. A wounded wildland firefighter from California and a struggling artist find solace and love in a small southern town. (978-1-63679-098-5)

The Artist by Sheri Lewis Wohl. Detective Casey Wilson and reclusive artist Tula Crane are drawn together in a web of passion, intrigue, and art that might just hold the key to stopping a killer. (978-1-63679-150-0)

The Inconvenient Heiress by Jane Walsh. An unlikely heiress and a spinster evade the Marriage Mart only to discover true love together. (978-1-63679-173-9)

A Champion for Tinker Creek by D.C. Robeline. Lyle James has rescued his dad's auto repair business, but when city hall condemns his neighborhood, Lyle learns only trusting will save his life and help him find love. (978-1-63679-213-2)

Closed-Door Policy by Erin Zak. Going back to college is never easy, but Caroline Stevens is prepared to work hard and change her life for the better. What she's not prepared for is Dr. Atlanta Morris, her gorgeous new professor. (978-1-63679-181-4)

Homeworld by Gun Brooke. Headed by Captain Holly Crowe, the spaceship Velocity's crew journeys toward their alien ancestors' homeworld, and what they find is completely unexpected—and they're not safe. (978-1-63679-177-7)

Outland by Kristin Keppler & Allisa Bahney. Danielle Clark and Katelyn Turner can't seem to stay away from one another even as the war for the wastelands tests their loyalty to each other and to their people. (978-1-63679-154-8)

Secret Sanctuary by Nance Sparks. US Deputy Marshal Alex Trenton specializes in protecting those awaiting trial, but when danger threatens the woman she's falling for, Alex is in for the fight of her life. (978-1-63679-148-7)

Stranded Hearts by Kris Bryant, Amanda Radley, Emily Smith. In these novellas from award winning authors, fate intervenes on behalf of love when characters are unexpectedly stuck together. With too much time and an irresistible attraction, anything could happen. (978-1-63679-182-1)

The Last Lavender Sister by Melissa Brayden. Aster Lavender sells her gourmet doughnuts and keeps a low profile; she never plans on the town's temporary veterinarian swooping in and making her feel like anything but a wallflower. (978-1-63679-130-2)

The Probability of Love by Dena Blake. As Blair and Rachel keep ending up in the same place despite the odds, can a one-night stand turn into forever? Or will the bet Blair never intended to make ruin their happily ever after? (978-1-63679-188-3)

Worth a Fortune by Sam Ledel. After placing a want ad for a personal secretary, a New York heiress is surprised when the woman who got away is the one interested in the position. (978-1-63679-175-3)

A Fox in Shadow by Jane Fletcher. Cassie's mission is to add new territory to the Kavillian empire—murder, betrayal, war, and the clash of cultures ensue. (978-1-63679-142-5)

Embracing the Moon by Jeannie Levig. Just as Gwen and Taylor are exploring the new love they've found, the present and past collide, threatening the future they long to share. (978-1-63555-462-5)

Forever Comes in Threes by D. Jackson Leigh. Efficiency expert Perry Chandler's ordered life is upended when she inherits three busy terriers, and the woman she's referred to for help turns out to be her bitter podcast rival, the very sexy Dr. Ming Lee. (978-1-63679-169-2)

Heckin' Lewd: Trans and Nonbinary Erotica by Mx. Nillin Lore. If you want smutty, fearless, gender diverse erotica written by affirming own-voices folks who get it, then this is the book you've been looking for! (978-1-63679-240-8)

Missed Conception by Joy Argento. Maggie Walsh wants a relationship with Cassidy, the daughter she's only just discovered she has due to an in vitro mix-up. Heat kindles between Maggie and Cassidy's mother in a way neither expects. (978-1-63679-146-3)

Private Equity by Elle Spencer. Cassidy Bennett spends an unexpected evening at a lesbian nightclub with her notoriously reserved and demanding boss, Julia. After seeing a different side of Julia, Cassidy can't seem to shake her desire to know more. (978-1-63679-180-7)

Racing the Dawn by Sandra Barrett. After narrowly escaping a house fire, vampire Jade Murphy is unexpectedly intrigued by gorgeous firefighter Beth Jenssen, and her undead existence might just be perking up a bit. (978-1-63679-271-2)

Reclaiming Love by Amanda Radley. Sarah's tiny white lie means somehow convincing Pippa to pretend to be her girlfriend. Only the more time they spend faking it, the more real it feels. (978-1-63679-144-9)

Sol Cycle by Kimberly Cooper Griffin. An encounter in a park brings Ang and Krista together, but when Ang's attempts to help Krista go spectacularly wrong, their passion for each other might not be enough. (978-1-63679-137-1)

Trial and Error by Carsen Taite. Attorney Franco Rossi and Judge Nina Aguilar's reunion is fraught with courtroom conflict, undeniable chemistry, and danger. (978-1-63555-863-0)

A Long Way to Fall by Elle Spencer. A ski lodge, two strong-willed women, and a family feud that brings them together, but will it also tear them apart? (978-1-63679-005-3)

Barnabas Bopwright Saves the City by J. Marshall Freeman. When he uncovers a terror plot to destroy the city he loves, 15-year-old Barnabas Bopwright realizes it's up to him to save his home and bring deadly secrets into the light before it's too late. (978-1-63679-152-4)

Forever by Kris Bryant. When Savannah Edwards is invited to be the next bachelorette on the dating show When Sparks Fly, she'll show the world that finding true love on television can happen. (978-1-63679-029-9)

Ice on Wheels by Aurora Rey. All's fair in love and roller derby. That's Riley Fauchet's motto, until a new job lands her at the same company—and on the same team—as her rival Brooke Landry, the frosty jammer for the Big Easy Bruisers. (978-1-63679-179-1)

Inherit the Lightning by Bud Gundy. Darcy O'Brien and his sisters learn they are about to inherit an immense fortune, but a family mystery about to unravel after seventy years threatens to destroy everything. (978-1-63679-199-9)

Perfect Rivalry by Radclyffe. Two women set out to win the same career-making goal, but it's love that may turn out to be the final prize. (978-1-63679-216-3)

Something to Talk About by Ronica Black. Can quiet ranch owner Corey Durand give up her peaceful life and allow her feisty new neighbor into her heart? Or will past loss, present suitors, and town gossip ruin a long-awaited chance at love? (978-1-63679-114-2)

With a Minor in Murder by Karis Walsh. In the world of academia, police officer Clare Sawyer and professor Libby Hart team up to solve a murder. (978-1-63679-186-9)

Writer's Block by Ali Vali. Wyatt and Hayley might be made for each other if only they can get through nosy neighbors, the historic society, at-odds future plans, and all the secrets hidden in Wyatt's walls. (978-1-63679-021-3)